VICTORY ON TERRA

BOOK TWELVE OF THE EMPIRE OF BONES SAGA

TERRY MIXON

YOWLING
CAT PRESS

Published by Yowling Cat Press ®

Digital edition date: 6/21/2023

Print ISBN: 978-1947376342

Large Print ISBN: 978-1947376359

Cover art - image copyrights as follows:

BigStockPhoto | Richter1910

DepositPhotos | Ragnarocks

Luca Oleastri

Donna Mixon

Cover design and composition by Donna Mixon

Print edition design and layout by Terry Mixon

Audio edition performed and produced by Veronica Giguere

Reach her at: v@voicesbyveronica.com

ALSO BY TERRY MIXON

You can always find the most up to date listing of Terry's titles on his Amazon Author Page.

Note: the links below (ebook only, obviously) redirect you to my website where you can click a button to go to Amazon. This allows me to participate in Amazon's associates program and earn a little more. Sorry for any inconvenience.

The Last Hunter

The Last Hunter

Bonds of Blood

Alpha Strike

The Enemy Revealed

Command Authority

The Grand Conspiracy

Shield of Humanity

Fog of War

Ships of the Line

Operation Liberty

The Empire of Bones Saga

Empire of Bones

Veil of Shadows

Command Decisions

Ghosts of Empire

Paying the Price

Recon in Force

Behind Enemy Lines

The Terra Gambit

Hidden Enemies

Race to Terra

Ruined Terra

Victory on Terra

When Luck Runs Out

Gunboat Diplomacy

The Imperial Marines Saga

Spoils of War

Imperial Recruit

Enemy Action

The Humanity Unlimited Saga

Liberty Station

Freedom Express

Tree of Liberty

Blood of Patriots

Single Novels

Scorched Earth

Storm Divers

The Vigilante Series with Glynn Stewart

Heart of Vengeance

Oath of Vengeance

Bound By Law

Bound By Honor

Bound By Blood

Box Sets

Want to get updates from Terry about new books and other general nonsense going on in his life? He promises there will be cats. Go to TerryMixon.com/Mailing-List and sign up.

DEDICATION

This book would not be possible without the love and support of my beautiful wife. Donna, I love you more than life itself.

ACKNOWLEDGMENTS

A special thanks to Jon Paul Olivier for his timely assistance with this book. It is deeply appreciated.

I also want to thank the folks that support me on Patreon. You got to read this book as I was writing it and that kept me working. You have my deepest thanks.

In particular, I want to thank those patrons that supported me at the $10 level and above:

Bryan Barnes
Dave Dolan
David Goldstein
Christian A. Michelsen
Dale Thompson
Clark Williams

Finally, I want to thank my readers for putting up with me. You guys are great.

1

Kelsey Bandar sat in the gritty, ancient tunnel, perched on a plascrete ledge just at the edge of the torch light deep beneath the horde city they'd just escaped from. The crash from the adrenalin high made her feel ready to collapse.

Dust still filled the air, and her eyes stung from the grit. The air was stale yet somehow managed to smell like something mechanical was burning off in the distance. It made her taste burnt toast.

That same dust had gotten under the primitive armor she wore and into her clothes. She itched all over. Parts of her felt like they were being rubbed by fine-grained sandpaper. It was like all the worst parts of making love on the beach without any of the awesome aspects.

Tired and sore, she scrubbed her face with both hands, trying to bring herself fully back to wakefulness. That probably ground more dirt into her pores and made her look like she'd been buried alive. Which, on reflection, wasn't that far from the truth.

Her hair had to be a nightmare. God, she needed a bath. No, two.

She ached from the efforts of the last few minutes. She hadn't broken anything—which was a good thing, since her medical nanites and the rest of her Marine Raider augmentation were still offline due to the EMP blast almost a week ago—but it felt as if several people had enthusiastically beaten her for hours.

After their flight from the vault where the horde had kept their scavenged Imperial technology, she'd used a plasma rifle built for marine powered armor to blow a massive hole through the stone walls that they'd used to plug an old tunnel leading to the ruined megacity they'd built their capital next to.

She'd fired a lot of plasma weapons over the last few years, so even without her enhanced strength, her graphene-coated bones and reinforced joints had taken the beating while she'd placed her shots just where they'd needed to go. It was her flesh that had paid the price in bruises and strained muscles.

Her ears, no longer protected by her augmentation, rang from firing the huge weapon. It was an annoying "squeee" that never seemed to go away and sometimes made it hard to understand what the others were saying. She hoped it wasn't permanent. That would totally suck.

Even if it was something that she had to live with, it had been worth it.

Two shots had utterly vaporized the barrier that the horde had put up to keep the inhabitants of the ruined megacity from sneaking under their walls. That had left her with a single shot left to fire into the vault's ceiling.

It had quite literally brought the roof down, fully sealing the area behind them. There could be no retreat now. The only path out of this mess was forward.

And going forward meant that they had to make their way underneath the ruined megacity once called Frankfort. She had no idea what they were going to find there, but based on the evident fear that the horde had about entering the old structures, it wasn't abandoned. There had to be people living there, and they would likely take her party's intrusion poorly.

Jared had brought down all of the people on board his destroyer before the AI had destroyed her. That had been more than two hundred people. When she added in the scientists and marines that she'd brought from *Persephone*, that number had grown to almost three hundred.

The electromagnetic pulse weapon that the horde had deployed had taken them all down when it had crashed their implants. The bastards had then slaughtered just about everyone. They were down to fourteen people.

Her mind still couldn't grasp the scale of their loss. It wounded her deeply that she'd failed so many people. It didn't matter that they'd had no idea the horde had that kind of weapon before they'd used it. All of those people were still dead.

The sorrow she felt was mixed with hot rage at the people who'd casually butchered so many innocent people. She hoped she'd killed a lot of their warriors in the fight they'd just finished, but it wasn't enough.

It would never be enough. Given a chance to exterminate them, she'd do so in an instant and deal with the trauma that caused her later. It wouldn't be the first time, though she'd hoped to never be in that mental place ever again.

Clarice Beauchamp, the warrior in charge of the first group of locals that they'd met, had lost all thirty of her warriors. Together, the survivors had made their way to the horde city, because retreat was impossible. The fires that they'd started during the fighting had cut them off, and they absolutely had to have some of the tools they'd lost to retrieve the override from the Imperial Palace.

Kelsey opened one of the survival rations that she'd recovered from the storage room where the horde had been sorting their captured gear. With what they'd found there, they probably had enough food for a week.

Whether that would be enough to escape the ruined megacity remained to be seen.

She ate slowly, looking around the hollow-eyed group. Each of them had been devastated in their own way, and this was the first chance they'd had to take a breath since the final fight had begun.

Hell, this was the first real break they'd had since they'd landed on this damned planet.

Talbot was off scouting with Clarice Beauchamp. That left Senior

Lieutenant Chloe Laird and Commander Kaitlinn Cannon managing security over the makeshift camp in the tunnel.

Huddled in a small circle around a couple of the torches that they'd propped up for light and heat were the remaining people in their group: Jared Mertz, Carl Owlet, Elise Orison, Olivia West, Commodore Sean Meyer, Austin Darrah, Ralph Halstead, Doctor Lily Stone, and herself.

And, of course, her doppelgänger, Julia, a version of herself from another reality. That was still a little hard to accept, but the woman was growing on her.

They were all ragged and worn because of everything they'd been through over the last few days. Not only the fighting, but the mad searching through the debris that the horde had scavenged while looking for any tools that could help them turn their implants back on.

Doctor Stone had found her spare medical kit, so she could get to the implants now. Then the struggle would be for Carl to convert a piece of equipment that he'd found to generate the exact frequency and charge needed to initiate a reboot of their implants.

Honestly, that was one of the first things they needed to do. Without her Marine Raider augmentation, she wasn't able to protect them. A lot of people had died because of her arrogance in thinking that their technology would keep them safe, but without her augmentation, they were working at an extreme disadvantage.

They needed to get their implants back online as quickly as possible, without rushing things to the point that they killed someone. And that process needed to start now.

She rose to her feet, futilely tried to dust her hands off for the umpteenth time, and walked over to Lily. "You said that you'd recovered enough of your medical kit to perform the surgery. Is that something we could do here?"

Lily shuddered. "I can theoretically sterilize the surgical zone, but this is an *incredibly* dirty area. The chances of something getting into someone's head—even with all of the precautions I can take—is greater than zero. If that happens and we can't get their implants back online so that their medical nanites restart, they could get an infection of the brain, and that would be fatal.

"Even if I perform the surgery successfully, the real work is going to be for Carl. If his modifications to the equipment generating the charge are flawed, it could fry the wiring in the brain and kill someone outright.

"All told, I suspect that working with this jury-rigged technology is going to put the first person at significant risk. Perhaps as much as a thirty percent chance of death or cerebral injury. And that's on top of the infection risk if the reboot fails."

"That's too high," Jared said, his voice echoing off the plascrete walls around them. "What can we do to bring it down?"

The doctor shook her head. "Absolutely nothing. I doubt that we're going to find a functional surgical center anytime soon, and at least Carl knows the equipment that he's modifying.

"If we find other equipment that could be used, it's going to be in questionable condition, and that would make the risk go up. As high as the chances of a negative outcome are, they're still probably the best we're going to get. The positive in this is that once we can assess the process, the risk goes way down for subsequent patients."

Before her brother could respond, Kelsey squatted down in front of the doctor. "I'm willing to risk those odds. If we don't get my augmentation back online, the chances that someone is going to kill us all will rise exponentially.

"You can bet that there are dangerous people in this city. People that had to have heard those explosions. Our time is running out."

Jared looked skeptical. "We're deep underground. They might've heard something, and they might even know that it came from the direction of the horde city, but they're not going to be able to know precisely which tunnel it took place in.

"Hell, the tunnel leading to the horde vault has been sealed off for a long time. This isn't going to be the first place they think of, if they even think that the explosion affects them at all. They may just end up believing that the horde did it to themselves."

"We can't take that chance," Kelsey said with a shake of her head. "We have to assume that the residents of Frankfort are going to come looking for intruders and that they're going to find us shortly.

"The question is, are they going to find us in a condition to resist or take us prisoner like the horde did? With their reputation, are we willing to chance that they won't torture and execute us like those bastards up there intended to do?"

Those were the million-credit questions.

Jared shook his head slightly. "Even with your augmentation, that's still not a guaranteed defense against attack. Yes, you've got all those unarmed-combat skills, but how far is that going to get us?

"We have no advanced weaponry. What if they do? This deep underneath the city, if they still have some kind of power generation, they may have functional Imperial weapons.

"The horde has to have something like that, or they couldn't have made the EMP weapon. If the people here bring something like that to bear, swords and bows are going to be useless."

They stared at one another for a few moments before she nodded. "There's something to what you're saying, but I think you're missing the bigger point. Our best bet is to negotiate passage if we run into the inhabitants. I believe that we have a better chance of doing that if we can prove our story of coming from the sky above, and my augmentation gives us a better chance of making that happen.

"I understand there's a risk, but it's one that I'm willing to take. When you get right down to it, this is relatively mild when compared to some of the chances I've taken over the years."

"One of these days, the odds are going to catch up with you," her brother said with a sigh. "I'd rather not have that happen today, Kelsey."

She smiled slightly. "Me either, but beggars can't be choosers. A thirty percent chance of death right now is better odds than a hundred percent if we're caught with our pants down around our ankles again. We've got to take the chance. I know it, and so do you."

"Talbot's not going to be happy about this."

"No, I'd imagine not."

Jared grimaced. "Do it."

* * *

CARL OWLET WATCHED NERVOUSLY as Doctor Stone made her first incision into Kelsey's skull. The small woman was unconscious due to the somatic stimulator attached to her forehead, which kept her in a state of sleep much more profound than any kind of anesthesia would have done.

He wasn't a big fan of the blood the incision caused, which Olivia West was wiping away with a sterile wipe, but this was far from the first surgery he'd witnessed. He'd worked with the doctor when they'd installed the new communications module in the princess's torso.

At least that had been with a full medical team in attendance and in a real operating theater. Doing this kind of thing in a filthy tunnel on a mostly dead world made him shudder.

Ever since they'd discovered the dead fleet crewmen aboard *Courageous* all those years ago, he'd seen a lot of implants inside skulls. It was still very much a gruesome sight but a familiar one.

After a few minutes of deft work, Doctor Stone had a small area behind Kelsey's right ear shaved, cut open, and a small section of bone removed. That exposed the node he needed access to inside his friend's skull.

He still wasn't exactly sure how the electromagnetic pulse had been strong enough to knock everything offline. That was supposed to be impossible.

Obviously not.

Unfortunately, that fact introduced a level of uncertainty into the procedure. Would this reset even work? Was the equipment in their heads so damaged that it wasn't going to come back online no matter what they did? Honestly, there was no way of knowing if he'd be able to make this work or fail miserably.

To make it work, he needed to use a piece of modified equipment to generate a charge on a specific frequency and with an extremely low amperage—a range of power output that the gear he'd recovered and modified had never been designed to generate quite so precisely.

As Doctor Stone had prepped for the surgery, Carl had made the needed modifications to his equipment. To the best of his knowledge, this was going to work, but it was still a gamble.

He had no way of measuring the output. If his modifications

didn't do what they needed to do, there was the possibility that he'd fry Kelsey's brain and kill her.

Lily turned to him. "Over to you, Carl. What can I do to help?"

Taking a deep breath, Carl held up the probe that he'd use to trigger the charge. "I'm going to need you to immobilize her head. In fact, if we can get everyone else to grab onto her and keep her from moving at all, that would be best.

"I know that the somatic stimulator isn't supposed to allow her brain to send any commands to move her body, but once I trigger her implants to reset, there's the potential that her augmentation will move her body without any input from her. Potentially at full strength.

"Even that should be okay, so long as she doesn't move her head toward me. I'll pull back as fast as I can, but if she moves too quickly, she could impale her brain directly on my probe. That would be really, *really* bad."

The rest of them grabbed onto Kelsey. Four of them had her head wedged as well as they could with their legs and hands. That was going to be as good as he could get.

If this worked, she'd be able to hold the next patient steady while he worked with absolute certainty that they wouldn't be able to yank their head around until he was clear. This was going to be the most dangerous operation of the group.

He inserted the curved tip of the probe into her brain tissue. He was moving directly adjacent to the implant node with a very thin tip, so it shouldn't have any adverse effect on her, but it still made him feel exceptionally nervous.

The location where he had to apply the charge was on the far side of the node, something that was easy to do in a modern medical facility but incredibly difficult with makeshift equipment down at the bottom of an ancient tunnel under a destroyed city.

Once he felt that he had the probe tip where it needed to go, he took one last deep breath. "I'm about to trigger the charge. I'll give you a count down from three and hit the button on zero. As soon as I deliver the charge, I'm going to retract the probe and get clear. Again, it's possible that she could seize with the full strength of her augmentation, so don't let her grab you. As soon as I'm clear, get well back."

If she got ahold of anyone at full strength, there would undoubtedly be broken bones and other serious injuries, so he hoped to avoid that. If his actions killed his friend, he wasn't sure he could ever get past that.

He took a deep breath and put his finger on the button that would send the charge. He made sure the tip of the probe was in contact with the implant node and looked around at the group one last time.

"Three… two… one… zero."

With the last word, he sent the charge into her implants and extracted the probe as quickly and carefully as he could. That took less than a second, and everyone else pulled back from Kelsey as he finished.

The only reaction he saw to what he'd done was her eyes twitching. Even that motion ceased a moment later. It looked like the somatic stimulator had kept her under.

She was still breathing, so she was alive. They wouldn't know the condition of her brain or her implants until she was brought out, though.

He sat back on his heels and watched Doctor Stone clean the exposed area, put the small sliver of bone back in place, and begin sealing it into place with surgical glue. Once that was done, the doctor used a portable regenerator to close the skin over the wound.

"We've done the best we can," Lily said a few minutes later. "I'm going to wake her up."

Carl watched closely as the doctor turned off the somatic stimulator and put it aside. After a few moments, Kelsey's eyes fluttered open, and she took a deep breath.

"How are you feeling, Kelsey?" Lily asked softly.

The blonde woman frowned up at the doctor. "Who's Kelsey? And who are you?"

2
————

J ared's heart leapt into his throat. He'd been an idiot to let this happen. He should've told her no.

God, how were they going to fix this? Then his eyes narrowed as Kelsey started chuckling.

"You should see your faces," Kelsey said with a smirk.

"That's not funny!" Jared snapped. "You scared the hell out of us."

His sister grinned as she slowly sat up with the assistance of Doctor Stone. "Blame Talbot. I think his sense of humor is rubbing off on me."

She stared up at the ceiling and blinked. "My implants are back online. My augmentation is coming up too. It's going to take a minute for me to do a complete diagnostic and make sure that everything is working, but this is a good start. A *really* good start."

Jared walked over to the ancient plascrete wall. His heart was still racing from the prank his sister had played on them. He wasn't going to snap at her, even though he wanted to tear a long, bloody strip off her.

"I'm sorry," she said, her voice contrite. "I probably shouldn't have done that."

He rested his forehead against the cold stone and sighed. "It's not really that big of a thing, I suppose. I'm sure that I'll be laughing about this in a couple of months if we make it out of here."

Jared walked back over to the group. "I'll agree that Talbot has really been a bad influence on your sense of humor, though. Are you going to try this on him when he comes back? If so, I don't think he's going to take it nearly as well as we did."

She sighed. "No, he wouldn't. It was a bad idea, and I'm very sorry that I made anybody worry. If it's any consolation, my implants are fully back online, and my augmentation is as well. Error checking is complete, and it looks as if there are no ill effects. My medical nanites are back in business."

His sister stood slowly, as if she were still cautious of how her body was going to react. "It feels weird having everything back online. It's interesting how deeply I'd become used to the changes. I've been fully enhanced for several years now and never had to deal with normal human strength or the lack of all the augmentation. Now that it's been gone for a few days, it feels weird coming back."

Lily put a hand on Kelsey's shoulder. "You're going to want to take it easy for a couple of hours and let yourself get reacquainted with your augmentation. Right now, we're not in a life-and-death situation, so there's no need to push the envelope."

The doctor turned her attention to Jared. "Since Talbot is keeping watch, I suggest we do Julia next. Everyone else's augmentation is significantly less intrusive than theirs, so I'm not nearly as worried about possible side effects. Based on how long it took to get Kelsey done, I'm anticipating that I can have all of us back in operating order in a couple of hours."

"If we have that long," he said. "We took a chance doing this, because the inhabitants of the megacity could come looking for us at any time. Let's focus on doing as many people as we can, starting with the most critical. Julia next, then Talbot as soon as he gets here."

Kelsey stretched and then took a moment to put her sword harness back over her shoulders and grabbed her bow and quiver of arrows. "It should only take me a couple of minutes to get him headed your way. I'll stay at the guard post and keep an eye on things while you work on him."

Without waiting for a response, she took off at a jog. In moments, she was lost in the darkness of the tunnel. Only after she'd left did Jared realize that she hadn't taken a torch with her.

"How can she see in the dark?" he asked. "Doesn't she need at least some light to amplify?"

Carl shook his head. "Her ocular augmentation is capable of seeing in both infrared and ultraviolet. It's also capable of using a weak scanner signal to generate input for her to see even in something like this. She's not going to get colors, and it's not going to work well at any kind of a distance, but she'll be able to move around without tripping over anything. Marine Raiders are pretty damn capable."

Jared supposed they were. He'd seen his sister in action numerous times and still hadn't delved into the full nature of her augmentation.

It had taken her years to get past her resentment about what had been done to her. Now, she'd learned to take it in stride but still didn't talk about it much.

Lily went to work on Julia while he was thinking. Based on how long it had taken to get Kelsey operational again, it was likely that Talbot would be back just after they finished with his sister from another universe.

There might even be time to activate one other person's implants before the marine made his way back to the group. Since he was in charge, he vowed that was going to be him. He needed every advantage to figure out how they were going to get out of this mess.

* * *

TALBOT STOOD in the darkness at the center of the tunnel, facing in the direction of the city of Frankfort. Or where it would be if they weren't a hundred meters under it.

The torchlight only went out a short distance, and then everything was lost in the gloom, so he really wasn't sure what lay beyond what they'd already explored.

The tunnel had several offshoots, small chambers that contained equipment that he wasn't familiar with that at some point in the distant past had once served the dead city above them.

Perhaps it was for power distribution. He suspected that any kind of long-distance power transmission would need boosting so as not to degrade, but only somebody like Carl could actually determine what the junk had once been used for.

Clarice Beauchamp stood near him, her hand resting on the bow that she held wedged against her boot. How she'd be able to shoot anything in the utter darkness was beyond him. Still, her presence made him feel better. The only weapon he had was a sword that he wasn't that great using.

Yes, sword work was part of what his wife had taught him of the Art, the martial form used by the Marine Raiders for thousands of years. That didn't mean that he was any good at it yet. He wouldn't cut off his own arms or legs, but a skilled swordsman would still have him at a significant disadvantage.

It was his augmentation that would've made the real difference in a fight like that. Without it, he was a rank novice. In fact, he suspected that Beauchamp could beat him handily with the sword on her hip. His larger size would do nothing to offset her skill with the blade and her lifetime of training.

He wondered what tips she might be able to offer him and his wife for enhancing their training with weapons. He'd have to look into it if they survived the next few days.

"How far underneath the city do you think we'll be able to go before they know we're here?" he asked softly, worried about how far his voice would carry.

"I suspect that they already know we're here," she responded matter-of-factly. "They'll have heard the explosion. It's possible that they could've felt the vibration of our attack on the wall down here. They may not be precisely certain where it came from, but they're going to be looking around to make certain that they don't have unwelcome guests."

She turned toward Talbot and raised an eyebrow. "What do you plan to do when they find us?"

He shrugged slightly. "I suppose that depends on how they engage us. If they attack, we'll defend ourselves. If they want to talk, we'll talk. If it's something in between, we'll have to see what happens."

"Hey, you two," Kelsey said as she stepped out of the dark behind them. "Lily wants you, Talbot. You should both go back, I think. I have this covered."

His wife wasn't carrying a torch, so either she'd staggered through the dark, or her augmentation was back online. She'd taken the risk of the surgery.

Of course she had.

He turned to face her. "I assume your implants and augmentation are back online."

"I'm good, though I should probably be taking it easy today," she said. "The circumstances aren't going to cooperate, I'm sure."

"I could overhear you talking from a little way back. You're right to be worried about how the inhabitants are going to react to us. That's why we need to get your augmentation online as well.

"Julia should be done by the time you get there, so send her back to join me. Even relatively untrained, she'll help keep any incursion at bay while you guys prepare."

"Are you sure you're going to be okay alone?" he asked, putting a hand on her shoulder. "You just had brain surgery."

She smiled, pulled him into a hug, and kissed him on the lips. "I'm fine. Time is probably going to be short, so you need to get moving. Get your ass back there and make it happen."

He grinned at his wife and grabbed one of the torches. "Try not to have all the fun while I'm gone."

With that, he took off back toward where the rest were waiting at a jog with Clarice Beauchamp at his heels. Kelsey was right in that the clock was ticking. When it reached zero, things would get ugly.

With Julia's implants back online, she and Kelsey could hold here if the weapons arrayed against them were primitive and the number of enemies low enough. She certainly hoped so, because they were only going to get one shot at surviving what came next.

3

Julia blinked as consciousness returned. It felt as if she'd only gone to sleep a moment ago. She tried to sit up, but Doctor Stone put a hand on her shoulder.

"Just give it a second," the other woman said. "Everything went fine, but I want to give you time to gather yourself back together."

That made her frown slightly. Her double hadn't required any extra time to get herself together. Why was she getting a little extra cushion where Kelsey hadn't?

"What's going on?" she asked. "What happened?"

"Your implant hardware reacted a little bit more than Kelsey's did. You thrashed around a little, and I want to make sure that everything has settled down before you try to get up."

Julia blinked a little at that and then looked at the faces around her. Everybody seemed to be okay, so she must not have hurt anyone, but Carl Owlet had a slight bruise on his cheek. Had she struck him? Or perhaps just knocked him back to the ground while he attempted to hold her down?

"Did I hurt anyone?" she asked quietly.

"It's just a bruise," Carl said. "I rolled and took up most of the impact. Nobody has anything serious, so don't worry about it."

Julia closed her eyes. "I'm sorry about that."

She had no desire to harm anyone, but specifically, she *really* didn't want to hurt the scientist. Though she hadn't developed feelings for him—he was a married man after all—she was fond of him and intended to seek out his duplicate in her universe once she'd returned there. It was growing more likely by the day that his doppelgänger would be her consort if things played out the way she hoped.

After a few more beats, she sat up and began examining her implants and augmentation. As much as she loathed the things, she needed them. Especially now. They'd all need them in the weeks and months ahead if they were to survive this horrible planet.

Her implants were back online, and her augmentation indicated that it was functional as well. She could once again fight if forced to. She wasn't trained like her doppelgänger or Talbot, but she'd do what needed to be done.

She'd also do whatever she could to bring death and destruction to the horde for killing Scott Roche. They'd slaughtered him even as he'd saved her life after the big battle. His sacrifice would not go unavenged.

The rage sparked by her memory made her clench her fists. She wasn't a violent person, but for them, she'd make an exception. She'd see them all dead if she could arrange it.

Julia blinked away the red that had formed in her vision and sighed slightly. As much as she wanted to make the horde pay, the smart move would be to escape the area entirely. They had to get away so that they could get the override from the vaults underneath the Imperial Palace. Then they had to escape Terra, rejoin *Persephone*, and get out of the system.

She waved the others away and got to her feet. If there was another glitch, she didn't want to be responsible for harming anyone. Her balance was decent enough to get her to her feet.

"I'll go replace Talbot," she said. "Everything seems to be working the way it's supposed to. Since we're working with makeshift equipment and we'll be running into things he'll have to help fix, I suggest you bring Carl's implants online soon. That can only help us as we go forward."

"Are you feeling okay?" Mertz asked, his tone concerned.

It shamed her a little when she found herself again questioning his sincerity, even though she knew better. This version of Jared Mertz wasn't the Bastard from her universe, but she still couldn't get past how much he looked and sounded like the man who'd killed her father.

That made perfect sense, since the two were identical in a physical sense. She'd seen how willing this version of Jared Mertz was to make sacrifices for his people, how much the loss of every single one of them tore at his soul.

She knew he wasn't a monster, but that didn't make it any easier for her to treat him differently. The habits of a lifetime were hard to overcome in just a few months. She was trying, but she wasn't certain that she'd ever fully succeed.

"I'm fine," she said curtly. "Now stop wasting time. We don't know how much of it we have left."

Without allowing time for him to respond, she took off down the tunnel at a slow jog. That would allow her time to become accustomed to her augmentation again. Her balance felt odd, and she knew that it would adjust itself.

Sadly, her artificial eye was still dead. That was irritating, but she'd work with the partial blindness. It had been far more bewildering when she'd lost her real eye, so this was a lot less disorienting.

The dark tunnel suddenly became lit as her ocular augmentation in her natural eye began peering into it. Everything was shades of grey and somewhat indistinct. Not because of distance, but from imprecision in the data she was getting back from her surroundings. Her implants were compensating for the gaps in data by extrapolating everything she saw. It was kind of eerie.

She'd have thought that after so many years, the thought of those machines inside her head would stop bothering her, but the violation never got any easier to live with. It was like rape, only worse. Counseling helped, but she still had a long way to go.

Somehow, her doppelgänger had adjusted and embraced what

had happened to her. Julia thought that was most likely because the other woman hadn't fallen completely under the domination of the implants in her head. She hadn't become a Pale One. Her Jared Mertz had rescued her before that horrible fate had befallen her.

She supposed that there was nothing like being an unwilling passenger in your own body as it fought for its life against others, killing and maiming, to twist one's soul like it had done her.

Those thoughts consumed her until she passed Talbot and Beauchamp on their way back to the others. The man gave her a cheery wave but said nothing.

Her doppelgänger had fallen in love with the man and married him. Personally, she didn't see the attraction. Their tastes had somehow varied quite a bit over the last few years. Julia didn't want a warrior in her life, not like that. Someone like Carl Owlet would suit her tastes much better.

She finally saw her doppelgänger ahead, slowed, and made sure that the other woman was aware that she was coming. Kelsey had the honed reflexes of a trained warrior, and Julia absolutely did not want to trigger any kind of surprise in the woman.

Kelsey turned to face her as she came to a stop. "How are you feeling?"

Julia shrugged. "I'm torn. I hate the implants and augmentation, but we need them to survive this mess. It feels like I'm addicted to them, like they're some kind of drug. That's really hard for me to take."

"I'd tell you that it gets easier with time, but I'm not sure that's exactly right. It does get easier to deal with the hardware but not the kind of baggage that yours have brought along for the ride. I didn't suffer like you did, so it's easier for me to accept what they've done to me. How they've changed me.

"I know I've said this before, but I'm sorry about what the AIs did to you. It was a horrible, horrible thing, and it makes me feel guilty that I avoided the worst of it and that you didn't."

Somehow, the other woman always knew the right thing to say. It was like she could see into Julia's soul. She supposed that was literally true.

"What do we do now?" Julia asked, putting the uncomfortable conversation behind her.

"You have a decision to make," an unfamiliar voice said from farther up the tunnel.

In the blink of an eye, Julia had her bow in her hand and an arrow aimed up the tunnel. But there was no one to shoot. No one showed up in her enhanced vision.

Kelsey also had a bow out and took a step forward. "Who's there? Show yourself."

There was the rumble of stone grinding against stone. It came from far closer than Julia would've expected.

Barely twenty meters in front of them, part of the wall slid back from the tunnel and then to the side. From the opening stepped a man dressed in armor similar to that worn by the horde but not identical. His had bits of chain mail woven into it.

He was a young man, large, fit, and strong looking. His face was impassive as it considered them.

"My name is Jebediah, and you are trespassers in the city of Frankfort," he said coolly. "I call upon you to surrender. Do so or perish."

* * *

Kelsey observed the man for a moment and then turned her auditory augmentation up to the highest setting that it could go to. Now with the wall open, she could hear the breathing of others behind it. That noise would've been too soft for her to hear with the plug closed.

That was a clever hiding place, one where they could safely observe the tunnel. It was just her bad luck that Talbot and Beauchamp stopped almost directly in front of it.

She only had a few moments to make a decision, and that choice was going to dictate how they proceeded. If she rejected the man's offer to surrender, they would be committed to a fight to the death against an unknown number of people. People that apparently knew exactly where they were.

On the other hand, if she surrendered, then they'd once again be prisoners of people that might very well want to torture information out of them and then execute them. Maybe they wouldn't use immolation like the horde, but death was still death.

Was there a third option? There was no way to go back, even if they could get past the horde. The tunnel had been thoroughly and utterly collapsed behind them. They were trapped against a place with no exits.

Or maybe they weren't. There was always the possibility that even while this man was talking to her, others were waiting behind similar hidden doors and observing the rest of her party. If she rejected their offer, they might come swarming out and kill everyone in sight.

With a sigh, she set her bow on the ground slowly. "We surrender. I'm going to have to tell the rest so that they don't resist, but I'm not going to fight you."

For a moment, she thought Julia wasn't going to follow her lead, but the other woman closed her eyes and then set her bow on the ground as well, raising her hands above her head.

"You have chosen wisely," the man said. He gestured, and men came boiling out of the hiding place behind the wall. There were dozens of them.

Even with her augmentation, though she could have taken them in a straight-up fight, it was entirely possible that they could've maimed or even killed her in the fighting. Primitive weapons didn't necessarily mean that they weren't a threat.

The men quickly and efficiently stripped her of all her weapons and then bound her hands behind her back. It amused her that she could snap those bonds with just a moment's effort, but that was something that she wasn't going to reveal to them unless she had to. If things went badly, she still wanted that ace up her sleeve so that they could escape, given the opportunity.

Julia raised an eyebrow at her and submitted as well. She said nothing openly but sent a message through her implants.

Are you really *going to surrender to them?*

I don't see that we have any choice. If they've got another group waiting back where the rest are, they could kill everyone. I'm not going to take that chance. I've talked my way out of worse situations, and until we know that these people aren't as brutal as the horde, we're going to give them the benefit of the doubt.

Her doppelgänger made a slight shrug to indicate that she would follow along.

Once she was thoroughly trussed up, Jebediah stepped over and scrutinized her. "You wear horde armor, but you're not of the horde. Where do you come from?"

"A planet far from here," she said, looking up at the large man. "You wouldn't know the name of it. It wasn't very well known even before the rebellion. What are your intentions toward us?"

"I'll take you to my father. He rules this city and will make the ultimate decision about your fate, but the fact that you have surrendered means that you will not be executed. Allow me to congratulate you on your cool thinking and wise decision-making skills."

"Save your congratulations until I find out whether or not this really ends up being a good decision or not," she said grimly. "I might just have thrown us out of the frying pan into the fire."

The man inclined his head slightly. "My father finds himself curious as to your story and how you managed to cause so much damage to the horde city. If you tell a good tale, he'll likely show you some mercy."

"You mean he might let us go?"

The man shook his head. "No intruder is ever allowed to leave Frankfort. Yet there are different levels of duty that you may be required to serve, and your cooperation and storytelling skills may influence my father in making that decision. Consider that well before you speak too harshly to him. Or me.

"Now, take me to your companions. So long as they also surrender peacefully, no one needs to be harmed today."

Kelsey allowed the man to take her arm and guide her back down the tunnel toward where the rest were waiting. Even though she had an extended-range com built into her augmentation, only Carl had a matching set. She wouldn't be able to warn the others about what was coming.

Hopefully, Jared would see the logic in what she was doing and stop the rest from putting up a fight. If they didn't have cool heads, there might still be a slaughter today. If need be, she'd snap her bonds and fight with everything she had, but she was praying that cooler heads prevailed.

4

Carl felt nervous. Doctor Stone had insisted that she go through surgery after Talbot, and that meant that someone with very skilled hands had to perform the work.

That meant it had to be him. His scientific duties often required him to do extremely delicate work, and while he'd never performed surgery, he felt confident that the techniques he used would carry across well.

At least he certainly hoped so.

Once the doctor was out, he very carefully removed the sliver of bone from her skull and set it onto a sterile pad. He then reset her implants before using surgical glue to put the sliver of bone back into place and seal it up. Once that was done, he ran the regenerator over the incision until it looked well healed. He then removed the somatic stimulator, and her eyes opened.

"How are you feeling?" he asked softly.

"Good," she said. "My implants are online, and I can even interface with my medical equipment. Excellent work, Doctor Owlet. Congratulations on your first major surgery.

"Swap places. You're next, so show me one last time how the equipment generates the charge."

"I'll stick with my PhD, thanks," he said dryly. "I prefer less blood and brains when working."

He lay down and went to sleep as soon as she fitted the somatic stimulator. It only seemed like a moment later when his eyes blinked open.

Rather than say anything, he quickly checked his implants and found them operational once more. That was an incredible relief because he'd grown used to the things over the years and had so much research and information archived inside them.

The additions that he'd made to his hardware also allowed him to work on Imperial equipment much more easily than would be possible without them.

There was a message waiting for him, marked as extremely urgent. It was from Kelsey. She'd sent it seconds after his implants had come back to life.

She'd had to have been continuously checking to see if he was receiving to do that, and that probably meant it wasn't good news. He played the message.

Julia and I were ambushed, and I decided the best course of action was to surrender. It's the city residents. We're coming down the tunnel, but I'm slow-walking them. Get all the surgeries done that you can because they'll almost certainly confiscate the equipment. Tell Jared we need to surrender without resisting.

"We have a problem," he said even as he acknowledged the message. "Kelsey and Julia have been captured by the residents and are on their way back. She's moving slowly but says we have to surrender once they arrive. She said that if we can't get everyone's implants online before they get here, they're almost certainly going to confiscate our equipment."

The doctor abruptly gestured for Admiral Mertz to lie down. "Time permitting, we'll move on to Lieutenant Laird and the remaining two of the three amigos next."

The three amigos were himself, Ralph Halstead, and Austin Darrah. Together, the three of them had overlapping scientific, computer, and technological skills that could potentially work miracles on any equipment that they found.

Carl wished that they could get everybody's implants back online, but with time working against them, there was only so much they could do.

Once Admiral Mertz was done, they moved on to Lieutenant Laird and got her back online. While she didn't have Raider augmentation, she was a trained marine, and that would undoubtedly prove useful going forward.

Ralph Halstead and Austin Darrah were next and quickly done. That left four people remaining: Commodore Meyer, Commander Cannon, Elise Orison, and Olivia West.

"No one make any hasty movement," Kelsey said from up the tunnel. "If you have a weapon in your hand, put it aside. Stand still and raise your hands over your heads."

Carl raised his hands. Since he had no weapons worth mentioning, he left them in the sheaths. No doubt the enemy would strip them from him.

A few moments later, a group of men pushed Kelsey into the torchlight. When they ascertained that no one was holding a weapon, they came forward in pairs and bound everyone's hands behind their backs. Once that was done, they stripped away every single weapon that they possessed.

Once again, they were prisoners. Hopefully, these new people wouldn't be as bad as the horde. He supposed he'd find out. It wasn't exactly as if they had a choice in the matter.

* * *

As TALBOT SURRENDERED, he took a good look at their captors. They were dressed like the horde fighters but didn't seem inclined to cause casual pain like the plain's dwellers.

His questioning at the hands of the crazy woman at the camp where Julia had rescued them came to mind. She'd had her men beat him and threatened to use a hot iron to brand him while telling him how she'd torture and kill everyone while he watched. She'd taken great pleasure in telling him so.

These people didn't seem to have the same worldview, and that was better than nothing.

There was no sign that they had any higher technology on them. No flechette pistols, no plasma weapons, and no stunners. They were seemingly just as primitive as the horde or Captain Beauchamp's people.

Once his hands were bound behind him, he allowed them to herd him together with the rest. He did manage to work his way over to his wife. He looked at the man standing next to her.

"She's my wife. May I speak to her?"

The man considered his words and then nodded. "Speak loudly enough that I may overhear. I have no interest in your personal business. My only concern is to make certain that you are not attempting to escape."

If he'd wanted to speak in a way that they couldn't hear, he'd have used his implants. He didn't have her long-range com, but his internal unit was good for a dozen meters without amplification.

This conversation was as much for their captors' benefit as it was for his own. If they were going to survive this, they needed their captors to see them as people. People that had something to offer when the time came and weren't the kind of threat that they needed to do anything strenuous to restrain.

"Are you okay?" he asked.

"They offered me a chance to surrender before they presented themselves, so I didn't overreact," she said. "Not that I suspect they would've taken me as much of a threat in any case."

"That's only because they don't know you as well as I do," he said with a slight smile.

Having said that, he didn't try to maintain his appearance of humor. Their situation was still grave, even if he didn't think it was immediately dangerous.

The man in charge had them bound together by a single rope and led them down the tunnel. Some of the others picked up all of the gear that he and his people had transported so far and brought it behind them. No doubt some of it would cause raised eyebrows and prompt pointed questions.

Operational technology would have to be scarce in a place like this. Still, living with even nonfunctional technology all around would make it obvious to them what kind of things he and his friends had in their packs.

He started to say something else to Kelsey, but she shook her head. "Just let it be, Talbot. We'll find out soon enough what they've got to say. I'm tired. It seems like we've been running for days. Maybe once they lock us up, I can take a nice long nap."

He had to admit that sounded good. The last week had involved a lot of hard riding and very little sleep. If they had a chance to eat and rest, that would be helpful.

The group moved along in silence for a while, and then he saw the opening in the wall ahead of them. He had no idea how he'd missed seeing something like that. It was inside the range of the torches that he'd leaned against the walls.

He eyed the door as they went through it and into the unknown portion behind the tunnel wall. Someone had gone to a lot of trouble to make a segment of wall on tracks that fit very tightly into the hole like a plug in a bottle. There must've been a seam, but without his enhanced ocular augmentation, he'd missed it.

That was sloppy and annoying. If Talbot had been writing his own efficiency reports, he'd ding himself for it hard.

Behind the fake wall was a series of tunnels that led away from the one they'd been traveling down. Unlike the abandoned one leading toward the horde city, this one showed signs of traffic. The dust on the floor had been disturbed numerous times, so it was probably an observation post where the city inhabitants kept an eye on the tunnel leading toward the horde.

Even though the larger tunnel had been plugged for decades or even centuries, it seemed that they still worried that the horde would try to sneak into the city through it. Considering how ugly the rulers of the horde and their warriors were, Talbot couldn't blame them.

Do you really think you can sweet-talk them? he asked Kelsey over their implants.

I'm not sure. No matter how we play this, they have the cards to trump us right now. We need to know more about them before we can make any decisions about how much to say or whether we need to fight or not.

Talbot grunted slightly in response. Everything she'd said made sense, but he hated being under someone else's control. These people might be just as monstrous as the horde but in a completely different way.

He supposed it didn't matter. Kelsey was the one calling the shots, and Admiral Mertz would back her up. So would he, for that matter. At this point, they were prisoners, so it didn't hurt hearing what their captors had to say. If nothing else, they might learn a little bit about what was happening in the area.

It was disconcerting realizing that they might never get to the Imperial Palace or access the vaults below it. Or if they did, it would either be with the help of the people now holding them prisoner or over their objections.

They reached a set of stairs and started upward. No matter what happened, they'd have their answers soon enough, he supposed. He might as well be patient and see if they got some good news for a change.

The thought of good luck almost made him chuckle. That wasn't their way. He'd just have to see what flavor of bad luck came their way. Then they'd figure out a way to overcome it.

5

Jared used the time that it took to climb the many stairs to figure out exactly how he was going to approach this situation. He had no idea how the locals were going to question them yet, but he knew the general approach that he intended to take. Everyone on this world hated the AIs. They hated the things that had destroyed their civilization.

If he could turn that hatred around so that these people became his allies rather than his enemies, that would be the best outcome. It would have to be done delicately, but he could at least start the conversation. The horde had doubted their story, according to what Talbot had said. Doubt was probably a mild word for what the horde had actually felt, honestly.

Now they'd have a chance to reframe the conversation, and he didn't want to waste it. Whatever he said, he had to make the most of this one opportunity.

While he had no augmentation like Kelsey, Talbot, and Julia, climbing the stairs didn't tire him as much as he'd expected. All of the riding had toughened his legs. If they got away from the city, he imagined that they'd all be tougher by the time they reached the Imperial Palace.

The stairs eventually let out into a large room that seemed to occupy the center of one of the buildings. Based on the height above their surroundings, Jared believed they were near the top of the building. There were large windows all around with what had likely once been a stunning view of Frankfort. Even in its ruined state, the city still commanded his attention.

He'd never been to a city like this before, but the recording of the building in Imperial City gave him a frame of reference. Even so, this structure had a way to go to reach even half that height.

The room was set out much like the throne room back on Avalon. This was where the ruler of the city received visitors or passed judgments. Based on what he'd heard about these people, he'd wager they didn't get many visitors, so this was where they conducted their internal pomp and circumstance.

The large room was devoid of decoration. The view of the ruined megacity seemed to be all the splendor these people needed. Contrary to his expectations, the room was spotless. No dirt or dust lay anywhere, and the glass was so clean that it sparkled.

He could see how they'd clean the inside, but getting to the outside of a building this high had to be terribly dangerous. Why risk someone's life just to clean the glass for this one room?

Jared turned his attention to the spot where the guards were taking them. There was no throne, only a large dais that held a table, behind which a single man sat. He was older, with a lined face and hair almost entirely white. He wasn't dressed overly formally, and the clothes he wore didn't seem ceremonial.

The man also didn't have anything on his head. No crown or circlet. No decoration of any kind from what Jared could see. Whatever his authority, he didn't feel the need for regalia to emphasize it.

In addition to the man, dozens of others stood along the circumference of the room. Men and women watched suspiciously as Jared and his people were led to the center of the room and stopped directly in front of the table.

Their captors lined them up so that they were all equally distant from the table. Then they stood behind them while the older man leaned forward and steepled his fingers as his eyes roved over each of them. He finally settled on Jared, and his eyes narrowed.

"I must admit that I have many questions as to how you came to be inside my city, but I think I will start my questioning with a simple and straightforward request. Do not lie to me. Whatever happens next is entirely within my discretion. Honesty and full disclosure will serve you best. Which of you is the leader of this group?"

"I am," Jared said before Kelsey could open her mouth. If things went badly, he wanted to make certain that she was as shielded as possible from the consequences. The more he could keep her to the shadows and not have her suspected of having more capability than she did, the better their options if they had to try something dangerous.

The man nodded slightly. "So I had believed. You may call me Leader Mordechai. Who are you?"

Jared thought about it for a moment and then took a single step forward. The guards didn't react. It seemed that so long as he didn't do anything rash, he had a little freedom of action.

"My name is Jared Mertz, and my title is Admiral. Before we get started with the discussion of who I serve, I want to make it absolutely and perfectly clear that I do not serve the computers that rule the Empire now. My people and I are here to overthrow them."

If his words threw the man off, it wasn't apparent at a glance. The older man simply stared at him, saying nothing.

"An interesting assertion," the man finally allowed. "And one wrought with danger for you. You claimed to have come from another world, according to my son. Considering the amount of damage that was dealt to the horde city, I'm certainly willing to entertain that statement.

"However, it's much more likely that you serve the computers and that you're here on some nefarious task. If so, your escape from the horde city will not save you. To work with the computers is death. Our penalties are perhaps not as draconian as those of the horde, but you can rest assured that they're just as final."

The man leaned forward, his expression severe. "I suggest that you measure your next words very carefully, Admiral Mertz. The story you tell will set the stage for what comes next."

Jared knew that he was taking a horrible risk. He could've made up some kind of story and maybe spared their lives, but then they'd be prisoners here, unable to complete their mission.

Yes, they might be able to escape later, but he'd rather find allies in this task, much like Clarice Beauchamp. In fact, she might be able to assist him in telling his tale.

He glanced toward the woman but decided this wasn't the right time to bring her into the conversation. He led off with his own story.

"About a week ago, the AI—the artificial intelligence—destroyed my ship, and our small craft crashed into the surface of this world. Perhaps your people saw something of that?"

The man nodded. "Our sentries did see a streak of fire coming from the heavens. You claim that was you arriving?"

"Yes. We came to Terra to retrieve something from the Imperial Palace that will help us overthrow the AIs. Our world was founded before the fall of the Empire, but crown prince Lucian retreated there during the final battles of the rebellion.

"He led us in recovering and gave us a message that brought us back to Terra five centuries later. The computers don't know that we exist. We're just too small for them to be aware of yet. But they *are* learning.

"As soon as we landed on Terra, we were caught up in the local fighting. It seemed that several groups were intent on retrieving the pinnaces that we came down to the surface in. They were too damaged to fly, but there were a lot of supplies in them."

He gestured toward Clarice. "Captain Beauchamp and her group of fighters arrived first. My oldest sister convinced her—at least preliminarily—that we were telling the truth. Enough so that her people were escorting us back to their outpost for further questioning when the horde overwhelmed us.

"They killed hundreds of my people and all of Captain Beauchamp's soldiers. Altogether, we had almost three hundred people, and those of us that stand before you are all that remain."

The man leaned back in his chair, slightly considering the group with a sweep of his eyes. "Captain Beauchamp, my people are at least somewhat familiar with yours. Your people have no love for the computers or the humans they control, yet you helped these strangers. Why?"

Beauchamp cleared her throat. "While it remained for my leaders to vet the truth of what they said, there was something about them that convinced me that they were telling me the truth. His people fought hard to save my people when we were outnumbered three to one in an initial skirmish. They revealed lost technology in a way that only an idiot would.

"I have to assume that they weren't trying to conceal their advantages because they had no idea what the consequences of revealing it were. That convinced me personally that they were telling the truth."

Jared couldn't argue with the logic of what the woman had said. What they were doing sounded insane. The people of Terra killed the servants of the AIs. He was taking a terrible risk in telling the truth, but he didn't think that he had a choice. Lies weren't going to help them now.

Mordechai considered him for a few moments and then shrugged. "I'm obviously going to have to consider your words most carefully. This isn't the time to make rash decisions."

The man that had overseen their capture stepped up behind Mordechai and whispered in his ear. The older man listened and frowned slightly.

"My son tells me that you were doing something to your people. You were cutting into their heads? Explain."

Jared had hoped that Kelsey had delayed them long enough so that none of the locals saw them reactivating the implants. That hope was obviously dashed.

"When we were fighting the horde, they used a weapon against us," Jared said. "We have equipment inside of our bodies that allow us to interface with computers and perform other work as well as store information. We were resetting that equipment so that it worked again."

"And how many of your people have these devices inside of you?" Mordechai asked.

"All of us, though some have not had theirs reactivated. The implants are similar to what the rebels used to turn humanity, but ours are protected against that sort of thing. Since the enemy uses them, we must use them as well to equal the fight."

"I see," the older man said. "Step over here so that I may see what you're talking about."

With a mental shrug, Jared stepped forward and pulled his hair slightly back, revealing the small shaved area behind his ear. With Doctor Stone's work with the portable regenerator, the scar there was probably barely noticeable.

The man probed it with his finger. "And this was done today? It looks as if it has healed for weeks."

"We have a device that is capable of speeding healing. If you'd like to see the process, I'd be more than happy to have our doctor demonstrate it for you. If you have injured, she might be able to treat them for you as well."

"You said that you had restored this machinery for most of you. Who remains yet to be done?"

Jared pointed at Sean, Commander Cannon, Elise, and Olivia.

"At this point, it won't hurt to allow you to finish the process, and it may provide me with information that helps me make a better decision about your fate. Proceed."

It took a couple of minutes for Lily and Carl to get the equipment that they needed from the guards, but once they did, it was a relatively quick and straightforward task to perform the reactivation surgery on each of the four that hadn't already received it.

In turn, each person went to sleep, had their implants reset, and then woke up—all under the close observation of Jebediah and his guards, as well as Leader Mordechai.

When the process was complete, the older man shook his head. "I've heard stories about some of the old technology and how it could do such miraculous things. Even seeing it with my own eyes, it's difficult to believe. What do these implants do for you?"

"That's a long story," Jared said. "One I'm certainly willing to tell, but my people and I have been running hard for a week and have suffered great losses. Is it possible that we could get something to eat and perhaps rest so that I can give you my best effort?"

Mordechai nodded to his son. "Take them to an appropriate place and guard them well. See that they are brought food, water, and allowed to bathe."

The younger man nodded and then started the guards herding everyone toward the stairs. They hadn't taken more than fifteen steps when there was a bright flash of light from outside the building. It was blinding enough to capture everyone's attention, and all turned toward it curiously.

"Kinetic strike!" Kelsey shouted. "Everybody down now! Cover your heads and faces!"

Jared had just thrown himself to the floor and covered his head with his arms and hands when the windows blew in. However durable they were meant to be, they weren't up to the task of stopping the shock wave.

The AI had finally decided to act. If Jared was right, it had just destroyed the two crashed pinnaces. The only positive to the situation was that the camp had probably been swarming with horde warriors. Maybe the AI would think it had killed them there.

Yeah, as if they were ever that lucky.

6

Julia felt shattered glass lash across her primitive armor. If she hadn't been protected, she was very much afraid that she might've been seriously injured. She certainly hoped that no one else in the city was going to be badly hurt but knew that outcome was extremely unlikely.

After a few moments, the air grew still, and the cries of the frightened and injured could be heard more clearly. She raised her head and looked around the room to find utter devastation.

All of the glass in the walls had blown out—on all four sides of the building—shattered by the shock wave from the kinetic strike. No single pane was in one piece. Many of the people closest to the strike had been killed or gravely injured.

Thankfully, the majority of the injuries elsewhere in the room would be less severe. That didn't reduce the gravity of the situation, but it did make the number of wounded people they were dealing with significantly lower than it could've been.

Julia leapt to her feet and raced to the area nearest the kinetic strike. Off in the distance, she could see a cloud of debris boiling into the sky. There was no longer any bright light, but it looked like a massive bomb had gone off.

In fact, one had.

When someone struck the ground with a tungsten rod weighing hundreds of kilograms moving at orbital velocity, it was more than enough to create the equivalent of a nuclear explosion.

She focused her attention on the people moaning around her. She had no medical training at all, but she could see that many of them were beyond help.

Before she could decide what needed to be done, Doctor Stone was standing beside her. The woman didn't seem disturbed by the amount of blood and death, though Julia knew that probably wasn't true. She just had better training to wall it away.

Stone started pointing at various people. "Get these folks over into the center of the room. Someone sweep an area clear of glass. I'll need my medical equipment set out for me. Carl, get it laid out."

The doctor turned to Julia. "Be as careful as you can, but get them there as quickly as possible."

Even as Julia was picking up the first person, a woman with her arm missing below the elbow, Kelsey and Talbot were there helping get others. With her augmented strength, lifting a single human being and carrying them carefully to where they needed to be was no strain at all.

Others were assisting even though they didn't have Marine Raider strength. Even their captors were following instructions and moving people as indicated.

Julia had very little time to see exactly what Doctor Stone was doing, but the woman had a small circle of observers as she used her equipment to staunch bleeding and save lives. Leader Mordechai, his son Jebediah, and several others were observing her actions, getting themselves bloody while helping as directed.

The guards had reformed and were watching the exits, so there would be no escape. There might have been a few minutes during the chaos that her party could have gotten out of the room, but no one had run. They'd stayed to help.

She certainly hoped that made a difference in how the locals treated them.

Once she'd finished moving the most seriously injured, she walked over to stand beside Jebediah as people that looked like healers had arrived to take his and his father's places.

"There will be other injured," she said. "You need to bring them here so that Doctor Stone can take care of the most seriously wounded. Or take her to where you're working on them, probably."

The large man considered her, his expression blank. "I don't know that we can trust you. My father seems inclined to allow you an opportunity to earn that trust, but I find myself doubting your story."

Before she could respond, Mordechai arrived and put his hand on Jebediah's shoulder. "My son is my chief of security. It's his job to be skeptical of everything that he sees or hears. I shall not gainsay him in this matter, but I will allow you to prove your willingness to help.

"We already have people scouring the city, looking for injured. It's going to take quite some time to get everyone to a central, protected location, but it will be done. Meanwhile, I find myself with more questions. First, what is your name?"

Julia considered telling him the truth, that she was Kelsey Bandar, but decided that no matter how honest they were being, some things wouldn't be believed. The fact that she was Kelsey's duplicate from another universe was a little bit outside the scope of the story they were telling. It would be far better to stick with the story of being twins.

"I'm Julia Bandar. You've undoubtedly seen that my older sister and I are twins. She's also the more experienced of the two of us."

It was galling to have to admit that her doppelgänger was more experienced, but it was something that she couldn't argue with. Kelsey had the air of someone who'd done far more than Julia had. Experience had left its mark on her.

The older man nodded. "Twins are not that unusual, but neither are they commonplace. You and your sister seem to have significantly more strength than I would have expected of someone of your... slight build. Explain that to me."

Well, that was going to be a lengthy explanation and one that had the potential to see them all in very deep trouble. No matter what Julia said, she was going to have to be truthful yet circumspect.

"A few years ago, I was captured by forces under the control of the

AIs. I had none of the implants that Admiral Mertz has spoken of before then. Also, everything that was done to me was done against my will and at extreme personal cost."

The man's eyes dwelt on hers for long seconds before he nodded. "I can see the shadows of the pain in your eyes. For the moment, let's say that I believe everything that you've told me. How does that explain the great strength that you've shown today?

"I've just watched you pick up person after person, some of them weighing almost twice what you do. You showed no signs that this even inconvenienced you. How is that possible?"

Julia gestured toward her head. "All of us have computer enhancements inside our brains. They've been modified so that we cannot be taken over by the computers, but the hardware is similar.

"Without a frame of reference, it's difficult to explain precisely what it does. Let's just say that it allows us to process information significantly faster than we were able to do before and in much more comprehensive detail. It also allows us to interface with technology that was built by the Old Empire.

"Unlike most of us, because I was captured by the enemy and transformed, I have significantly greater physical augmentation than you would believe, I think. So do my sister and her husband. None of the rest has anything like this. It's not common.

"One of the benefits of this change is that I have artificial muscles woven through my biological ones. They grant me significantly more strength than you'd believe possible.

"Picking up the injured and moving them is just one example. I can also run faster and jump higher than anyone you've ever seen. As difficult as it is to believe, the equipment inside my body was designed to turn someone into one of the premier warriors of the Old Empire."

Mordechai pursed his lips. "We've heard tales of such. Fantastic warriors that had abilities far beyond those of us with normal bodies. Marine Raiders, they were called. Is this what you speak of?"

Julia nodded. "Yes. I never received any training to be anything like that, but that's the kind of hardware that's inside my body. It seems that when the AIs rebelled against the Empire, they took whatever civilians they could catch and forced them to become horrific fighting machines. They used the Marine Raider template to manage that."

She thought about it for a moment and then asked a question of her own. "If you don't mind my asking, what have you heard about the Marine Raiders? How is that possible when they all must've died out centuries ago?"

The man waved his hand dismissively. "That's a long story. We're going to have plenty of time to get to know one another, and I'll share it with you at some point. I appreciate your candor, and in exchange, I will warn you not to attempt to escape.

"Do not mistake the goodwill you have earned for clemency. While I'm forming an opinion of you and your people, I'm not yet swayed. Take things slowly, because rushing might mean unfortunate things happening to you and your friends."

That wasn't the news that Julia had wanted to hear, but it beat being told they were being turned into slaves without a hearing. Even having told him her secret, that didn't mean that he fully understood the scope of what a Marine Raider could do. That organization had been *very* secretive about its capabilities and methods.

"What happened to the horde city when we escaped?" she asked. "I seem to get the impression that there was a significant disruption of some kind. Those people killed hundreds of our comrades. I hope we caused them some pain in return."

"You lost friends," Jebediah said, his voice low. "I can hear your rage, though you try to hide it. Allow me to compliment you on the quality of your enemies. The horde is a blight upon the face of Terra. Come with me."

He led her to the far side of the room and gestured for her to look out. They could only get so close because the wind raging outside the building was a real danger. A fall from this height would kill her just as surely as being at the site of the kinetic strike.

Below her, she could see other buildings that had suffered from the blast wave. Off to her right, she could see the wall of the horde city and its makeshift buildings. It seemed to have taken some damage from the kinetic strike as well, but the most noticeable difference was the *large* pit in the center of the city.

Where the palace had once stood, there was now devastation. It looked as if the cavern that Kelsey had collapsed had drawn it in. The death toll was probably hideous.

The thought made her smile coldly.

"It couldn't have happened to nicer people," she murmured. "You're right about me hating them. They killed one of my closest friends. If I could slit all their throats, I'd do it. My sister wouldn't understand, but I'm thirsty for their blood."

Jebediah turned his head and examined her closely before nodding slowly. "That's the first thing one of you has said that I don't doubt at all. The horde is filled with those willing to torture and kill. The fact that they live so close to Frankfort sickens me. If we had the forces to do so, I would drive them from this place."

He gestured with his chin for her to turn back. "It's time for you to return to your fellows. We will take you to a place where you may rest and recover from your arduous fight. Your doctor will be returned to you unharmed as soon as she has finished her work. You have my word."

Julia had to admit that she could use the rest. Without her augmentation, she was exhausted. Now with it activated, she was feeling refreshed but famished.

"I don't suppose we could ask for some food. It galls me to say, but I eat like a horse, and I'm starving."

The large man smiled slightly. "I will see that each of you is given as much to eat as you desire. The quality is perhaps not as fine as you're used to, but I assure you it is filling and will sate your hunger."

"That's all a girl can ask for."

While they hadn't escaped the trouble all around them, she had to leave tomorrow's problems for tomorrow. None of them had died, so this would have to be chalked up as a win. Once they'd had some sleep, perhaps they'd be able to talk their way into better accommodations or convince their captors that they might be able to work together to further their mutual ends.

She wouldn't be doing the talking when it came to that, but she was confident that Mertz and Kelsey could sway the old man given enough time. He seemed relatively reasonable, all things considered.

It would have to do.

She joined the others and allowed the guards to lead her away.

7

Once the prisoners had been taken away, and the situation seemed to be in hand, Mordechai returned to his office under the city. As he walked, he considered his new prisoners and the events that had impacted his city today.

As spies went, these people were—at best—incompetent. Not only had they failed to sneak into the area they were supposed to observe, they'd gotten into several large-scale fights with the horde and been massacred.

Then, to escape the horde, they'd used Imperial weapons and destroyed the horde palace, along with the treasure vault underneath the city. He had no idea how many of the ruling class there had been killed, but the number must be significant.

The horde was still roiling and trying to establish new leadership. That seemed to be a bloody process. With any luck, the most powerful factions would be bled dry, and the horde would be crippled for decades to come.

While decisive, that blow apparently hadn't been the goal of the group that he'd captured. All they'd been trying to do was recover some of their equipment and escape. So what did they do next?

They'd walked right into his trap. Not only that, they'd also surrendered immediately.

They then proceeded to tell him all of their deepest secrets. The woman he'd spoken to had to have suspected that the type of implanted hardware she was speaking of was an automatic death sentence. Yet she made no effort to conceal… anything.

As crazy as it sounded, he believed them. He wasn't certain what their real goals were, because they hadn't been very specific, but even the destruction of their vessels by the AI lent credence to their words.

If the AI was trying to slip people into the local population, it could've come up with a far better plan than what he was seeing. No. Whoever they were, whatever they were hoping to accomplish, they didn't work for the AI.

Minutes after he'd arrived in his spartan office, a knock brought him out of his reverie. Jebediah stepped through the door and took a seat without being asked. One of the prerogatives of being his son.

"I believe them," Jebediah said without preamble.

Mordechai raised an eyebrow. It was his son's job to be suspicious of *everything*. He was the one always spouting conspiracy theories and plots that had to be foiled. He saw shadows lurking just around every corner.

And, sometimes, they were even there.

Such a statement from a professional paranoiac was… notable.

He leaned forward and smiled slightly. "Did one of them perhaps slip you a drink spiked with some type of drug? Surely this cannot be my Jebediah, the man who trusts nothing and no one."

His son's face flushed red. "I understand that I'm not usually so gullible, but after having spoken with Julia, I don't think that they mean us harm. As insane as their story sounds, I believe that it's true. They've come to Terra on some type of mission to harm the computers.

"We'll need to question them more deeply to find out for certain that they aren't pulling the wool over our eyes, but at this point, I doubt that they're working in the best interests of the machines."

"I'm inclined to agree," Mordechai said. "This is not a group of warriors. Those most enhanced to do the fighting seem ill suited to do so."

The two of them discussed everything that they'd seen and heard. Mordechai focused on the story of Julia, the woman captured by merciless computers and forcibly implanted with their hardware.

It was an interesting tale. If only three of the people that they'd caught had full combat enhancements, the twins made no sense. If the intent was to fool someone into thinking that they were harmless, it made for poor policy to immediately reveal your capabilities at the first crisis, particularly when you weren't actually attacking anyone.

He had mentioned the Marine Raiders to her, and she'd known what he was talking about. His information about them came down through stories. A group of Marine Raiders had once been stationed here in Frankfort. After the rebels struck the Empire down, the Raiders had acted as guerrilla warriors to cause harm to the invaders.

Sadly, they didn't last for more than a few decades. One day, they went out on a mission and never returned. Undoubtedly, they'd been slain somewhere in a desperate fight.

His grandmother had told him many stories about those men. Some of the incredible feats they'd been capable of and some of the modifications that had been done to their bodies to make them the premier warriors of the Empire.

He could hardly envision a woman as small as Julia being capable of that type of mayhem. Or her sister, for that matter. Frankly, the one called Kelsey seemed to be the more forward of the two. If one of them had the enhancements of a Marine Raider, it would be Kelsey.

Julia made no sense. She asserted that she wasn't a warrior, and Mordechai was more than comfortable in accepting that as truth.

"I want you to get to know these people better," he told Jebediah. "I don't know if I fully believe their story, but I've heard enough to allow them the opportunity to try and convince me further."

He smiled a little shrewdly. "They seem to have a mixture of people. Their doctor obviously has true Imperial medical skills. Some of their people seem like they are technicians or mechanics of some kind. Show them some of the malfunctioning equipment and see if they can assist in restoring it. That way, we learn something about both them and the old technology."

Jebediah nodded. "I'll see to it. What of their leader?"

"Leave him to me. As one leader to another, we shall speak. You focus on the twins. If they're deceiving us in any way, your suspicious nature will be our tripwire. While we may hope that they tell the truth, it's wiser to plan for finding out that this is all some kind of trick."

"If it's a trick, they're going to wish they'd never tried it," Jebediah said grimly.

* * *

KELSEY SLEPT FITFULLY and woke groggy. Now that her implants were reactivated, her need for sleep had been reduced, but her body was confused. She didn't blame it. Her head felt like it was stuffed full of cobwebs.

The "cells" that they'd been placed in were of significantly better quality and spaciousness than she'd expected. Over the years, she'd been locked up in a wide variety of locales, and this one certainly didn't rank near the bottom of that list.

That wasn't to say that they were free to roam about. They weren't. They'd been taken deep underground and placed in a series of rooms behind some substantial doors. She wasn't sure what the original purpose of this area had been, but it was more than sufficient to keep them penned in.

She had no doubt that she could force one of the doors. But it was only the first of several. They'd hear her, and then she'd walk into a lot of trouble. Common sense told her that they were taking her capabilities seriously and that she just needed to wait.

At least the area had a bathing room with large containers of water and what looked like a gas heater with some kind of vent to take away the fumes. It had been a *long* time since she'd cleaned up, and she'd been too tired last night to take advantage of the situation.

She considered waking Talbot up and having him join her, but that would probably lead to other things, and that wasn't going to be happening in such a public location. The tub was in a small side room blocked off by a curtain made of some type of woven material. Everyone could hear what happened in there, and anyone could walk in at any time.

There was a second room further up in the suite where a primitive toilet was secreted behind a similar curtain. That kept the smell down to a manageable level, but she imagined it was going to have to be emptied regularly to keep the rooms from smelling like a pigsty.

When she had the tub full of hot water, she found what passed for soap and began stripping off her clothes. She'd gotten about halfway through that when the curtain slid aside, and Julia stepped into the room.

The other woman froze and then started to back out, but Kelsey gestured for her to come forward, not bothering to hide her body from the other woman. "I haven't got anything that you haven't quite literally seen many times before. The tub is big enough for both of us, so let's not waste the water."

The other woman stood there, her eyes wide, for a moment. "How can you be okay with getting naked in front of *everybody*?"

Kelsey chuckled. "When you have no choice but to armor up in front of marines, you pick up their habits. They don't segregate by biology, so you lose your body modesty pretty fast. Once you get used to it, it's not so bad. Nobody is staring at you. They've got their own things to be doing. And even if someone does take a peek, what harm is there?"

She finished stripping off her clothes and slid into the hot water. It felt *wonderful*.

While her doppelgänger continued to struggle with the idea of taking her clothes off in front of her, she started lathering up. Perhaps it would help the other woman if she couldn't see anything.

Julia sighed, turned her back, and started stripping off her clothes. Even though the other woman had been through a full sequence of regeneration, Kelsey knew Julia had been chewed up pretty hard. There were no scars now, no real injuries, other than the artificial eye. Lily Stone knew her business.

Then it occurred to her that from the way that Julia was moving, she had a blind side. Her mechanical eye hadn't been reparable, at least in the short time they'd had with tools.

She made a mental note to have Carl do something about that if he could. That might not be possible, but she owed it to the other woman to try.

Moments later, Julia was in the tub, and Kelsey handed her the soap. The other woman took it gratefully and began lathering up.

"I saw you talking with Jebediah while we were helping the injured," Kelsey said. "He was listening to what you were saying, and I think you might've formed a connection with him. Tell me about it."

Her doppelgänger shrugged. "There's not much to say. He asked me how I could be so strong, and I explained how the computer had captured me and forcibly implanted the Marine Raider augmentation inside me.

"He said they already knew what Marine Raiders were, just based on tales told by the older generations. Since you and Talbot were busy showing off your own strength, I told him that you were the other members of our team that had augmentation. I stuck with the story that we were twins simply because it's a lot easier to understand than the truth."

"That works," Kelsey said as she started washing off. "You were looking out the other side of the building toward the horde city. What did you see?"

"It looked like there was fighting taking place, and Jebediah said that there was some type of power struggle to replace the leadership, so maybe they won't be looking for us for a while."

Kelsey smiled at that. She hated the horde as much as anyone, but she knew that Julia loathed them. There was a kind of bloodlust in her that Kelsey had never developed. It was somewhat worrying, but in this case, she thought it was understandable. Perhaps even laudable.

"What do you think the best course of action is that we can take to make friends with these people?" Kelsey asked as she began lathering her hair.

Julia shrugged and followed suit. "Be honest. The truth will serve us better than some story. Other than the fact that I'm you from another universe, the truth is the best story that we can tell.

"Then that's what we'll do," Kelsey said right before she ducked her head under the surface of the water.

Once her hair was thoroughly rinsed out, she climbed out of the tub, grabbed a rough towel from where they were stacked nearby, and wrapped it around her hair. In consideration of her doppelgänger's body modesty issues, she turned her back as she dried off with another towel. Then she dressed once more.

They'd have to see about getting their clothes washed. Hers smelled, and she felt dirty again almost immediately. Now that she'd cleaned up, she could smell her stink in the cloth. Perhaps they could get some clothes from their captors. She'd have to ask.

By the time she was done, Julia was out of the tub and drying off with her back turned.

Once they were both ready, Kelsey gestured toward the curtain. "Let's wake Jared and Talbot. They can clean up, and then we'll go see what our captors have to say. The sooner we start forming bonds with these people, the sooner we can be on our way to the Imperial Palace. And the sooner we can get off this damned planet."

8

J ared sat up when Kelsey woke him, rubbing his eyes. The bed that he'd slept in wasn't anything to scream about by Imperial standards, but it beat the hell out of the ground. The past week had certainly taught him that.

Even with the thin cushions that they'd recovered from the horde, sleeping on the ground was brutally hard on one's body, particularly when their medical nanites were disabled.

He gratefully took advantage of the hot water to bathe and was exceptionally pleased when Elise joined him. That made the bath take a little more time than it should have, but they didn't hog it for unduly long, as hanky-panky was out of the question. While rank had its privileges, he didn't want to be standing between the rest and being clean for longer than he had to.

Even though Kelsey had been urging them to get ready and go out and meet their captors as soon as possible, Jared insisted that everyone get a chance to bathe first. He didn't know exactly what his plans were going to be, but he didn't want to be rushed into them.

Lily still hadn't returned. He wasn't shocked at that. With the sheer scale of the carnage, it had to be like fighting the tide. He'd ask about her and check in on her as well if he could.

His sister was smart enough to realize that she couldn't argue with him on this subject just yet, so she sat beside her doppelgänger while the last of them took baths, discussing the general parameters of their imprisonment.

They also talked about how the AI now knew about their presence and undoubtedly suspected that they'd failed to deliver the Omega Plague that it thought would eliminate humanity on Terra.

That was going to have long-term consequences, but he wasn't sure what they would be or when they would occur. It had taken years and a lot of money to secretly develop the virus. Lord Oscar Fielding —the man that had created the deadly pathogen—had claimed that he'd destroyed the actual research and tampered with the recipe that he'd given the AIs because he had no desire to see such a weapon spread beyond Terra.

Jared wasn't willing to give Fielding much credit, but he believed the man had no desire to die with the rest of humanity. That hadn't stopped the bastard from growing enough of the Omega Plague to kill the remaining population on Terra.

Once the rest of his people had bathed and dressed, he let Kelsey make her pitch.

"I think that we should form a small delegation to meet with Leader Mordechai," she said, moving her gaze evenly around the group. "Julia, Jared, Sean, and I would be a good start. We need to convince him of our sincerity about fighting the AIs. If we can do that, there's every chance that he'll not only let us go but provide us with valuable intelligence to help us get to the Imperial Palace."

Jared immediately shook his head. "I agree in principle, but I think you've picked the wrong people. They've seen how heavily modified you and Julia are. They're going to be distrustful of you and what you have to say. Admittedly, the rest of us are modified as well— except for Clarice—but I think that's going to give us a better chance to have an open and honest discussion.

"I think Elise and Olivia would be a better choice. They have the most experience as leaders in our group. I understand that you're not exactly lacking in that area, Kelsey, but I think you should focus your attention on Jebediah.

"He's going to be suspicious of everything we do, and I think you and Julia can help allay his fears. Sean and I could round out the delegation."

He looked around the rest of the group, and his eyes settled on Carl. "And that brings me to you, Carl. I think you, Ralph, and Austin would be an excellent delegation to see if any of the equipment in Frankfort can be repaired. I understand that you don't have much in the way of tools, but there must be a lot of things lying around inside this megacity that the inhabitants don't understand anymore. I'll bet you can rig up something to make their lives a little easier."

He paused for a moment to let all that sink in before continuing. When no one argued, he went on.

"The remainder of you get what rest you can and be prepared to assist any of the teams that need an extra hand or two. Our captors are exceptionally suspicious of us, and we're only going to get one chance to make a first impression."

"I agree with everything you've said, but I want to make one change," Kelsey said. "Julia has formed something of a bond with Jebediah. What you're saying about her talking to him makes absolute sense. But I'm the leader of the political side of this conversation, and I'm going to be going with you, Elise, and Olivia. Sean can help Julia. I think he'd bond well with Jebediah."

Jared considered that and slowly nodded. Her change wasn't that drastic, and he could live with her modification.

"Then we have a plan. Everyone be on your best behavior, and try not to get us all killed."

* * *

Talbot decided to include himself in the group that was going to see Jebediah. If, of course, the man was willing to let them out of their cells long enough to talk with him. Julia was the one leading the effort to have a conversation with him. They'd finally decided that Commodore Meyer, Commander Cannon, and himself should come along for the meeting.

Their captors had decided on an interesting way of providing security for them without endangering too many of their people. The rooms where they were being kept were isolated in a hallway with multiple heavy doors that one had to go through. Just outside the first set of doors was a pair of guards. This grouping was duplicated in each and every set of doors so that none of them could be taken out without the rest being aware of the attack.

Julia spoke briefly with the guards, and they passed the word to the next set of guards that she wanted to speak with Jebediah. Twenty minutes later, the man himself arrived to hear what she had to say.

"If you don't mind, I'd like to have a private conversation with you and a few of my people," she said. "We talked yesterday, but I feel as if we could expand on that and let you know more about ourselves and what we're trying to do."

The large man considered her for several seconds and then nodded. "My father is still uncertain whether we should believe what you've told us. Because of that, I'm inclined to agree.

"None of the other groups that we've captured have gotten this level of access, so you should feel honored that you're getting a chance to at least try to convince us that we should let you go. I want to caution you that that possibility is still unlikely, but it's not completely off the table at this point."

He gestured for her to follow him. "As you are probably ignorant of our way of life here in Frankfort, I feel as if I should give you a tour to show you what kind of society we have. Even though those who intrude here are not allowed to leave, we don't do anything like what the horde does to its prisoners."

Jebediah led them out of their prison suite, and fresh guards fell in all around them, staying at a distance to keep an eye on them without being in what they perceived to be danger themselves.

Talbot knew that they were underestimating the capabilities of Julia and himself. If they genuinely wanted to, the pair could reach the guards and disable them.

Since the guards weren't using projectile weapons, they risked getting cut in that fight, but there was no real doubt that they could disarm or kill all of the guards in just a few seconds with their bare hands.

Not that they'd ever dream of doing that. They already had one large group of bloodthirsty warriors itching to torture them before setting them on fire. Having a second group on the warpath would be suicide.

No, convincing these people that they could be decent allies was a much smarter play. Not that it would be easy, he suspected.

Rather than going up, Jebediah led them to a broad set of stairs that descended even farther under the city. Before they'd come down to join Admiral Mertz, he and Kelsey had wondered how far underground a megacity might have extended before the AIs suppressed all civilization on Terra. He suspected it was very deep indeed.

He doubted that would protect from something like a kinetic strike, but the illusion of security allowed people to live what life they could with some joy, so perhaps it was worth it.

Talbot's guess was proven correct when they continued on for quite some time. So deep, in fact, that they had to switch stairwells to continue down. With his implants back online, he could tell pretty well how far down they'd come. The level they exited on wasn't the lowest that the stairs could reach.

"I see that the stairs keep going down," Talbot said, giving in to his curiosity. "Is there more below us, or are we near the bottom?"

The large man smiled back at him. "Frankfort wasn't the largest megacity, but it was fully developed. We aren't in the lowest reaches of the underground tunnels. Those go so far down that the air is tainted, and no one can venture there. The explored portions that we've reached go down at least as far as we've already come."

That was a long way down, Talbot had to admit. Depending on what was down there, the air could have been tainted with any number of things once life support failed. It might be a naturally occurring gas coming through cracks in the walls. Methane perhaps. Or it could be some industrial chemical from work being done deep underground that had leaked out of its storage containers after the power went out.

Going everywhere with torches provided its own form of air pollution. The smoke made Talbot's nose itch and occasionally made him cough. The ceilings were coated with soot from generations of people that had used torches to light their way.

It was also possible that the use of so many torches had depleted the oxygen deep below. Not a pretty way to go.

Thankfully, that wasn't his problem.

"If you don't mind my asking, without any power, how is it that the air down here is still any good?" Julia asked. "After all this time, the air should be bad, shouldn't it?"

Their captor gave her a slight smile and a nod. "There's some truth to what you say, but we're in the right place for me to give you an example of why that situation isn't occurring."

With that, he stopped at a large double doorway with two guards posted outside it. The two men opened the doors for the party. Talbot stopped in his tracks as soon as he made it inside.

The large room in front of them certainly appeared to have formerly been used for life support. The massive air circulation machines were an obvious clue to that. Their original intent must've been to pull air from the surface and move it around the underground portions of the city.

A large wooden structure had been built around the circulators, and about forty people were sitting on what looked like exercise equipment, peddling gears set at the level of their feet. He wasn't sure what they were supposed to be doing, but it obviously served a purpose.

Julia scrunched up her face in disapproval. "Those people are peddling to drive gears inside the equipment, probably to rotate fans and pull fresh air down into this area, right?"

Jebediah gave her an approving glance and nodded. "The process also circulates the air to areas that we use on this level and above. The people you see driving the air equipment are primarily citizens of the city, but some of them are prisoners. They don't work any longer hours than our own people do. If you want to steal from us, then you can deal with the consequences."

He gave them all a stern look. "Unless you can convince us that you can grant us some benefit that outweighs the crimes you have committed against us by intruding into our privacy, work like this is the fate that awaits you. I suggest that you be convincing. My father is not one to take intrusion lightly, and neither am I."

Julia smiled at the man and nodded. "I think that we can come to some kind of arrangement once we convince you of our sincerity. Is there a place where we can sit down and have a frank discussion?"

The large man gestured for them to continue on into the industrial space. "There is a conference room attached to the offices just across this room. I believe it will suit our needs."

Talbot saw the doors to which the man gestured and started walking that way. He really hoped that Julia was better at talking her way through problems than Kelsey was. Fighting wasn't going to save them this time. They had to solve their problems with reason.

Not that his wife was unreasonable, just impulsive. For his love, far too many problems looked like nails, so her solution ended up being a hammer.

Or, as could be said after she'd made him watch an old entertainment vid called *The Fifth Element*, she negotiated like Korben Dallas.

The vid had proven far more humorous than she'd intended, and for entirely different reasons. Talbot had taken great pleasure in pointing out all the similarities between her and Dallas.

Her sudden consternation seemed genuine, so she probably hadn't even considered that aspect of the vid. His high point of the evening was telling her she was a pint-sized Bruce Willis.

After that, they'd watched *Die Hard*, which had proven his assertion decisively, much to his wife's annoyance.

Unable to help himself, Talbot grinned at the large man and Julia as they came in behind him. This should be... interesting.

9

Kelsey walked up the stairs slowly, since not everyone had her stamina for climbing what seemed like an endless number of steps. Now that her Marine Raider augmentation was back online, she could do this all day. And she meant that quite literally.

Her artificial muscles took up the majority of the strain, while her medical nanites kept her biological muscles working at peak efficiency. As long as she wasn't pushing things, everyday activities like this could be continued until she ran out of steam and had to eat.

The same wasn't true of Jared, Elise, Olivia, or Clarice Beauchamp. Hell, it wasn't even true of the guards that were trying to look tough as they escorted the prisoners up to meet their leader.

Their captors tried to put on a good show, but Kelsey could tell they were exhausted by the time they reached the tip of the spire high above the dead megacity.

With her implants active again, she could keep track of little details, like how many levels they'd passed and how high off the ground they were, but after a certain point, that just became a matter of keeping score.

Yes, this building was significantly smaller than the one that had dominated Imperial City, but it still rose more than three hundred levels from the surface and had a dominating view of the landscape around them.

When the guards escorted them into the single large room that filled the spire of the building, she could tell at a glance that it was once a restaurant of some kind. Many of the tables were still stacked by what was obviously a door to the kitchen.

Interestingly, the kitchen was situated in the center of the room right next to the stairwell and defunct lifts. The exterior of the room was one large circle with a panoramic view of Frankfort. Even from the center of the room, it was breathtaking.

The windows here had suffered just as severely as in the large room they'd been in yesterday. All the glass was gone. The gusts felt even stronger than in the level below, and Kelsey could strongly smell wood burning. That probably came from the horde city.

It was also chilly, even now during the summer. She imagined that this kind of wind would kill in the winter.

Someone had obviously taken the time to sweep the debris off the floor and to break out the rough shards that had remained in the frames. They'd also rigged up a makeshift rail along the outer edge of the room to keep anyone from getting too close to a lethal fall.

The winds might just snatch the unwary off their feet and send them out into the void. That included her, so she'd be cautious and keep an eye on her friends.

Seemingly unconcerned about all of that, Leader Mordechai stood beside the railing, gazing out at the horde city. From her current vantage point, she could see a good number of smoke plumes, so the blazes were severe.

At their arrival, Mordechai half turned and gestured for them to join him. They all did so, moving carefully.

"Thank you for taking the time to meet with us, Leader Mordechai," she said as she stepped up beside him, grasped the rail firmly, and got a better view of the horde capital.

The fires were worse than she'd expected. At a guess, maybe a fifth of the city had already been consumed by flames and was now just a smoldering pile of rubble. The active fires seemed to be burning out of control amongst the poorer sections of the city, where most of the construction was of wood.

Even the buildings made of a mixture of wood and stone seemed to be suffering. Whatever they had for a fire brigade was obviously overwhelmed and unable to deal with the scale of devastation they were experiencing.

Under other circumstances, she'd have felt sorry for those killed or rendered homeless by the flames. She didn't, though. Those people had killed almost three hundred of her people and their allies.

While specific individuals below might be innocent of wrongdoing, collateral damage was a sad fact of war, and that's what this was. She'd used the weapons she'd had at hand to escape their captivity before they could torture and murder her and her friends.

No, she had no sympathy for them at all.

"While my knees don't appreciate the climb to get here, I don't begrudge you your meeting," the older man said. "I realize that I could've done so in my offices below, but I do so love the view from up here. It's also good exercise to climb those stairs every day and overlook the city of my ancestors.

"I mean that quite literally, by the way. I can trace my lineage back to the Imperial mayor that ruled Frankfort at the time the computers crushed Terra a century ago. Even before then, our family controlled the city in the name of the emperor for generations, though I couldn't tell you precisely how many."

He turned and gazed toward her, his expression serious. "Like those that have come before me, I take my responsibilities to this city and its people very seriously. The rule until this time has been that any who dare intrude are never allowed to leave.

"Another rule is that those who work for the computers are to be executed. I must determine if you fall into that latter category. I will tell you now that I'm of two minds on the matter. Yet I will not rush to a decision. I will give you a chance to convince me of your honesty and expand upon why you've come to Terra.

"If I decide that you're telling the truth and that it serves our interests in assisting you, I'll not only allow you to depart in peace, but I'll do what I can to assist you in your task.

"That doesn't mean that it will be easy to convince me. My son and I have discussed this, and we believe that the only way to determine your mettle is to put you under pressure.

"So there will be some tasks that we want you to complete. Tasks that only someone with your evident technological skills could manage. They will not be easy, and they may yet prove impossible. Yet how you proceed with them will tell us much about you. I suppose you could consider them quests, just like in the old stories."

Part of her was excited to hear this, but the cost of failure could be drastic, so she was wary of being too pleased. "What kind of work are we talking about?"

"It's my understanding that you have three individuals with high technological skills. Is this correct?"

Kelsey nodded. "We have one man who is a specialist with hardware, another who is a specialist with software and computers, and a third who is brilliant at making breakthroughs in all of the above and more.

"I have to warn you though, we don't have a lot of tools with us. Only what we could recover before we had to flee the horde city. I'm not certain what you have in mind, but without the correct equipment, it might be impossible."

Mordechai smiled thinly. "We shall see. I will send guards to summon your remaining people to a meeting that Jebediah is already holding underneath the city. It's best if I gather you all together before I tell you what I have in mind. My apologies, but that will be quite far under the city, so you have more exercise ahead."

Kelsey almost smiled at how her companions' expressions fell. Now, after having climbed all those stairs, they'd have to go right back down and then even deeper under the city. She wondered if that was some kind of test as well.

"Whatever your tasks, we'll do the best we can," she said with all the assurance she could muster. "You have my word on that."

They really would give it their best effort. This was the one chance they had to leave Frankfort peacefully. If they failed, they'd have to fight their way out against a foe that knew the ground a lot better than they did. She'd like to avoid that if at all possible.

* * *

CARL SAT in the large room with his associates. He'd known Ralph Halstead since Kelsey had captured the man and his parents during an operation inside the Rebel Empire. Unlike the man's aunt, Ralph had passed the test given to him by Fiona, the newly constructed AI they had aboard *Persephone*.

He'd been working with his aunt, spying inside an Imperial research facility that Kelsey had raided. Carl had to admit that running into someone else stealing from the Rebel Empire while they'd been doing the same thing had been unexpected. Circumstances had demanded that they take Ralph, his aunt, and her husband with them when they left.

They'd turned Ralph's aunt and uncle over to the resistance. Not that he expected that they would deal harshly with them. They'd only been engaged in industrial espionage against the Rebel Empire, something the rebellion probably approved of.

But those people were better positioned to keep an eye on the aunt. She was wily. If it was worth money, she'd try to sell it, so maybe mercenary was a better word.

Ralph, on the other hand, had jumped at the chance to go with Kelsey and the rest on their mission to Terra. He'd passed multiple loyalty tests since then and was seemingly becoming well integrated with the science teams.

Carl was glad he'd survived the horde massacre. There'd been an inordinate number of research personnel on the mission because they'd expected to explore the Imperial Palace. All of them were now dead. It tore at his heart. Deep down, he wanted some payback, but he just wasn't sure how he could manage to get any.

In any case, Ralph was a hacker. While Carl could claim to know a lot about computers and programming, he was wise enough to admit that Ralph was his master in that arena. His friend had grown up inside the Rebel Empire and had learned from masters in the field at cracking and hacking into Imperial technology via software. Then he'd practiced that art for most of his life.

That put him almost completely at odds with Carl's other new friend, Austin Darrah. Unlike the lowly born Ralph, Austin had been a member of what the Rebel Empire called the higher orders. Their version of the nobility. His family meant something inside the upper strata of the Rebel Empire.

Not that that had interested Austin in the slightest. He'd found himself drawn to understanding how mechanical items worked due to the influence of his uncle when he was young. Oscar Fielding had owned and controlled a shipyard supplying the Rebel Empire version of Fleet and various civilian interests.

Sadly for Austin, his expertise in working with virtually every kind of Imperial hardware meant that he'd been forced onto the mission that was supposed to deliver a lethal virus to Terra: the Omega Plague.

Even worse from Austin's perspective, his uncle was neck deep in the project. He'd not only overseen the teams that had developed the weapon, but he'd also been the one that had sicced the AIs into pressganging his nephew.

The older man sounded like a real ass to Carl. He was glad that he hadn't had to meet the bastard. It amused the hell out of them that Admiral Mertz had found a way to maroon Fielding without a good chunk of his money after the guy had double-crossed the AIs and tried to do the same to the admiral and his crew.

So Carl now had both a software expert and a master of hardware. Combined with his own flair for working with Imperial tech, he felt confident that the three of them could do just about anything when it came to Old Empire machinery.

And that was what probably brought them to this meeting. He'd expected their captors to keep them in the quarters assigned to them, but they'd been led deep under the ground beneath Frankfort.

The group that had gone with Julia had already had some kind of meeting with Jebediah, the son of the ruler of this ruined megacity. They had joined them.

Considering the hodgepodge of work that was being done with the air-handling system just outside this meeting room, Carl was confident that they'd be tasked with doing something to improve the efficiency of moving the air.

Not that the man was talking about the work that he wanted them to do just yet. He seemed to be waiting for something.

A minute later, Carl figured out what the holdup was when Kelsey, the admiral, and the rest of their people walked into the room. Everyone except Doctor Stone, who was likely still struggling to save lives.

Along with the last group came another bunch of guards and Leader Mordechai, the ruler of this city. It looked as if this was going to be it. Whatever was going to happen, they were going to find out about it now.

Part of him almost didn't want to know. It seemed like the last week had been filled with tragedy following disaster. Almost nothing had gone right for them. In fact, it was hard to imagine how things could've gone *worse*, other than them all dying in the process.

Once everyone was seated, Mordechai joined his son at the head of the table. The overhead panels were dead, so the room was lit with oil-filled lamps. Those had a peculiar smell that wasn't wholly unpleasant, but it certainly wasn't something Carl would have sought out.

"I'm sure you're wondering why I've brought you all together again," Mordechai said solemnly. "As I told Kelsey Bandar and Admiral Mertz, my mind is not yet made up about your sincerity and truthfulness. I've decided that a test is in order. Perhaps the first of several. I'm told that some of you have particular gifts with mechanical items and old technology."

As he said that, he looked right at Carl. Not sure what to do, Carl decided to respond directly. He rose to his feet and softly cleared his throat as he put his hands behind his back.

"Yes, sir. Two of my associates and I have the skills you're talking about. What kind of task did you have in mind? Something to improve the air handlers outside the room?"

"No. Something significantly more dangerous. Deep beneath the city, at levels that have not been accessed in almost a hundred years, lies the fusion plant that once powered Frankfort."

The older man smiled slightly when Carl blinked in surprise. "Oh yes, I know what a fusion plant is, at least in general terms. My father saw to my education when it came to Imperial technology and how the city used to work. The diaries kept by my ancestors have much information about what equipment worked and what didn't, as well as how such items could be maintained in a general sense.

"The fusion plant was shut down before the AI struck. The level of resistance against the computer's occupation had reached a plateau that the Imperial mayor felt would invite retaliation. So when the number of ships orbiting around Terra began to rise precipitously, she decided that lowering Frankfort on the list of potential targets would be wise."

His expression grew dark. "My great-grandmother was a brilliant woman. I knew her briefly as a child before she passed. According to the words she wrote in the leaders' diary, the fusion plant was shut down in good order, and they had even incorporated shielding to keep it from being detectable from above ground. What I want you to do is venture deep, deep under Frankfort and bring it back to life."

Carl grimaced. That wasn't going to be an easy task, particularly with only the equipment he had available. He couldn't trust that anything down there still worked. Imperial technology was very long-lived, but components failed, and a century was a long time.

Still, it wasn't exactly as if they had a choice in the matter. If he and his friends wanted to earn their freedom, he'd have to find a way to make this work.

"I'll do my best, but I can't promise success," Carl said. "I'm going to have to look at what's down there. Even getting to the fusion plant is going to be tricky, because the air is probably foul. I'm not exactly sure how we can protect ourselves."

The older man smiled thinly. "If it were easy, it wouldn't be a suitable quest. I'll grant you access to all of the equipment that we have. Perhaps something among it will allow you to construct some type of protection.

"But make no mistake: your success will reflect upon your compatriots. As will your failure, should success elude you. I would suggest that you do your absolute best."

Yeah. No pressure at all.

10

Julia stared at their captor. "Are you crazy? The AI can sense that kind of thing. I don't care what kind of shielding you have. If you reactivate it, lights all over the city are going to come back on, and *somebody's* going to notice. Hell, *everybody* is going to notice! The least bad thing that will happen is that the horde is going to come looking for what's going on."

Mordechai nodded. "That's certainly a possibility, but I'm counting on your people being knowledgeable enough to disconnect all of the power lines into the city itself until you can figure out which ones can be energized safely. That is within your control, is it not, Mister Owlet?"

"If we can get the system operational, we can certainly isolate it," Carl agreed. "If it has shielding like you say, then it probably won't be detectible on the surface, much less in orbit. So long as there are no visible indications above ground that power is back on, no one should be any wiser.

"The problem is going to come in when you decided that you want something specific powered up. Even if the equipment is operational—which is not guaranteed—then you're going to run into the problem of there being other things on that circuit.

"There are far too many connections through the power linkages in the city to be certain of turning everything off if you want to energize power to the basement of this building, for example. It's just not going to be that easy.

"It will take a lot of work to be absolutely certain that everything on a line is disconnected. Then rechecking it, probably with a separate set of people to bring fresh eyes to the work. And, considering the risk, probably a third group. It'll be time consuming and dangerous."

"And that's only the beginning," Julia added, already thinking of other potential problems. "What about the danger down there? You're talking about going into an area where the atmosphere is going to be full of carbon dioxide and perhaps other chemicals that were released once the power went off.

"It's not exactly like you have access to vacuum suits, Carl. How do you intend to stay alive long enough to even reach the fusion plant? Putting that aside, let's say that you do. How are you going to be able to stay there long enough to do any work?"

"I have a few ideas on that," Carl admitted. "If we search the area around us on this level, I'll bet we find some emergency lockers that have air bottles. Many of them are still going to be charged, at least to a degree. We'll have to make certain the equipment still works, and it's going to be something of a gamble, but I think that problem can be solved.

"Once we get the fusion plant back online, I feel pretty confident that we can at least set up some of the life support down below to get the toxic elements cleaned out of the air. The scrubbers should still be intact, even after all this time. The components aren't meant to break down over time to the point that they degrade past their useful operational life."

Julia wasn't convinced, and she was pretty sure that her expression conveyed that. Not that her opinion was likely to deter the pigheaded scientist.

"I can't stop you from going, but I think it's too dangerous. Is it really worth the risk?"

Mordechai raised an eyebrow. "Is your potential freedom worth the risk? Because I can assure you that without completing this task, you will not leave this city.

"And before you start to think that your enhanced physical attributes are going to make a difference in that, we have areas that we can isolate the three of you that have that capability and be certain that you won't escape. I'd rather not do that, but if you choose to be recalcitrant, then I won't have a choice."

Julia threw up her hands. "Of course you do! You're making the active choice to force us to do this work in exchange for our freedom. We haven't done anything other than trespass on your property.

"We had no choice in where we went when we escaped the horde city. You have every option in how you react to our presence and in how you help or hinder us in our actions against the AI.

"If we do this, you let us go. No other little tasks you want us to do. Once and done. Then we're friends, not intruders."

Almost everyone around her was aghast at how she'd confronted Mordechai. It was a risk but one that needed to be taken. If they just did everything he said, they'd never be free of the old man. No, there had to be a line drawn in the sand.

If her words disturbed Leader Mordechai, he didn't show it. He only smiled at her response.

"I suppose it's good to have limits on one's behavior. Now that we've settled what the limits are on what we'll each tolerate, I suggest that we get back to the problem at hand. My city will only have this one opportunity to take a quantum leap toward getting its old technology functional again.

"You don't understand what it's like living next to the horde city. Those people are monsters in human form. If you think we're xenophobic, then you don't know them very well. We don't wantonly torture or kill.

"I needed to make clear to you that armed resistance would have severe repercussions so that you wouldn't feel the desire to try to use your greater strength to try and overpower us. Our two groups *can* work together to achieve something that neither alone could do. Perhaps you haven't considered the options thoroughly.

"If power can be restored to Frankfort, that means that power can be used to reenergize the old trains that once carried people and cargo from city to city. Traveling over the surface to escape the area is asking to be chased down and murdered by the horde. What if you could just climb aboard a train and take it all the way to your destination?

"I don't know for a fact that the tunnels lead directly to the Imperial Palace, but the old stories certainly talk about them reaching Imperial City. Even though that wondrous place no longer exists, I'd wager that coming out of the ground near Imperial City would put you within striking distance of the Imperial Palace. Wouldn't you agree?"

That was certainly something to think about. Julia raised an eyebrow at Carl, who shrugged. He wasn't saying that it could be done, but he wasn't rejecting the idea out of hand. That meant that it was a possibility that they could cut the trip that would've taken them half a year down to a day, or perhaps even a few hours. That would certainly be better than walking the entire distance and fighting whoever they interacted with.

Still, even if they *could* restore one of the trains to functionality, the tunnel might be blocked, or the train might run out of power partway. Would the air inside the tunnels be toxic? She had no idea.

But she supposed that it was worth examining in greater detail, and that meant that they had to have power in order to check out the systems on the trains themselves.

"I think we can probably stop throwing threats around at one another," Mertz said, cutting into the conversation. "You're right that that would help us greatly in our mission, so we're going to help you get your fusion plant back online, so long as it's not going to draw the attention of the AI.

"That's one thing we have to avoid at all costs, particularly now that it knows we're down here. That kinetic strike destroyed our pinnaces, but you can bet that it's examining the general area with whatever resources it can bring to bear. It's going to look at this city and at the horde city, too.

"If it thinks we're here, it might be inclined to drop another kinetic strike on Frankfort just to be sure. That would be the death of all of your people, and we've got to avoid that. Right now, it can't be sure. We've got to keep it that way."

Mordechai opened his mouth to respond, but the door opened abruptly. One of the guards stepped into the room and bowed slightly. "Leader Mordechai, something is happening at the horde city. It looks like a number of their warriors are exiting their walls and heading toward Frankfort."

The older man stood. "It looks as if some of our options have just been taken off the table. The horde must believe that you have fled to our city. You've definitely kicked over the anthill, and now they seem determined to sting you. I will allow that the kinetic strike may have also played a role in uniting them.

"They will regret that decision quite soon, but even though they're monsters, they're canny fighters. The defense of Frankfort is going to be important. I ask that you contribute your three trained fighters to my forces.

"If you would like to use your enhancements to your benefit, now would be the time to do so. If we don't stop them, not only are you again at risk of death, but you can rest assured that they'll never let you escape the area and complete your mission."

Mertz nodded grimly. "Talbot, you and Lieutenant Laird will assist with the scouting and in any other way that the local forces request. You actually have full military training, so it makes more sense for you to be on the sharp end of the stick."

He turned toward Julia. "You have the ability, but no training. I'd prefer that you help Carl. His work is going to be important, and your augmentation could save him if something goes wrong."

Mertz turned toward Leader Mordechai. "Kelsey has skill with swords and her augmentation. She could directly join your defenses. I'd like to request that the three that will be fighting be returned their weapons.

"I understand that you're concerned about whether or not we're going to stay under your control, so I'm not asking that the rest of us be rearmed."

The older man nodded at once. "I agree. The remainder of you can stay down here. There are additional quarters available that we can station guards at, but the odds of the enemy incursion reaching this level are small.

"You can assist your technical people in preparing for their mission. If I understand what they need correctly, they'll want to search for specialized equipment that might be refurbished. We can send individuals to escort you, so your time will not be wasted."

Julia wasn't sure how she felt about being kept out of the fighting. She knew that she didn't have the skills that Kelsey had, and so part of her was grateful that she wouldn't be directly involved.

The other part of her was still filled with rage and wanted to kill as many of the horde warriors as possible. That part of her was severely disappointed.

It was difficult to balance those emotions, so she didn't even try. If the incursion was as strong as they'd indicated, she'd get her chance to spill the enemy's blood at some point. She'd never be able to kill enough of them to pay them back for what they'd done, but she sure hoped that she had the opportunity to try.

For now, she had to focus on helping Carl do what he needed to do to earn their freedom. No matter how dangerous and foolhardy that turned out to be.

* * *

WHEN THEIR CAPTORS returned his weapons, Talbot accepted them gratefully. He really wished that he had something more modern, considering that the horde just never seems to stop coming, but he'd take what he could get.

Arming them showed a promising level of trust. He hoped Kelsey and Admiral Mertz could transition that into something more solid once this little problem was dealt with.

Talbot had used "little problem" intentionally, minimizing what he knew was going to be a significant incursion. If the horde felt it necessary to enter a place like the abandoned megacity, there would be a lot of them. This place's reputation demanded they use as many warriors as they could lay hands on.

Talbot wondered what that meant for the power struggle inside the horde city. After Kelsey had destroyed their palace and probably killed most of their leadership, there'd been fires scattered throughout the city and signs of fighting. They'd seen that from the towers. That had probably meant different groups had been vying for control of the horde and literally killing off the competition.

The fact that the horde was now invading Frankfort meant they'd almost certainly settled that particular struggle. Someone was in charge now, and he had blood in his eye.

Talbot's group consisted of Chloe and two guards, a man and a woman. The man identified himself as Richard and the woman as Lydia. No last names were given. Based on how well the two worked together, he suspected they were a couple.

The four of them entered a ruined building that was maybe a quarter of the size of the large tower they'd been in before. It was still a significant structure, but it was nowhere near the league of the big boys.

What it did possess was an unobstructed view down a broad boulevard that had once been a major thoroughfare in the city. Talbot could imagine the wide gap filled with grav cars moving in regimented order through the sky between the buildings as people went about their daily lives or walked through the gardens that once filled the ground level.

That sort of thing was still relatively new on Avalon, but he'd seen recordings of Imperial City, and it was truly mind-boggling. Imperial City had once housed over a billion people. Frankfort was much smaller but still far more extensive than anything on Avalon.

The four of them went up the stairs and only stopped when they reached the fiftieth floor. They were maybe halfway to the top of the structure. The door to the stairwell led them into what had once been a wide corridor, but the walls had decayed, giving occasional glimpses into the rooms beyond.

Their guards led them to windows, where they could see down the boulevard. These, like many others in the city, had been shattered by the nearby kinetic strike. Thankfully, there'd been no rain since the event, so there were only the glass fragments on a dry floor to deal with. Slipping in this could be very bad.

A quick search found an ancient broom that they could use to clean the small area where they'd be lying low and watching for the enemy. Once all four of them were stretched out on the floor, Talbot glanced at Richard and Lydia.

"What are we expecting? We're going to have a decent view of them coming, but we're so high off the ground that we're not going to be useful against them."

"With only four of us, that's probably a good thing, don't you think?" Lydia asked. "All we're doing is gathering information. You may not have seen it, but there's a mechanical telephone back at the stairwell.

"Basically, it's run by batteries that we charge via solar power and capable of sending short-range transmissions down a hard line that we've run underground. When we do, the leadership will decide where our major forces will strike. We're their eyes."

"What we need to do is give our leaders some decent information," Richard said in agreement. "The horde usually sends about thirty or forty people when they want to scavenge. That's not a problem if we can ambush them in a worthwhile manner.

"Even so, horde warriors make terrible prisoners. Most of them would rather die fighting than surrender. Even those we do capture alive will do their damnedest to force us to kill them. Frankly, it's better for everyone if we just end them in an overwhelming ambush.

"This is going to be a very different kind of fight. They're coming in force, and that means there's going to be hundreds of them in any group. Maybe thousands. We have plans in place to deal with a full invasion, but we've never had to execute them. What did you people do to piss them off?"

Talbot shrugged slightly. "As part of our escape, we brought the roof down on their treasure vault, and their castle collapsed with it. So not only did they lose all the treasures they had stored down there, but they lost their honchos.

"Based on the look I got at the city earlier, they were having some kind of succession war. Now that they've settled it, they've obviously decided that we came here, and they want to get us. I'm kind of surprised that you haven't at least considered handing us over to them to make this problem go away."

The man gave him a shrug in return. "Leader Mordechai doesn't cooperate with intruders. Well, until your arrival, at least. He'll never give in to the horde, though."

"I see something," Chloe said. She'd kept her focus on the ground below.

Talbot used his optic augmentation to zoom into the area she was watching. There were indeed a bunch of warriors creeping through the open ground between trees and high grass that had grown up over the century since the AI had suppressed Terra.

It was hard to get a firm count when you couldn't see the enemy clearly, but he suspected he was looking at a minimum of forty people moving through the foliage. They'd just entered the boulevard and were quite a distance away. He passed that information on to their guards.

The two guards seemed impressed. From this range, they probably couldn't see the enemy at all, much less count them. He was surprised that Chloe had seen anything. She didn't have any ocular augmentation, so she must've had truly excellent vision.

He was about to say something along those lines when the movement at the end of the boulevard increased significantly. It seemed that those forty were scouting for a larger force, and soon the number of people moving through the foliage left little doubt that there were hundreds of horde warriors down there.

When they finally broke into sight, Talbot saw that none of them were mounted. These were infantry. They had bows out, swords at their hips, and were moving in a well-drilled formation. They looked as if they were expecting an ambush.

He supposed being evil bastards didn't mean they had to be incompetent or cowardly. Pity.

Talbot passed that information along, and Lydia excused herself to go report. He turned his attention to Richard.

"How are you going to handle that many people? Do you have a large enough force to attack something like that?"

The man smiled grimly. "Just because we've lost the old

technology doesn't mean we're helpless. We have a few tricks up our sleeves that will hurt them.

"My concern is that this isn't their only incursion. If they're really coming in force, they'll have sent every warrior they could muster. Many of the people that became the horde were expelled from Frankfort because they weren't suitable to have as neighbors.

"They've long wished to regain what they believe we stole from them. We've been preparing for this day for many years. We won't lose this fight."

Talbot certainly hoped the man was right because if the city fell, they were in real trouble. They'd never escape overland now that they'd stirred the hornets' nest. Their only hope of survival was getting the fusion plant online and taking a train toward the water-filled crater where Imperial City once stood.

Based on the information he had in his implants, there would probably be a station within a hundred kilometers of the Imperial Palace if there wasn't a trunk line that would take them most of the way to their ultimate destination. Supplies had obviously needed to get to the palace, and not all of them would come in via grav car.

Of course, none of those plans would mean anything unless they survived this fight.

Talbot didn't know what the city's defense plans were, but he vowed to make sure they succeeded. With the capabilities that his Marine Raider implants and augmentation gave him in a fight like this, he might be able to make a real difference.

He only hoped that Kelsey would be okay in the brewing fight. If she fell, it would be like he'd been killed, too.

11

J ared opened a metal door set into the wall of the passage. Its faded markings identified it as containing emergency supplies. If it was like the others he'd seen today, it wouldn't have been disturbed in the last century.

They held basic medical kits, air bottles, face masks that covered the nose and mouth, and other emergency gear that might be required in an area where industrial equipment was in operation.

The priority for him was air, though he did take the medical supplies as well since he figured that Lily was going to need as much help as she could get once the fighting actually started.

She had a full kit, but if they had hundreds of casualties, that would use up the supplies they had on hand almost immediately. The Imperial medical establishment had made supplies that would last for decades, and even though these were far beyond their expiration dates, many of them were still useful to her.

The air bottles were more problematic. Some still claimed they had a full charge, but most had lost some or all of their contents over the intervening years. Probably one tenth of the ones that Jared had found had a full charge. Of the rest, maybe thirty percent had anywhere from twenty-five percent to seventy-five percent. The remainder were empty or only held a fraction of a charge.

They'd have to test the equipment to make sure that it worked before they relied on it to keep someone safe. If anyone could determine how functional this gear was, it was Carl and Austin. Between the two of them, they understood the mechanical side of Old Empire tech very well.

Jared had found a wheeled cart that he was using to hold his haul. It was just about full, so he turned back the way he'd come.

He hoped the others had found more bottles because even those that were rated as full would only last for fifteen to twenty minutes, and if multiple people were going to work down below, they'd need a lot of them.

Since there'd be four people going down—Carl, Austin, Ralph, and Julia—they'd need four times the air. Thankfully, Julia could haul quite a bit, though he doubted that she'd enjoy being the group's pack mule.

Carl and the others in the technical squad were busy testing bottles and masks when he arrived back in the air handler room. They were making notations on each cylinder with different colored markers. He noted that perhaps half of what had been brought back was simply thrown into a bin. Their lack of care with them meant that the discards weren't going to be useful.

"All right, I've got my first load," he said as he pushed his cart up to them and started unloading it. "How's it looking?"

Carl glanced over as he tossed another bottle into the disposal bin. "The gauges are unreliable. Basically, if it says its below fifty percent, it's probably useless. If it says that it's around seventy-five percent, it's probably going to have maybe ten minutes' worth of air. If it says it's full, fifteen minutes is all that we can count on.

"The gauges weren't designed for this type of long-term use, and they've failed in a linear fashion. At least that allows us to make some estimates by looking at the indicators."

Jared looked over the stack of supposedly full bottles. There weren't that many of them.

"How long are you expecting to need to be down there?"

Carl shrugged. "Until we get there, I can't make any guesses. If the shielding is actually in place, we may only need to service the reactor before bringing it online. I don't want to commit to that without seeing things, though.

"I think this first trip is going to be an exploratory one. We'll just make it down to where the fusion plant is, make an assessment, run diagnostics if possible, and then return to this level to work out a battle plan.

"There are a lot of air bottles being brought in, and in a city this size, I suspect we're going to have more than enough. It's just going to take time to gather them.

"Right now, you're only bringing in the ones closest to the air handler room. To get more, we're going to have to move farther out, and that's going to take additional time and effort."

Jared thought about that and nodded reluctantly. "I can shepherd the search for more air. How long until you've got enough for the four of you to start down and make an assessment?"

Carl considered that for a moment. "I think we'll have enough in about an hour. We won't really know until we see how far it is to the fusion plant and what the obstacles are. We're going into this with a decent margin for error. If we use forty percent and we're not at the target, we're going to turn around and start back up."

"That's a good idea," Jared said. "I want all of you to be *very* careful. Not only are you irreplaceable as friends, but you're also the only technical support we're going to have when we get to the Imperial Palace. You're doubly important, and I don't want you to take any unnecessary chances. If you run into trouble, abort the mission and come back up. I'll deal with our captors if it comes to that."

Carl looked over at the guards. "I sure hope you're right about that because they seem determined to get the fusion plant online."

Jared considered the armed men watching them and nodded. "They are, but diplomacy is the art of the possible. We have to give this everything we have because that's the simplest way to get us out of the city and on our way. If the fusion plant is functional, then we can start looking at the trains and make an assessment of how far they can get us. All I'm saying is to do the best you can and be careful."

With that, Jared grabbed his now-empty cart and started back to get some more supplies. He really did hope this plan worked, because the horde would never let them ride away. Their only chance of escape was underground.

If Carl failed to get the fusion plant online, they might very well be trapped here for the rest of their lives. However short a time that might be.

* * *

THE RALLY POINT for the defensive forces was a large room at the base of one of the massive towers toward the center of the city. Kelsey thought it might once have been an indoor sports arena, based on the movable stadium seating.

The gathering included more people than she'd expected. Her implants calculated that there were probably seven hundred and fifty defenders gathered in the vast space.

She had no idea what the population of the dead megacity was, but if this was their defensive force, then the overall population had to be lower than she'd anticipated. Of course, there could be other gatherings. She had no way of knowing.

As far as the armament that they had available, they had the usual primitive weaponry that was commonplace in these days without technology, but that wasn't all.

Arrayed against the rolled-back seating were tables holding a sampling of intriguing weapons. Some held what looked like grenades. Others held primitive firearms, similar to those used in the prespaceflight wars on Terra: pistols, short rifles, and long-barreled weapons. Even what might be simple rocket launchers. In all, a respectable arsenal.

Kelsey wished she had more time to examine them, but a short woman with gray hair motioned for everyone to gather around her.

The woman didn't bother introducing herself, which made sense since everyone beside Kelsey probably knew who she was.

"We're going to go with defense plan Charlie," the woman said with no preamble. "We'll fan out to meet the incoming groups at the designated ambush zones for their path of advance. If we can push them back, fine. If not, we fall back and strike them again at the secondary locations."

The woman turned in a slow circle to examine everyone as they absorbed her words. There was far less murmuring than Kelsey had expected. These people knew what they were about. That boded well for them all.

"Our goal is to bleed them," the woman continued. "If we inflict enough casualties, they'll retreat. At least that's the theory. If it doesn't work out that way, we may end up fighting hand to hand. In that case, reducing their numbers is going to be critical because they'll outnumber us badly if we don't.

"I don't have to tell you how important this is. If we want to keep our families and friends safe, we have to stand between them and the horde. I expect everyone to give this everything they have. Group leaders, take command of your forces and fight like hell. Dismissed."

A thin man with fringes of reddish hair around the base of his bald skull gestured for Kelsey to join him. It looked like a hundred people or so were gathered under his metaphorical banner.

"My name is Charles Davis," he said to Kelsey. "I want you to stick near me while we do our thing. Leader Mordechai has indicated that we're to trust you with your weapons, but I want you to know that I'll have my eyes on you. If you try to betray us, we'll kill you. Do you understand?"

"I'm not going to betray you," Kelsey said firmly. "We want to make the horde pay just as badly as you do."

The man considered her for a moment and then nodded with seeming satisfaction. "Excellent. I understand that you're trained in the use of Imperial technology. None of what we have available is of that caliber, and it will have to be explained to you. Step over to the table so that I can show you what we'll be working with."

He picked up one of the grenades and showed it to her. "This metal ball contains explosives, and the shell becomes shrapnel. To use it, one pulls the pin and throws the grenade. The spoon is spring loaded and flies up when you release it, lighting the fuse.

"Once you pull the pin, Mister Grenade is no longer your friend. You'll have roughly seven seconds before it explodes. The lethal radius is about ten meters, so keep that in mind. Aim for clusters of the enemy, and avoid your allies. It's quite effective if one can throw it far enough."

He examined her critically. "I'm not certain this is an appropriate weapon for you. To get one on target requires pinpoint accuracy and a bit of upper-body strength if one doesn't want to be too close to the target."

She smiled toothily. "I'm a lot stronger than I look, and my aim is exceptional. Trust me when I say that I'll be better at getting those on target than many of your own people."

He didn't seem convinced but didn't argue. Instead, he set the grenade down and picked up one of the metal tubes Kelsey had decided were rocket launchers. With a tug, he extended the tube even farther and revealed that it was about a meter long at that point. Two small sights popped up along the top as well.

"This is an antipersonnel rocket. They're constructed much like the grenades, as far as the explosive goes, but each has a chemical charge that propels the payload to its target. Basically, you take the tube that you've extended, rotate it onto your shoulder, line your sights up with the target, and then squeeze down this trigger along the top surface. It requires firm pressure to depress and is a one-shot, throwaway model. Once it's done, it's done.

"You'll want to be certain that no friendlies are behind you, as the propellant will kill at close range and maim for a distance beyond that. Best to make sure by calling out 'backblast area clear' and waiting for a positive response unless you are absolutely certain that no one you care for is behind you."

He did something to the tube and collapsed it back down again. Once that was done, he set it on the table and picked up one of the primitive firearms. It definitely looked like something out of one of the World War II movies that she'd seen in vids.

"This is a chemically based firearm. They're based on something we found in a museum after Terra fell. Basically, when you pull the trigger, a striker pin sets off a small priming charge that is built into the bullet, which in turn ignites gunpowder inside the brass case. That pushes a lead slug coated with copper down the rifled barrel, which imparts rotation.

"It's a fairly significant weapon at short range and can penetrate horde armor. Each of us will be issued one of these and several magazines of ammunition. More ammunition will be provided by people that are keeping us supplied during the fighting.

"We have short rifles that can fire very quickly, firing until you release the trigger or the weapon is empty. We call them submachine guns. In tight spaces, they are quite lethal. Also, very loud. They use the same ammunition as the pistols.

"In fact, the magazines will fit in either weapon, though the submachine guns will empty a pistol magazine in a few moments. The submachine gun magazines will work for the pistols but make them somewhat unwieldy. The pistols require a trigger pull for each round fired.

"Finally, there are longer weapons, but they are hard to make and difficult to form in a way that makes them accurate. The few we have will go to our snipers. They'll help us disorganize the enemy and make it so that we can perhaps attack them without them using their full capabilities in turn."

He focused his full attention on her. "They have rockets of a sort that are much more powerful. They are designed to penetrate Imperial armor."

Kelsey felt her face close down. "We've encountered them, and I've lost friends to them. I'll make sure those bastards die first."

The man smiled for the first time. "That's a plan that I can get behind."

He issued her a submachine gun, a pistol belt, and ammo for both and returned her swords. She settled everything into place and stuck close to his side as he started gathering his people and heading out.

She didn't have the same bloody rage that Julia did, but she also had a score to settle with the horde. Killing their leadership wasn't enough. She intended to send them racing back to their city with their tails between their legs today.

Those she didn't manage to kill. They'd pay for what they did today. On the souls of her dead people, that she swore.

12

Carl hefted the makeshift harness that held his equipment, making the air bottles rattle in their mesh. He felt a little overloaded. Well, better that than dead.

The others were similarly arrayed. Ralph had more air than Austin, but that was only because the hacker didn't need to worry about having that much equipment. Everything he required was in his implants, and all he needed was the appropriate gear to be able to link in with whatever he was going to be accessing.

Austin carried a lot more equipment. If they needed to work on anything, it would require a separate tool. That meant that the rest would have to carry sufficient air for him.

Thankfully, Julia would be able to carry a hefty reserve because of her augmentation. The woman, though small, was heavily laden with air bottles and gear. Carl figured they had enough air to stay down there for a couple of hours before needing to return to the safer levels.

"Are you boys ready to go?" Julia asked, her voice tinged with impatience. "I'd rather get this underway now so that we can get back up here sooner. If there's trouble, I don't want to be caught down there."

Carl didn't disagree. The sooner they dealt with any problems with the fusion plant, the sooner they'd be able to get on with their real business. If the horde managed to overwhelm the defenders, he'd rather not be caught down where he couldn't even breathe without assistance either.

"Let's do this," he agreed.

From what Mordechai had told them, they'd need to go to the nearest stairwell leading down—which his son had already pointed out to them—and start the process of entering the lower levels. They'd need to switch stairs below, as this one didn't go deep enough.

As they grew closer to the target, there would be signs indicating where to exit the second set of stairs. The older man had no idea how far down that was, but the old stories had indicated that it was quite some distance.

Once the four of them had entered the stairwell and started down, Carl began checking the air quality. For the first dozen levels, it held at about the same as it was in the area where they'd been.

That changed once they reached a certain point, and the carbon dioxide began climbing fairly rapidly. The oxygen levels were also falling. Within a couple of levels, the air quality had become bad enough that Carl was glad they'd brought air with them.

They stopped at that point, slid their masks into place, and turned on their air before continuing down.

Once they reached the bottom of that first stairwell, they exited into the corridor. The lower ceilings made him nervous about the torches they had to use. Even those weren't providing enough light as they flickered badly in the bad air.

They were pretty deep at that point, and the air quality would have been lethal to an unprotected person. Even their medical nanites weren't going to be enough to clean out someone's blood at this point.

They followed the directions given to them and were quickly at another stairwell leading downward. This one had a sign indicating the level that the fusion plant was on. It was almost twice as deep as they'd already come. Whoever had decided to build it down there had made certain that it was well protected.

Every five minutes, they each checked the air remaining in their bottles, discarding any that were too low. Best not to take chances. It took them half an hour of slow moving to reach the designated level.

The air there was so bad that the torches were almost dead. Carl pulled out one of the few battery-powered flashlights they had and turned it on.

To his surprise, the stairwell continued down. There was stuff below this incredibly deep location. He'd had no idea of the complexity and scope of the underground support system that made it possible to live in such a large city.

They ran into their first roadblock about five minutes later. It was a security door that had a keypad on it to keep unauthorized personnel out. It was dead, but they had an actual, physical key that Leader Mordechai had provided to bypass it.

That was certainly something one didn't see every day.

Carl fitted the key into the lock. It stuck a little, but he finally got it to turn and heard a loud click as the lock opened. He pulled the door wide and looked into the dark corridor beyond. Once again, it looked like every other section down underneath the megacity: dark, somewhat dirty, and cold.

A sign on the wall indicated that they needed to take a specific set of turns to get to the fusion plant. This level, even though it was very deep beneath the city, was enormous. Most of it seemed dedicated to the maintenance of the fusion plant and the distribution of power generated by it.

He immediately noted that the support system wasn't intact. A lot of panels were open, and it looked as if specific power conduits had been either removed or jury-rigged in some fashion. It was going to take a *lot* of work to get the fusion plant back to providing power to the city like Mordechai wanted.

The next security door was going to be more difficult because it had been computer-controlled, but there was no power. It was built with a battery to support itself during a blackout, but that would've drained long ago.

They were going to have to use a little brute force and ignorance, as Kelsey said, when they reached it. For that, Julia would come in very handy, indeed. As would the axe that she'd recovered from a fire station they'd passed.

Only when they reached the security door, it was wedged open. Leader Mordechai had been confident that it had been secured.

Carl led the group through the door and deeper into the power generation center with a sense of growing dread. His premonition proved dead on when they reached the area housing the fusion plant itself.

It was gone.

"Isn't there supposed to be a fusion plant here?" Julia asked, frowning.

Carl played his light around the large room and began cursing. Since he'd worked closely with the marines for years, the range and scope of profanity had become quite extensive.

When he finally ran out of nasty things to say, he headed for the cabinets along the periphery of the room that would typically contain the spare parts and tools needed to work on the fusion plant. As he began checking them, it quickly became evident that they were empty as well.

"Someone stole it," Carl eventually said. "Either that, or it was never here to begin with. Maybe Leader Mordechai got it wrong. Perhaps his ancestors moved the fusion plant to a lower level to protect it better, and that's where they installed the shielding."

"I don't think so," Austin said from where he bent over the area the fusion plant had been removed from. "The amount of corrosion on these bolts isn't all that great. Even with the low oxygen levels, I'd expect to see more rust and tarnish. These are almost bright. If I had to guess, the fusion plant was probably removed no more than a couple of years ago. Perhaps as little as six months."

He looked over at the rest of them and shook his head. "It seems to me that Leader Mordechai and Frankfort have been robbed. And without the fusion plant, I'm not sure how we're going to get out of this city either. Even if they still let us go, how will we power a train?"

"Who the hell could've taken it?" Ralph asked. "And how did they get in past all the guards up there?"

Carl started to answer, but Julia beat him to it by pointing downward.

"If they couldn't get in from the surface and the train system wasn't functional, there has to be something down lower that provided them with access. They also had to have a means of surviving in this awful atmosphere.

"Not only that, they had enough people, equipment, and training to safely disassemble and remove the fusion plant. Whoever they were, they knew *exactly* what they were doing and how to do it. We need to figure out who they were and where they went."

* * *

JULIA CONSIDERED the situation and did an inventory of the air bottles she carried. They had used maybe thirty percent of what they'd brought with them. They had a little bit of time that they could spend looking around, but they didn't have the air to go hunting extensively for where the equipment had been taken.

Thankfully, the people that had stolen the fusion plant hadn't taken any effort to hide their tracks. A lot of the equipment they'd taken was cumbersome and had left obvious marks on the floor. The series of scratches and scrapes led deeper into this level rather than back the way they'd already come. That gave her a direction to go looking for answers.

"We've got enough air for a little bit of searching," she said as she headed off.

The others didn't seem convinced, but they didn't argue against her plan either. They were undoubtedly as curious as she was.

Following the scrapes and gouges in the floor quickly led them to what could only be a service lift. Based on the doors, it was large and probably had a very high capacity. That would've allowed the intruders to get the fusion plant—suitably broken down into sections —moved to a different level.

What she didn't understand was how it could've been used without any power.

She pressed the button to summon the lift, and to her surprise, it illuminated. A minute later, the doors opened, and a large lift car awaited them. One with operational overhead lighting that dispelled the gloom all around them.

It was downright spooky. All the scene needed was some intruding mist and disturbing background music.

"How is this working?" Carl demanded. "This isn't possible. It's not designed to have an internal power supply."

"Could another fusion plant be online?" Austin asked.

Carl shook his head. "Cities aren't designed like warships. They have one fusion plant. Two would be an unneeded expense. Maybe Imperial City or the Imperial Palace had more than one, but not a mid-sized city like Frankfort. The technology is too reliable to need a spare. If well maintained, there would never be a need to shut it down. They were built for continuous operation."

"Is there any way we can tell which level the lift went to?" Julia asked. "If we can get to that level, maybe we can find out exactly how they did what they did and where this power is coming from."

Without bothering to respond, Austin opened the panel beside the buttons inside the lift and began pulling equipment from one of his pouches. He quickly had a cable attached to the internal systems and was looking at the small screen in his hands.

"We're at the highest level this lift services. It looks as if it's made a lot of trips down to the very bottom level. And, by the way, that's *really* far down. I had no idea that the city went so deep. Hell, it may go down farther if there are other lifts or stairs."

"There's no real way to know unless we look," she said.

Carl shook his head. "No. What do we do if the lift stops working? If we get trapped down there, we're dead."

Without bothering to argue, Julia pressed the button for the lowest level. The lift doors slid shut, and it started down with them all inside.

Carl glared at her. "Have you lost your mind?"

"If the lift has made as many trips as you say, the odds of it breaking during this one trip are pretty damn low."

The other three didn't seem convinced, but it wasn't as if they had a choice at this point. Julia had committed them all now.

13

Talbot watched the advancing forces and was impressed with the numbers he saw. For such a primitive people, the horde fielded quite a few dismounted fighters. He supposed that shouldn't surprise him, as warlike as they were.

When they'd had the opportunity to walk through the horde city, they'd only seen a small area. There had been a lot of civilians, merchants, and other noncombatants, but the number of troops they'd passed had been relatively large. Most of them hadn't been mounted, and neither were the forces arrayed against them now.

He wondered if that meant that the mounted forces were scouring the plains around the two cities. Did that mean that a large group of mounted riders was fanning out to make sure that they didn't escape?

Probably.

The group below the tower in which he was perched seemed to have grown to around a thousand people. That was quite a force. If they had more than one group penetrating the city, this was going to be a tough fight for the locals to win.

When Lydia returned from passing on what they'd seen, he broached that subject with her. "Is there word on other forces? Are we looking at multiple groups with this many people, or is this it?"

The woman grimaced. "There are three groups. This seems to be the main one, but two others parallel it. Our best guess is that we're dealing with maybe three thousand unmounted warriors, with possible reinforcements coming in behind them."

Talbot raised an eyebrow. "And do you have the defensive forces to resist that?"

She shrugged. "We've never been invaded on this scale before. When the horde first formed, they were a much smaller group. In the last sixty years, as they built their city, they've enslaved many from other groups and now have a large number of young warriors.

"Can we fight them head to head? No. We're going to have to use all the advantages of being a defender and knowing the terrain grants us. Some traps and ambushes will reduce their numbers.

"We'll start that process here. Before the building lost most of its glass, we'd break out a window to use for our attack, which might have given us away beforehand. Now that the glass is gone, we can pick any vantage point that we want and reduce their leadership while forcing them to keep their heads down."

"What kind of weapons do you have that will be accurate at this range?" Chloe asked. "For a bow and arrow, it's going to be impossible to hit any particular individual. There are enough people down there that the odds of you hitting *someone* are fairly good, but we must be seven hundred meters up and a few hundred from their lead elements. Add another hundred or more to reach their leadership if we can even identify them at this range."

The woman grinned at Chloe and went to a nearby closet, opening it to reveal a long-barreled weapon. It didn't look like a flechette weapon. In fact, it bore a striking resemblance to weapons used in war vids that Kelsey had made him watch from the prespaceflight era.

"This is a sniper rifle," the woman said. "It uses a chemical propellant to fire slugs of copper-sheathed lead. With an appropriate aiming mechanism like this magnifier and some skills, you can hit a human target at this distance.

"Admittedly, firing from such a high angle makes targeting a problematic concept because the bullets travel in an arc. When they're fired, they rise, and then they fall as influenced by gravity. They're also subject to deviation caused by the wind, which at this height is something to consider.

"We have other primitive weapons at the ambush sites that are going to make them pay for every meter they push into the city. At some point, they're going to get tired of being killed and turn around. If we don't decisively engage them, they can't inflict the level of casualties they'd need to make us submit."

Talbot nodded. "That makes sense, but what if they settle in? If they take over a set of buildings, you'll be at a disadvantage pushing them back out. With those kinds of numbers, they'll be able to come in and keep reinforcing themselves. The disparity in forces is going to make it difficult to kick them back out again."

Richard shook his head. "With the forces and weaponry we've managed to put together, we can take any building from them. All the structures are connected to the underground levels, and if we can get access to them, we can strike into their midst even though they think they've secured all access.

"The Imperials were quite clever about figuring out unobtrusive ways to get services into their buildings. These people will probably not be able to defend any building they try to hold."

"If you say so," Talbot said with a shrug. He didn't bother masking the uncertainty in his voice. These people might know their city better than him, but he knew that pushing out a determined force that outnumbered you was a tricky business.

"So, when are you going to start using that sniper rifle?" Chloe asked.

"If I was confident of my aim, I might try now," Lydia said. "We've been authorized to engage them, but they're still too distant to accurately hit their leadership."

Talbot held out a hand. "This might be a situation where my Marine Raider augmentation can be useful. Let me take a look."

She considered him for a long moment and then handed the weapon over. "Okay, we'll give it a try. I don't think that you're going to be able to target single individuals at this distance, much less hit them at this angle, but it'll be interesting to watch you try."

Talbot cleared broken glass away from the area nearest a shattered window that had a decent view of the enemy and knelt. The window had once gone from floor to ceiling. Now the opening allowed him to aim down as much as he liked without exposing himself overmuch.

Not that he expected that the enemy was going to be able to effectively return fire. Even their antiarmor weapons weren't all that accurate at any range at all. Bows wouldn't have a chance of hitting him since the arrows couldn't get this high.

The weapon had a primitive scope attached to it. It was a long tube that held what looked like very small crosshairs inside and provided a significant magnification of the objects being viewed. Of course, even at this distance, the magnification was insufficient to provide any real detail.

"Can we take this off?" he asked. "I need to have a direct look at what I'm going to be shooting at. I hate to say it, but my augmented vision is better than what you're getting through this scope."

Richard looked at Lydia and then shrugged. "It will need to be sighted back in once you're done, but I'm willing to give this a try because I'd also like to see you in action. Hand it here."

Talbot passed it over to the man, who quickly removed the scope and handed the rifle back.

"It has five shots in the internal magazine," Lydia said. "Once you've fired them, hand it back to me, and I'll reload one time. I'm not willing to squander more than ten rounds. The ammunition is quite time-consuming and costly to make. They're worth killing the enemy leadership with but shouldn't be wasted."

Talbot grinned. "Oh, I think you'll be pleased with how well this is going to work. How do I tell which of them are leaders?"

He looked down the fixed sights as he aimed at the horde warriors, using his augmented vision to zoom in on them.

"All of the officers have colored stripes on their shoulders. If you see color there, you're looking at an officer. The lighter colors are lower ranks, and the darker ones are higher. A deep red is pretty much the best kind of target if you can find one."

Talbot swept the sights across the approaching enemies. Spotting a bit of red, he focused in on the man and saw that this one was dressed in armor that was of much higher quality than the people around him.

His first shot was going to be an educated guess, so he lined up with the man and made an estimate of where he thought the shot would go. He kept his focus reasonably wide so that he could tell where the bullet hit and squeezed the trigger so as not to jerk the weapon.

The kick against his shoulder was surprisingly sharp. Luckily, his augmentation made the recoil manageable.

His first shot went somewhere beyond the target and caused everyone below to duck a little, but they didn't scramble for cover as the weapon ejected a piece of brass off to the side. It seemed ready to fire again, so Talbot lined up his next shot more carefully and lowered his point of aim.

The recoil was much easier to deal with the second time. This shot also went long, but Talbot saw its impact point as a puff of dirt a bit to the side and behind the target. The combat computer in his head made a few calculations, and he lowered his weapon to match where he thought he needed to aim to hit the target in the chest. Then, for the third time, he fired the weapon.

Blood blossomed from the target's chest, and the man fell backward. Based on the way he lay, Talbot was pretty sure he was dead. Even if he wasn't, it hardly mattered. He was out of the fight.

"Got him," Talbot said. "Now, let's see if we can make these bastards pay a little bit more before we have to relocate."

* * *

THE GROUP that Kelsey was assigned to set out through the labyrinth of tunnels under the city. Their destination was the ground floor of a large building halfway across the city.

Once they arrived, she saw that it didn't have windows on the ground level. The bottom floor had been thoroughly cleaned out and turned into another marshaling area and defensive redoubt. One with some peculiar features.

The leader of Kelsey's attack group quickly arrayed their forces behind a ramp of dirt that went all the way to the ceiling. There were depressions that people could fire their weapons through, but the holes were small, only as wide as a person and less than half a meter from the ceiling.

Without waiting for permission, Kelsey scrambled up the embankment and took a look for herself. Someone had driven a lot of metal rods between the dirt and the wall to keep it from collapsing once the wall was breached, she noted.

Against the exterior wall at intervals, placed away from the openings the people would use, were explosive charges linked by wire. She suspected they were shaped charges, designed to send most of their force outward.

It was going to be interesting to see whether it worked like the defenders imagined or if the dirt collapsed under the shock wave. Dangerous but educational.

Satisfied, Kelsey climbed back down and made her way to where the man marshaling their forces was standing. "How far away is the enemy, and how much time do we have before you blow the walls?"

The man shrugged slightly. "The observers say we have about ten minutes before the first group arrives. We're attacking the rightmost of the three prongs.

"The plan is simple. We set off mines buried outside the building to disrupt them, blow the walls, cause as much havoc and death as we can, and then retreat back underground.

"I'll arm self-destruct charges underneath the floor here as soon as we're clear. They'll trigger them when they pursue us, and the explosions will kill many more of them as we make our way to the next fallback position and repeat the process."

Grateful that she knew what was happening next, Kelsey found a place behind the embankment and waited for the fight to start. She hoped the piled dirt really did manage to stop the blast.

Even if it did, it was going to be impressively loud. Many of the locals would suffer permanent hearing loss, even if they stuffed their fingers in their ears, as was likely. There was only so much human flesh could do to stop the shock wave.

She hunkered down against the hard-packed dirt and examined

her weapons more closely. When the time came to use them, she needed to know how everything worked. Some practice would've been a lot better, but she'd just have to make do.

The submachine gun was definitely handmade rather than constructed off a machined template, but the gunsmith had had real skill. She ran her fingers across the smooth metal and decided that it was an impressive piece of work. She confirmed that the safety was engaged and that she knew how to quickly make it ready to fire.

She'd seen weapons like this in a number of the old vids, so she had some idea what was going to happen when she used it. It would obviously have a fair amount of recoil because the stock was made to deliver it to the shoulder. Each of the magazines was filled with brass cylinders that contained copper-sheathed lead slugs. Such pretty things for being so deadly.

It was similar—if far inferior in quality—to the Pirone Nitro Express 18 millimeter semi-automatic hunting rifle she'd used to kill the assassins that had come for her at the Imperial Retreat on Avalon. The bullets used by the submachine gun were also far weaker.

Still, the experience of using the massive weapon—which presently graced the wall in her quarters with Talbot aboard *Persephone* —gave her confidence that she could use these without any problem.

Unlike flechettes, these wouldn't cause massive damage due to their slow speed. She didn't think they'd be very good at penetrating armor either. Without testing, there was no way to be sure. She supposed she'd find out shortly.

The pistol was of a similar make, obviously a one-off by a professional. It was even more of a work of art than the submachine gun. She wished that she had the time and knowledge to disassemble both of them so that she could better understand how they worked.

Once she got off Terra, she'd double-check the databases on *Persephone* and see whether or not she could build weapons like this herself. They wouldn't be the most effective choice for combat, of course, but they'd make for interesting pieces to hang on her wall with the Pirone.

Or maybe she could take these with her when they left Frankfort.

The examination of her weapons successfully distracted her, so it only felt like a couple of minutes before the man in charge made a series of hand gestures, and everyone crouched lower, plugging their ears with their fingers.

Kelsey did the same, even though she knew that her auditory augmentation would protect her. Sometimes it was best to look like everyone else and not raise questions.

Once everyone was prepared, the man held up a hand with five fingers showing. Then he pulled his thumb in, showing only four. Three... two... one...

Kelsey squeezed her eyes tightly shut and hunched as low as she could right before a massive explosion shook the ground she lay upon. It felt like she was tossed up into the air, but when her eyes snapped open, it was only the ground having jumped, bouncing her a bit.

A second blast went off, and dust flew through the perforations in the dirt embankment. That would be the wall of the building being blown clear so that they could fire. Now sunlight was filtering through the airborne debris, and the people around her were scrambling up the incline with their weapons leading the way.

Kelsey did the same, settling in with her submachine gun. The street outside filled with horde soldiers. A lot of them were down, either wounded or dead. The ground had smoking craters where the bombs had gone off underneath their feet.

That didn't seem to deter the survivors, who were already turning their weapons toward the wall to face Kelsey and her companions. Many of them were armed with bows, and they began firing at once.

Thankfully, the blasts had affected their equilibrium, and their aim was crap.

Even as the enemy was acting, everyone around Kelsey opened fire. The din of the primitive weapons was almost as bad as the charges had been. Kelsey was glad that her hearing was adequately protected. She could only imagine what this must've been like for people without augmentation.

The weapon's stock slammed against her shoulder, and fire shot from the muzzle of her submachine gun. With so many soldiers in front of her, she could hardly miss as she swung her weapon back and forth, spraying the enemy with bullets.

In what felt like just a few seconds, the large magazine was empty. She hastily removed it and fumbled a replacement into place. When she squeezed the trigger again, nothing happened, and she realized she had to release the bolt to chamber the first round. She found the catch, and the weapon clattered a bit as the slide locked into place, and it was ready to fire again.

The death and destruction caused by these weapons, particularly at short range, were merely horrific. Again, it wasn't the same as using flechette weapons, but for something put together by a relatively primitive people, it was outright deadly.

Kelsey resumed firing even as the enemy charged her position. She immediately realized that there wasn't going to be enough time for the people around her to retreat in an orderly fashion. There were far too many enemies about to overrun them.

Somewhere behind them, the man ordered a retreat, but Kelsey already knew that they were going to end up fighting the horde inside the building. She fired for as long as she could and then slid back down the embankment only when she was forced to.

She was on steady footing when the first of the enemy warriors came through the opening above her. Apparently, the embankment wasn't as hard to climb as the defenders had hoped. Now the building was going to become an abattoir filled with blood and death.

Kelsey allowed her submachine gun to drop, held only by a strap around her neck, and drew her swords. In close quarters like these, they'd make far better weapons than her pistol. As soon as the first enemy slid down the slope in front of her, she leapt forward and struck.

Her hull metal blades easily cut through the warrior's sword and his body. With her enhanced strength driving the blow, it barely even slowed her momentum, and she was already striking at the next person coming down the embankment even as the first one fell.

With her strength restored and her preferred weapons in her hands, she was a whirling dervish of mayhem. The problem was that there were dozens of new fighters climbing over the embankment to face her every single second.

They were going to be overrun no matter what she did. They had to retreat as quickly as possible so that the man could arm the traps under the floors.

"Retreat!" Kelsey shouted. "Run while I cover you!"

The enemy was pressing the people around her heavily, and the line couldn't retreat, but those to the rear of the room were able to dash for safety. Those that were heavily engaged would have to back up step by step while holding the horde away from their retreating friends.

Kelsey never doubted that this was what she had to do. The only question now was whether she'd survive defending these people and escape herself.

14

Once he'd gathered more air bottles, Jared found himself at a little bit of a loss as to what he should do next. Everyone else was assisting an exhausted Lily in setting up a makeshift triage station so that she could use her advanced equipment and have semiknowledgeable hands to help her when the inevitable stream of wounded began coming in.

He'd decided to assist in that, but when he arrived, the guards redirected him to the upper-level tunnels. It only took him a couple of minutes to realize that his ever-present minders were taking him to the same building where they'd last met Leader Mordechai.

His legs were aching by the time he was halfway up, and he was out of breath. He made a mental note to exercise more and maybe even start working out with the marines once he got off this damned planet. Being a Fleet officer was just a little too sedentary.

Once he'd reached the very top of the building, he found Leader Mordechai standing fairly close to the makeshift rail, arms casually arrayed behind his back as he stared out over the city he ruled.

Jared could faintly hear the sounds of battle below. The pops of gunshots—he could thank Kelsey and her preflight Terra entertainment vid fetish for knowing what those were—that echoed between the buildings and through the cavernous canyons that made up the city. He was sure there was a lot of shouting and swordplay as well, but they were too high for that to be audible.

Without windows, the wind blew into the building, gusty and strong. It also howled as it went through various openings in the buildings around them, creating a kind of subliminal growl.

He stepped over to stand beside the old man. Two guards stood nearby, undoubtedly making sure that he didn't do anything untoward with their leader. The two guards that had accompanied Jared for the last few hours quickly joined them.

After Mordechai failed to say anything, Jared felt the need to fill the silence.

"I can hear that the fighting has started."

Mordechai nodded without looking over at him. "Indeed, it has. This is a day that I'd hoped would not come during my lifetime, but now that it has, we shall crush our enemies. Or, I suppose, die trying."

Having said that, he turned to face Jared. "Some of your people are involved in the fighting. Are you concerned about them?"

"Of course," Jared promptly responded. "Even one bit of bad luck might see them injured or killed. That's the risk that even the very best of them take, even with all of their advantages. Every time I lose someone like that, it hurts. I want to see them all come back safely."

Mordechai nodded and smiled grimly. "Your feelings do you credit. That's how a leader thinks. You've obviously commanded people for some time to have developed those instincts."

"It's not really a matter of how long I've been in command of others," Jared said with a grimace. "I've seen people with similar authority view them as game pieces to be expended where needed to gain some tactical advantage.

"My views on the subject are a lot more complicated. My people's lives are something to be hoarded and treasured. I hate having to send them into fights where I know that some of them will die, but circumstances force my hand on occasion. It hurts each and every time."

He took a deep breath and let it out slowly. "How's the fighting going? Have you got any word on how we're doing?"

The older man nodded. "It seems the enemy is more resistant to ambush than we'd hoped. I'd forgotten how deeply ingrained their ferocity was. The majority of the people that we're facing are young and have been trained since birth to fight for the horde. It's almost as if they don't care whether they live or die, so long as their teeth are in the throats of their enemies.

"One of our ambushes has already gone bad. I don't have many details at this point, but our people are withdrawing from the areas as quickly as they can while a rearguard holds the horde back. I'm afraid that's the group where your sister Kelsey is."

Jared could feel the other man eyeing him to see how he responded to that. All he could do was shake his head slightly. Of course Kelsey was involved with something like that. How could she *not* be?

"I'm not surprised. If there's a desperate fight to be had, she's going to be in the middle of it. The only thing that's going to work to her advantage is that, with her Marine Raider augmentation, she's more than a match for any group of people that wants to kill her. Give her half a chance, and she'll get out of there in one piece, even if she can't win the fight."

Mordechai seemed to consider that for a moment and then nodded. "That matches well with the stories that I've heard about the Marine Raiders as I grew up. They were gone long before the computers crushed Terra, but the stories of their exploits were passed down through my family.

"Raiders were based here in Frankfort, though I'm certain they weren't the only group. They lived deep down underneath the city in places that none of the enemy collaborators would've been able to find them. My ancestors kept their secrets and hid them until the time came for them to take the fight to the enemy."

The older man wrapped his fingers around the railing and stared out over the city. "Those men and women fought against the invaders for decades. From what I understand, those were strange days.

"The troops that the rebels sent down at first seemed insane.

They'd scream and shout, begging for death even as they carried out the will of their masters. Very few people saw how crazed they were because simply seeing them meant that you were either taken into their number or killed. They left very few alive and free in their wake.

"There were other collaborators who seemed completely normal. They came down and took over for the leaders that the Emperor and his people had put into place. That was later, though.

"My ancestors vanished into the population then, hidden by the very citizens of the city, much like the Marine Raiders. I suppose if the enemy had been quick enough—or Frankfort important enough—they would've been taken to join whatever madness was taking place elsewhere. A number of the citizens were taken away to fight for the enemy and never returned."

The older man rubbed his face tiredly and looked over at Jared. "The Marine Raiders fought, and—even though their abilities were legendary—they weren't sufficient to win the day. Within two decades after the fighting had started, they were gone. They went out on a mission and never returned.

"Our ancestors waited for them, hoping that at least some of them would make their way back, but they were never seen again. I'd imagine that they ran into a force they couldn't defeat and were trapped. They likely died in a final desperate fight for survival. One they lost."

The two of them stood in silence for several minutes, listening to the faint sounds of fighting below. Eventually, the older man looked over at Jared.

"I understand that happened all too often in the Empire after the rebels won. I've heard many stories about ships that fought similar battles. You indicated that your rank is admiral, so you've commanded ships. Perhaps a large number of them. Yet you come to the city with a dozen people and no fleet. How is that?"

Jared sighed. "It's a complicated story. The truth is that I'm new to flag rank. Only a few years ago, I was in command of just about the smallest kind of warship that could travel through the flip points.

"The rebels missed the planet we came from during the fighting. Rather, I should say that they never invaded. They used EMP weapons five hundred years ago, just like they did against Terra. They also destroyed our capital and spaceport with kinetic strikes like the one you saw here.

"It took us a long time to get back into space. Even once we did so, our ships were nothing compared to what the Old Empire had. The only thing we had going for us was that we were independent.

"I suppose that we were also blessed by the fact that Emperor Marcus sent his son Lucian to our world. The warships that came with him defeated the force that was sent to occupy us. They all died except for Lucian and some civilians that they rescued along the way. With the emperor's line unbroken, Lucian led us, driving us to get back what we'd lost."

"After that, we began exploring to see what had happened to the Old Empire. After all the stories passed down throughout the years, we were certain that it was dead. It turned out that we were wrong."

He stared out over the city for a minute, letting his mind roam back over all that had happened in the last few years. When he finally spoke again, his voice was firm.

"My expedition found a derelict ship, the battlecruiser *Courageous*. The crew was long dead, but the computers on board that ship gave us the true history of what had happened at the end of the Old Empire.

"Once we knew the stakes, we set out to finish what our ancestors had started. The true story of the AIs was lost to us because it had been kept secret by the emperors and only passed down to the heirs when they were old enough to understand. That proved to be a mistake.

"Boiled down, the last few years have had a lot of fighting and more than our share of adventures, but we've found a lot of ships that could be repaired. Those now form the nucleus of the fleet that protects what we call the New Terran Empire."

The older man nodded slightly. "I'm sure there's a lot more to that story, but I really don't have time to hear it. So, now you had a fleet whereas before you just commanded a small ship?"

"That's right," Jared agreed. "Promotions came rapidly after that. I suppose that's not so surprising since our original fleet was tiny. With so many more ships being brought into service, rapid promotions were unavoidable. My original crew and I had a lot more experience using this new technology than anyone else, so we got promoted faster and sooner than many of the others.

"Personally, I'm not certain that I was ready. It wouldn't have been something that I'd have chosen to do on my own, but needs must when the devil drives."

Mordechai gave him a curious look. "And why would you say that you weren't ready?"

"I suppose that would require me explaining a few other things. The emperor is my father, but I'm a bastard child. Everyone in Fleet has always either gone out of their way not to show any favoritism toward me at all or been actively hostile. It's been… challenging.

"Kelsey and Julia are his legitimate daughters. Needless to say, they weren't huge fans of mine to begin with, and in the case of Julia, I still have some more work to do to convince her that I really don't want to steal the Imperial Throne.

"Their older brother saw me as a threat, and that made my life very hard. Getting promoted to command a destroyer was hard enough. Imagining more for myself? I hadn't bothered. Basically, I thought that was as high as I'd ever go."

The older man gave him a tired smile. "I think you'll find the circumstances of your birth don't dictate how well you do in life, which I believe you already know. So, where is your fleet, Admiral?"

"I went on a short mission into enemy space to gather information and deliver a report. We reprogrammed a computer-controlled destroyer for the ruse. The goal in that was to keep them from looking in the area of space where we were operating.

"The fleet that I nominally command was following at a safe distance. Our intention was to come to Terra afterward as a group. Only once we arrived to deliver the report, the Rebel Empire commandeered the destroyer and sent it off to Terra via a different route.

"My fleet was unable to follow. Honestly, I'm not sure that they're going to be able to even get here. They might have been forced to turn back.

"We hid aboard the destroyer and overpowered the people they'd put aboard. Their original goal was to pick up a lethal virus to deploy here at Terra and kill everyone on the planet. We disposed of that, and it will hopefully take them quite some time to figure out what happened."

Mordechai's face paled. "If they tried such once, they'll try again. The next time, they might succeed. How can my people fight against something like that?"

"You can't," Jared said bluntly. "We've got to stop the AIs before they can make another attempt. The design for the virus was supposedly destroyed, so they're not going to just be able to cook up another batch. If my people and I can get what we need at the Imperial Palace and get back to the ship that brought Kelsey here, we'll have a decent chance of ending this war. That's why we need your help in getting out of here."

Mordechai didn't say anything for a long while. He gripped the railing with his hands tight enough to turn his knuckles white as he stared out over the city and listened to the faint sounds of fighting below. At long last, he turned and faced Jared.

"Trust doesn't come easy to my people, Admiral Mertz. We've been under the heel of the computer for a very long time. Yet your story is so implausible that I have to give it credit. Honestly, I believe that you're telling me the truth. What are you hoping to find at the Imperial Palace, and how can it help you win this war?"

Jared considered whether or not he should tell the truth. They were only going to have one shot of getting the override. If he screwed this up, they might never get out of Frankfort. In the end, he decided that the truth would serve him best.

"There are vaults underneath the palace. Inside of them is a device called an override. It's a piece of hardware that was designed to shut down the master AI. If we can get into the space station where this thing is, all we need to do is plug it in, and the war is over.

"We can order the AI to send out instructions to every unit that it controls, telling them to stand down. If we can get our hands on the override, then we only need to find a way to get back into space so that we can use my sister's ship to escape the Terra system."

"That sounds like a daunting task," Mordechai said with a grimace. "If you have no small ships to escape Terra with, how will you ever get off this planet? Even if you do, the computer waits above. How will you stop it from just destroying you?"

"I'm not exactly sure," Jared admitted with a shrug. "No matter what happens, it's going to be complicated. We're taking a risk, but we can't afford to just give up. Even if the odds are against us, we must succeed. If the AIs have decided that killing humanity on Terra is a good idea, how long before they decide to do it everywhere?"

"The idea of the computers exterminating humanity is even more shocking than them enslaving us. Frankly, it's terrifying.

"I know nothing of the worlds beyond Terra. Let me be honest. I know little about the areas of Terra distant from my own city. I'm not certain how much assistance I can be to you in this matter."

The man's expression firmed. "What I can say is that I'm not a man given to blind trust. Yet everything you've told me has rung true, and I'm an excellent judge of character. I've decided that I will do everything within my power to assist your people in getting to the Imperial Palace. The computers cannot be allowed to win this fight."

The man's words were a relief to Jared. This was the kind of breakthrough that he'd been hoping for. The only problem was that they had to win this fight before any of it mattered.

If they lost, the horde would occupy the ruined megacity and hunt them down. With them controlling the plains around the city, there could be no escape that didn't involve getting the fusion plant back online and using the train system to escape the area. They couldn't fight all of those mounted warriors.

Everything was resting on Carl. He really hoped the young man and his companions were making progress because they really needed some good news right now.

15

When the lift reached the bottom of the shaft and the doors opened, Carl saw that it let out into a long, dingy corridor lit by functional overhead lights. Proof that this area was powered. Somehow.

The scrapes that they'd followed into the lift were still visible, heading directly down the corridor. There were side corridors, but none of them were illuminated. For the moment, it made the most sense to track the quarry they'd come after.

Julia moved to the front of the group, seemingly ready to defend them if there was any trouble. Carl was more than confident that she could do so with her Marine Raider augmentation, even though she was unarmed. Anything that she had in her hands was a deadly weapon, including the heavy bag filled with air bottles that she now hefted.

The sight of the bag made him pause to check his equipment and to determine what the atmosphere around them was like. To his surprise, it was breathable. The carbon dioxide levels were only slightly elevated, and the oxygen was normal. Unlike the floors above them, life support was online down here.

"There's breathable air," he said as he took off his mask. "We need to conserve our air."

Julia didn't look convinced, and neither did the others.

"It's safe," he assured them. "I'll let Ralph carry the tester, and he can check as we go. I'll set it up so that the alarm will go off if the carbon dioxide levels start going up or the oxygen levels drop.

"Someone took the time to refurbish the life-support systems down here. More interestingly, they had the knowledge to do so. It takes a lot of know-how to disassemble a fusion plant without destroying it, and their work on the life-support system only confirms that whoever did this has training. Based on the fact that the power is still on, we can't assume that they're gone, so we need to be careful."

Julia seemed to consider that for a moment before nodding. "Stand still and let me listen. If anyone is working around here, I might be able to hear them with my enhanced hearing."

After about thirty seconds, she shook her head. "I can hear the air handlers, but that's about it. I honestly don't think that anyone else is down here. We're seeing what they left behind after they finished taking the fusion plant. I'll wager they left the lights on in case they needed to come back."

"Why would they do that?" Austin asked. "If they've got a power supply, why leave it here? Somebody might come down and find it. Like, for example, us."

Carl gestured around them. "This is a bubble of good air. Everything above us is lethally toxic. That's one hell of a barrier to people without technological know-how. The locals would never have made their way down here on their own.

"And only the fact that Julia is insane got us into that lift. Honestly, any sane human being would think that this level had the very worst atmosphere. It's only pure luck that it's not. Seriously, the chances of anyone actually finding this place were very low."

"So let's take advantage of the situation," Julia said as she started walking forward. "Let's find out what's down here."

Carl expected her to keep walking forward until she found whatever was at the end of the scrape marks, but she didn't. In fact, she stopped and looked inside the rooms as they passed. Each and every one of them was filled with unmarked boxes and what looked like salvaged equipment. Nothing belonging to the fusion plant from what he could see.

"Let's get a decent idea of what we're passing by," he insisted. "A few minutes isn't going to cost us anything."

The room that he selected seemed to be mostly filled with parts from a power distribution system, undoubtedly from somewhere above them. It looked like whoever was stripping the lower levels of the megacity had been thorough. They'd taken everything that wasn't nailed down.

Leader Mordechai was going to be seriously pissed when he found out. Thankfully, that wasn't something that he or his friends had screwed up. Hopefully the man wouldn't hold it against them.

After a few more rooms, Julia grew impatient and strode ahead, forcing the others to hurry to keep up. Carl didn't blame her. They were almost certainly going to find parts and equipment stripped from the megacity in all of these rooms. They'd have plenty of time later to do a more thorough inventory once they found the fusion plant.

Where the hell had these people taken it? Why disassemble it and then move it all the way down here? He supposed it would make sense if they intended to hide out at this lower level and make sure that no one came looking for them, but Julia hadn't heard anyone. Where had they gone?

Honestly, this wasn't making a whole lot of sense. There had to be some aspect of the situation that he just didn't get yet.

As they walked, he started wishing that they had a map of the lower levels. There was nothing in this corridor to give them a clue what they were headed toward. Admittedly, there were lots of plaques over the doors that had letters and numbers, but their meaning was obscure without an index. He supposed it was only meant to be helpful to maintenance teams.

Thankfully, they had the scrapes on the floor to follow. Tracking them to their ultimate destination took about twenty minutes.

When they finally reached the end of the corridor, he wasn't really all that surprised to find a maglev train platform. Just exactly the sort of thing that Leader Mordechai had promised that they could get working and use from one of the upper levels. This station must've been used for maintenance purposes.

He'd seen stations just like this on other worlds in the Rebel Empire. The trains could go down the tunnels at high speed, reaching their destinations in relatively short periods of time.

Unlike the more public stations that he'd seen before this, this one had none of the amenities one would expect to see when the general public would be using it. That only confirmed his guess that it was meant to serve the people that kept the city running.

The other thing of note was that there was no train sitting at the platform. There was also no fusion plant.

"This has to be where the power is coming from," Austin said. "Whoever energized the system to get here needed to keep this online so that they could be certain that they could come back for everything else they salvaged. The cost of keeping a limited portion of the life-support system online wasn't that much in the bigger picture."

"I don't see a train," Julia said. "Is there a way to summon one?"

"There's going to be some kind of control room where we could probably do that, but the question is whether or not we should," Carl said. "Rather than doing anything hasty, we should go back upstairs and report what we've found. There's going to be some fallout when Leader Mordechai hears what's happened. It wouldn't surprise me if he wants to come down and take a look at everything himself.

"Well, he might be a little old to make that trip, so he could send Jebediah instead. In any case, they don't seem like the kind of people that'll take this lying down. They're going to want their stuff back, and they're going to want to make somebody pay for taking it."

Julia shook her head. "They've already got the horde to deal with, so they're not going to go after another group of people while the fighting is still taking place."

Carl sure hoped that she was right, but he wasn't completely convinced. He only hoped that they could convince them that a technologically advanced group of people were probably armed with weapons that would stop them cold. A fight with people wielding flechette weapons would be a bloodbath.

It was probably a forlorn hope. There was going to be a reckoning at some point. Carl only hoped that he and his friends didn't get caught up in the middle of that particular fight, because it wasn't going to be pretty.

* * *

KELSEY FOUGHT for all she was worth, slashing with both swords at any horde warrior that came near her. She used her augmented muscles to jump into their midst from distances they didn't expect and killed with single strikes.

If the enemy's numbers hadn't been growing so rapidly because they were rushing the position, that might have made a difference. Unfortunately, for every person she cut down, three more climbed through the openings from the street.

They were being overwhelmed.

She dumped Panther into her system, letting the combat drugs take the rough edges off the world, seeming to slow everything happening around her. In actuality, her nerve and cognitive speed had been increased, giving her more time to assess and react to everything around her.

Kelsey wasn't a fan of how the drug made her feel—particularly when she came down from it—but in this kind of fight, it might just save her life.

She ducked under an enemy warrior's strike and jammed one of her swords into the man's torso. With her now free hand, she plucked a grenade off of the belt of one of the dead defenders at her feet, grabbed the metal ring in her teeth, and yanked it out.

She threw the grenade into the largest concentration of enemy nearby and retrieved her sword from the dying man's chest, slashing at a woman trying to cut her down from the side. She took off both the woman's hands in the same strike.

The explosion of the grenade shocked even her system, but the break in the enemy's attack was just what she needed.

Resuming her two-sword attack, she pushed the horde warriors back and allowed the remaining defenders a chance to retreat. Many of them had already died trying to hold the line, but a few of them managed to extract themselves.

With a break in the number of attackers around her, she quickly sheathed her swords and grabbed more grenades from the bodies of defenders. Keeping in mind the lethal radius, she began hurling the grenades into pockets of the enemy inside the building.

She knew that there was always the chance that she'd catch a piece of shrapnel, but that was a risk she was going to have to take. Combat wasn't safe. Everything was a calculated risk, and if she didn't take chances, they were probably all going to die.

The explosions killed many of their enemies and stunned everyone still in the room. Everyone except her.

Kelsey followed the rest of the defenders out of the room and turned to protect the retreat down the corridor. That came in the form of a large metal barrier that slammed down when the man leading the raid manipulated a lever beside the door.

The horde warriors immediately began pounding on it, but they wouldn't be able to break through before Kelsey and the rest escaped. This was the break they'd needed.

"Where do we go now?" Kelsey demanded. "Where did the rest go?"

The man, bleeding from a cut across his forehead, gestured down the corridor. "This takes us directly to the stairs. We go down three levels, and then we exit. There's a trap set up on the fourth level, so anyone going that far gets blown up."

Having said that, the man smiled cruelly. "There's also some bombs buried underneath the floor in the room behind us. As soon as we get out of the area, watchers in other buildings will set them off and kill as many of those trying to follow us as they can."

Kelsey nodded her approval. Working with the rest, she helped move the injured down the stairs and into the appropriate tunnels on level three. There was only a small group of defenders waiting to see if anyone else escaped, but it was enough to get everyone that needed a hand someone to lean on.

Once they were sure that no one else was coming, the defenders armed the booby traps, and everyone fled down the tunnel.

As they ran, Kelsey flushed her system of the Panther, and the world became duller as her senses seemed to slow. The world seemed so much drabber now.

Honestly, that was what she hated the most about Panther: having to let go of the almost god-like feelings it brought. The damned stuff was addictive.

Fifteen minutes later, they'd been through many twists and turns and even changed levels multiple times, so Kelsey knew that even if the enemy had come through the booby traps waiting to stop them, they'd never be able to track them in time to make a difference.

That wasn't to say it was impossible. A number of the people with her were injured, and they were leaving a blood trail that a determined enemy could follow.

When they finally gathered at the new location, the man in charge grimaced. "It looks like we've lost almost half our people. That wasn't what we were hoping for, but the enemy was more ferocious than we'd imagined possible. We're going to have to combine forces with another attack group because we just can't defeat a force this size by ourselves."

"Aren't they already engaged?" Kelsey asked.

The man shook his head. "None of the other ambushes have kicked off yet. This was the first group to arrive at a suitable location. I've heard your husband will soon be on his way to assist another such group. If you'd like to join them, I have no objection to having one of our people take you.

"I'm going to take the rest of our force and merge with another group. Our numbers might make a difference there. We might have failed to stop this particular force, but if we can exterminate the other two, that'll give us an advantage in pushing the remaining invaders back."

Kelsey considered turning down the offer, but if Talbot was about to get into a fight like this, she wanted to plant her back against his so that they could cover one another. She trusted her husband to stay alive, but in a melee like this, one inattentive moment could mean death.

"That sounds like a plan," she said grimly. "Let's be about our business."

16

By the time he'd run out of ammunition for the sniper rifle, Talbot had made quite an impression on the horde forces below them. After the first few kills, the enemy had realized that he was able to hit them effectively and sought better cover.

While he didn't manage to kill a lot of enemy officers, he convinced them to keep their heads down. That delay might prove useful for the defenders when it came to fighting off the other groups.

Richard and Lydia seemed *very* impressed at his accuracy.

"I can't imagine how having a machine in your head allows you to shoot so well, but I'm glad you're here," Richard said with a grin. "I wish we'd brought more ammunition. We've kept their heads down longer than I'd expected. That's going to help the ambush groups."

Talbot was pleased, but fighting from a distance wasn't his usual style. He didn't object to it in principle. After all, keeping the enemy from attacking friendly units was a positive thing. The longer they managed to keep the horde at bay, the better their eventual chances of winning this fight. Still, he'd rather be in the rough and tumble.

"Any word on the other ambushes?" he asked. "In particular, the group my wife is with."

The way the two locals glanced at one another made him uneasy. Something was wrong.

"Trot it out," he ordered firmly.

For a moment, it seemed as if they were going to keep him in the dark, but Richard finally sighed and nodded. "The ambush didn't go as planned. From what I've heard, they engaged the enemy, but the horde swarmed their position. They charged right into the ambush site.

"Your wife and the rest managed a fighting withdrawal, and she wasn't hurt, but it was a close thing. She's on her way to the same ambush site that we'll be moving to, although she's going to be down in the fighting zone, while we're going to provide long-range covering fire. I'm sorry that we didn't insist that she come with you."

Talbot laughed before he could stop himself. "You don't know my wife. No one can stop her once she's made up her mind. And don't mistake her small size for a lack of ferocity. If she wanted to, she could thrash me in a stand-up fight. She's had her augmentation for a lot longer than I have and can fight in ways that none of us can really imagine without having seen it. Just trust her to do what needs to be done."

Once they'd digested that, he continued. "So, now that we all know that I'm not going to rush off to save my retiring flower of a wife, what's the plan?"

"We're going to head down into the tunnels and move to an observation site across from the new ambush zone," Lydia said. "The setup is going to be very similar to the one your wife was just at. They'll be inside a building so that the horde can't see them and will attack them just like this last time.

"I've made arrangements to have access to more weapons at this location so that we can utilize your specific talents more effectively. The plan for the ambush is going to be modified so that the engagement time is shorter for the people on the ground. They're also going to use heavier firepower to kill more of the invaders and keep additional distance between the groups so that they can escape more readily.

"Our job will be to provide both a distraction and kill off as many of the enemy as possible before they can get into the building. We're going to be the people that make sure your wife and the rest can effectively disengage when they're ready to."

Talbot slowly nodded. "That sounds like a serviceable plan, but I'd have to see the specific layout before I can make any suggestions for improvement. If you have any explosives that can be thrown, I'm pretty accurate with those as well. In any case, whatever you've got, I can probably use it better than whoever you originally planned to fire it."

She smiled at his response. "I've already taken that into account. We're gathering everything we can think of to take advantage of your specific skills and abilities. Unlike this observation post, others are going to be adding their fire to yours at this new site, so your friend doesn't have to feel like a third wheel this time."

"Chloe is used to me hogging all the glory."

His subordinate punched him in the arm. Hard. "Don't listen to this guy. I want my turn. Big guns for the win!"

"Then we'd best be about it," Richard said. "We don't want to be late to the party."

In the end, it took them about twenty minutes to get into position in the new building, and Talbot was both impressed and satisfied with the arsenal they'd gathered. Not only were there sniper rifles, he now had access to primitive grenades and even some rocket launchers.

Those would be an ugly surprise for the horde warriors, though how he was going to fire them effectively remained a mystery. He'd seen weapons like them in use in some of the vids that Kelsey insisted that he watch from prespaceflight Terra. An era called World War II.

This kind of weapon funneled burning propellant out the rear of the tube, and the exhaust would be lethal. As he was inside a building, Talbot wasn't sure how he'd make that work.

He supposed that they wouldn't have brought the weapons if they didn't have a plan. He'd just have to wait for them to explain it to him.

Chloe took her share of the weapons and went to a different section of the building. She'd be providing support in much the same way he would, he was sure. She might not have Raider augmentation, but her implants and experience would be more than enough to make her lethal at this range.

The ambush hadn't kicked off yet, though Richard assured him that the horde was very close. The building across what was like a deep valley from the building he was in rose five stories from the ground before it had any windows. The lower levels appeared to be natural stone. It was beautiful and would make excellent shrapnel when it fragmented.

Like the rest of the city, many windows were shattered, though there was more intact glass than he'd expected. Perhaps that was because the lower levels were closer to the ground and better shielded by the buildings around them.

Lydia had explained how the ambush group would use explosive charges to knock holes in the wall so that their people could fire through them at the enemy. There were also explosives buried in the ground just in front of the ambush site to take out any of the invaders unlucky enough to be caught in the blast area.

Based on how the horde had reacted the last time, that wasn't going to be as effective as the defenders had hoped. The horde warriors would countercharge and get in among the ambushers as quickly as they possibly could. Engagement time might be minimal.

Well, then, he'd just have to make the most of the opportunity. His efforts might mean the difference between life and death for the ambushers, including his wife. He'd damned well do whatever it took to see this work, no matter how dangerous it was.

* * *

JULIA and the rest had finally decided that they'd gathered all the information that they were going to get and made their way back to the lift. Once they'd affixed their air, they boarded and began the ride back up. It only took a couple of seconds for the atmospheric readout equipment to start announcing that the air had grown toxic.

Arriving safely on the level the fusion plant had been taken from, they walked to the other set of stairs and began the long trek back to the occupied levels. By the time they reached breathable atmosphere again, they'd used up about two-thirds of the air bottles they'd brought with them.

They found a group of guards waiting for them, and Julia asked to be taken to see Leader Mordechai. Thankfully, they didn't have to go to the stupid building where they'd visited him the last time. Even with her Marine Raider augmentation, she'd done a lot of climbing today and wasn't in the mood to do any more.

Instead, they met the man in the air handler room. Seated beside him was his son Jebediah.

The older man leaned forward expectantly. "We were beginning to worry. I hope you have good news. What is the condition of the fusion plant?"

"Missing," she said flatly. "Somebody stole it."

The two men across the table blinked at one another before Jebediah frowned at her, his voice a low rumble filled with disapproval. "What do you mean by that?"

"I mean that the fusion plant and all of it shielding aren't there anymore. Someone disassembled it, dragged the pieces to a maintenance lift, and took it down to the very lowest level.

"The lift still had power, so we took it down and discovered that they'd stripped the lower levels. They stashed a lot of equipment and parts in various rooms, but they took the fusion plant to a maglev train station on the lowest level.

"There weren't any trains present, so I have to assume that they just left the power on in case they wanted to come back and pick up more stuff. They also fixed the life-support systems on those lowest levels."

Everyone sat in silence for a full minute as they digested what she'd said.

Finally, Mordechai leaned forward. "How did they manage any of this?"

Julia shrugged. "Whoever they were, they obviously had some level of training with Imperial equipment. Disassembling a fusion plant isn't something that just anybody off the street is going to do, even on a world that hasn't lost access to technology. Someone knew exactly what they were doing."

"It looks like they took the fusion plant sometime between six months ago and a couple of years ago," Carl said. "The rooms on the lowest level are stuffed full of boxes and salvaged equipment. The places we checked had supplies and spare parts.

"It's obvious that they were systematically stripping as many levels of your city as they could. They wouldn't have just left the train system powered unless they intended to return for everything at some point."

Mordechai leaned back in his seat. "If this is true, it's extremely disturbing. Jebediah, I want you to accompany them back down and discover the truth of the situation for me.

"I want the rest of you to know that it's not that I doubt your word, but I want to hear that this terrible thing has happened from a source that I trust completely. Once my son has verified what you say —which I have no doubt that he'll do—then I'll decide what needs to be done next."

"We don't have enough air to take us all back down," Carl said with a shake of his head. "If you want the entire group to go, we'll have to gather some more before we start."

"Then don't take everyone," Mordechai said evenly. "It's not as if you're repairing anything at this point, so it seems that Julia could accompany my son."

"I'd like to go as well," Mertz said from the door behind Julia.

"Why?" Mordechai asked with one eyebrow raised.

"Because if that's the direction we're going to have to go, I want to see what it looks like for myself."

Mordechai considered Mertz's words for a few seconds and then nodded. "Very well. The three of you shall depart immediately if you have enough air to see you through."

Julia shot a questioning look at Carl.

The young man frowned slightly, thought for a few seconds, and then nodded slowly. "If Julia takes the partially filled bottles that we left here in the air handler room, that should be enough for the three of them to make the trip down and back, so long as they don't dawdle."

"Excellent," Mordechai said. "Then I won't delay you any longer."

Before they started down, Jebediah led Mertz and Julia to an area where they could eat. Once they'd done so and secured extra water for the journey, the three of them retraced the path to the stairs that led down.

Without any of the others to tell her when the air got bad, Julia relied on her olfactory augmentation to continuously sample the air quality and have her implants keep a running tally so that she could see what they were dealing with. When it became necessary, she told the others to don their masks.

She wasn't sure why she hadn't thought of using her built-in equipment the last time. Perhaps it was because she just wasn't used to using the implants and augmentation at all. She had to keep reminding herself that she was capable of doing a lot of things if she just thought about how she could use her equipment.

Once they reached the level the fusion plant had been taken from, Jebediah insisted that they spend some time examining the reactor room. After a few minutes, he grunted and slowly nodded his head.

"The evidence here fully backs up what you've said. I can see where a large machine was removed, and it's evident to me that it could not have been done just by the four of you in the short amount of time that you were gone.

"Also, the scratches on the metal plate where it rested have rusted. Trust me when I say that I have an excellent idea of how long it takes something to rust. Based on the level of corrosion, your guess of between six months and two years seems plausible.

"Now, let's go see what they've done below. I have to admit that I'm very interested in seeing this lift. None of the ones in the city above have been functional for a century, and I'm curious what the experience of traveling in one will be like."

Julia led the man to the lift and pressed the button. Since the lift car was on this level, the doors promptly slid open.

Jebediah stepped into the center of the lift and turned in a slow circle, examining everything under the artificial lights in the ceiling above his head.

"The light seems unnatural," he finally said. "Too steady, and it almost wavers in my vision. It's definitely not like sunlight or torchlight. I have to admit that this experience is somewhat disconcerting."

She grinned at him. "If you think that's disconcerting now, just wait until the lift car starts going down. You're going to feel a sense of motion. It's not going to be too bad, but you need to be aware in advance that it's going to happen. The trip will take a minute."

Once he'd nodded, she and Mertz piled into the lift behind him, and she pressed the button to take them to the lowest level. The doors slid shut, and down they went. No one said anything until they arrived at their destination.

When the doors slid open again, Jebediah stepped out and looked back into the lift. "That was an amazing experience," he admitted. "I can only imagine how much time and effort something like this would save me on my daily climb to the top of my father's building. I'm a fit man, but all those stairs wear on a person. I can't imagine how the old man does it every day."

Julia laughed. "That's just how old men are, vexing us young people. Come on. I'll show you a couple of the rooms where they stored some of the salvaged gear so that you can see what they've been up to."

She proceeded down the hall, opening doors and showing the two men all the boxed goods and salvaged equipment. Ten minutes later, they stood on the platform at the maglev station.

Jebediah put his hands on his hips and scowled. The overhead lights here were much brighter than in the lift or the hallway. Even he had to see that there was no way that they'd missed anything.

"Everything you said is true," he growled. "Someone has stolen from us. My father will not stand for that. I can assure you that he's going to make absolutely certain that whoever did this pays. Come, we must return to the surface."

They retraced their steps to the lift, and Julia pressed the button to take them back up.

Nothing happened.

Frowning, she pressed the button again. Still nothing. It

illuminated when she pressed it but went dark as soon as she removed the pressure. Only the overhead lights indicated the lift still had power.

"That doesn't seem very promising," Mertz said.

What had started as a short jaunt was now a survival situation.

"It looks like we've got a lot of walking to do," she said, pressing the button to open the doors again and gesturing at the stairway door to the right. "It's a good thing you've gotten all that practice in, Jebediah. We're going to have to get through the toxic air in a hurry, so all that exercise is now going to save your life."

With her augmentation, she wasn't going to have any trouble making the trip. If anyone was going to slow them down, it was going to be Mertz. She hoped he could keep up because she wasn't looking forward to having to carry the man.

Yet if that was what it took, she'd do it. For whatever reason, Kelsey loved him, so Julia wouldn't leave Mertz behind.

As much as part of her really wanted to.

She sighed. Maybe one day she'd get used to him. Unlikely, but possible.

With that, she opened the stairwell door. The sooner started, the sooner done. At least so long as nothing else went wrong.

17

"Hold up," Jared said. "We should salvage air bottles from this level before we try heading up, just to make sure we've got enough."

If they ran out of air, they'd die. There were dozens of levels above them with bad air, and that was only to the old fusion plant room. There were even more above that. They could breathe now. Best to gather what they could while they had time.

"Good idea," Julia said with a nod, though her tone was grudging.

They headed back toward the maglev station. Unfortunately for them, the first safety compartment they opened was empty. So was the second. And the third.

Whoever had stripped this level had taken *everything*. The missing air bottles were likely in one of the rooms around them. He couldn't imagine them being worth hauling off for these people.

Jared passed along his thoughts and then considered their options. If they spent the time looking for the air, they were extending their stay in the area that was subject to dangers that they might not understand.

Even if they decided to search for air in the extended stash, only pure luck would allow them to find it. Nothing was labeled, and the rooms were stacked deep, with almost everything small placed into boxes.

"I understand what you're saying," Jebediah said when Jared explained his thoughts. "Even so, we're not going to get another chance once we start back up. Let's at least look into every single room and see if we get lucky."

Giving in to the inevitable, Jared acquiesced. A quick search of all the rooms along the corridor leading to the maglev station didn't find anything that they could use. It was mostly salvaged equipment that wasn't labeled. None of the boxes had anything on them to identify their contents.

They were going to have to do this the hard way.

"We're going to have to make a try," Jared said grimly. "If we can get part way up into the area where the atmosphere is bad, we might be able to find some air bottles they didn't take. Or we could just do the smart thing and send Julia up with all of the ones we have and let her bring back help."

Jebediah shook his head. "I don't believe any of us should go off alone. There's no telling what she'll find on her way up. If there is some kind of trouble, she'd need someone to help pull her out of it."

Julia's eyes narrowed. "Not to be a pain in the ass, but that's a sexist comment. I can extract myself from any kind of trouble that you can, probably even better than you."

The large man raised his hands in a gesture of surrender. "Giving that impression was not my intention. I simply meant that any one of us can fall victim to a situation where two people would allow survival for both. What I said about you I hold equally true for myself or Admiral Mertz."

The prickly princess gave the man a long, hard look before she nodded curtly and opened the stairwell door. It was lit, which was good, though they had a hand light for when the air became too foul to allow for the torches.

They made it up five levels before the lights no longer worked. This must be the boundary for the power the thieves had linked into the city.

He turned the hand light on, and they made it two more levels before they had to switch to bottled air. Once they were safely protected, they resumed their trek and almost immediately ran into their first roadblock.

In this case, roadblock was the perfect word for the situation. The stairwell was closed off by a metal door with a mechanical lock.

It was probably intended to keep anyone from getting down into the lowest of maintenance levels, and it looked extremely sturdy. Without a key to open it, their options fell to brute force and ignorance, as Talbot was fond of saying.

Unfortunately for them, while Julia was fully augmented, her hands and feet were still made out of flesh. Beating on metal wasn't going to do her any good. She needed a tool with leverage to bring force to bear on the problem, but the door was smooth and looked like it would be hard to get through.

She shook her head. "If I had a knife, I might be able to make this work, but I'm not able to get enough leverage to pry it open. We're going to have to find another way."

"Before we go back down, let's spread out and see if there any air bottles on this level," Jared said. "Since the life-support system wasn't activated here, it's more likely that we'll find something."

Sadly for his optimism, the safety compartments on this level had been stripped as well. They were going to be trapped unless they found another way up or took a chance in the lift shaft.

The latter was a risk that he wasn't willing to take. The former was problematic because they hadn't seen any other stairwells servicing this section of the underground.

"I think our best bet is to find some kind of tool that will let me force my way through the door," Julia said. "It's also possible that we can find the air bottles that they scavenged."

"Without food or water, we're not going to be able to hold out for more than a few days, but they'll have noticed that we're missing by then," he said confidently. "They'll send Carl and the others to find us, and when they find that the lift isn't operational, he'll know what to do."

Jebediah scowled. "I don't like relying on others for my safety. Unfortunately, I don't see that we have much choice.

"I think you're correct that we can productively search through some of the boxes and other storage areas to find items that have been packed away. Perhaps we'll get lucky and find something to point us to where these people came from."

As the group started back down the stairs, Jared sent up a prayer that Carl and Mordechai would quickly realize that they were missing and send help. Unfortunately, with the fight going on above, it was all too likely that other events would be holding their attention.

For the time being, they were on their own.

Lost in his own thoughts, he almost missed the flash of something shiny on the stairs as they went back down. It was wedged into the corner of the stairs, and he'd only spotted it because he'd been worried about placing his feet incorrectly and had been looking down.

He picked it up and found himself holding a metal pin with an enameled image on one side. The image made both of his eyebrows rise. He'd seen it before. It was the emblem of the Marine Raiders.

* * *

WHILE CARL WAS WAITING for Julia, Admiral Mertz, and Jebediah to return from their trip down, he busied himself by securing more air bottles. That meant that he, Austin, and Ralph had to venture fairly far afield because they were becoming hard to find close to the air handler room.

Not being as rushed this time, he only selected the ones that read full. That allowed him to carry a fair number back for their use without being overburdened.

Even though the process was easy, it wasn't quick. By the time they'd returned with all the air bottles they could scavenge and had finished sorting them out, almost ninety minutes had passed.

Carl knew that Mordechai and the rest would be focused on the fighting, so he wasn't surprised to discover that there was only one guard in the air handler room. What did surprise him was that those that had gone below hadn't returned.

That was concerning. There was no reason they couldn't have made the trip down and gotten back by now.

"Something might have gone wrong," he told the others. "We need to go below and find them. Gather up your gear and split up the air bottles."

"Shouldn't we get extra help?" Austin asked uncertainly.

Carl shook his head. "These people are in a fight for survival, and they need every hand they can get. Search and rescue is going to be up to us. Come on."

Since they'd made the journey down once before, it didn't take them very long to get to the room where the fusion plant had once been located. Once there, they quickly made their way to the maintenance lift. When Carl pressed the button to summon the car, it lit but went dark as soon as he released the pressure. He tried again with the same result.

That wasn't good.

"They've either got the doors wedged open below, or it's broken," Austin said. "From up here, we can't really tell which. We're going to have to go down another way."

"We need to get these doors open," Carl ordered. "Look around and find something that we can use to pry them apart. Once we get it open, we'll start making an assessment about how safe it would be to go down the shaft."

The three of them spread out, searching for tools. Unfortunately, they found nothing of value. Whoever had taken the fusion plant had stripped the level. In the end, they had to venture much farther afield to find a locked maintenance room on a separate level.

Inside, they found a pry bar and a locker full of reinforced rope. They'd have to test it to be absolutely sure it was any good, and even then, Carl was going to braid the strands to provide added strength.

With the help of his companions, he wedged the prybar into the crack between the doors and they put their shoulders into it, forcing the doors open.

Being very careful with his footing, Carl looked down the shaft. He couldn't see the bottom, but that was no surprise. The shaft was lit, but the panels were somewhat dim and mounted far apart. If memory served, there were at least four dozen levels between him and the bottom of the shaft.

Definitely not the kind of thing one wanted to fall into.

There was a ladder on the inside of the shaft. It was made of metal and thus really couldn't be trusted. With the amount of time that had passed, it was sure to have weakened.

"Help me braid some of this rope together," he ordered. "I'll have you anchor me as I go down. Once this strand runs out, you'll need to tie more on. Can you do that?"

Austin nodded. "I can, but I don't think this is a good idea. There's a stairwell right there. All we have to do is go down and get them."

"If it was that easy, they'd have walked back up themselves," Carl retorted. "There's no way that something down there incapacitated all three of them. With the lift out of service, that means they can't get back up through normal means. We've got to go down through the shaft.

"But you're right that it's dangerous. I'll keep my hands on multiple rungs and try to use the ladder's sides as much as possible. You'll need to wrap your end around one of the supports up here. It might take several lengths of rope to get to the bottom, but we can do it.

"When I get down there, I'll find out what's going on and pass it back up by shouting. Then we'll figure out what we need to do to get them out."

"This is insane," Ralph grumbled. "We should just get help and go down once we're better prepared. They're going to be fine. The atmosphere is good down there."

"In a perfect world, that would be true. This world is far from perfect, and sometimes we've got to take chances. They're worth the risk."

Without giving them any more time to argue, Carl gestured for them to secure the rope. Only then did he gingerly climb onto the ladder.

Once he was fully situated, he started down slowly and carefully. He made it three steps before the rung he put his weight on snapped off and went clattering down the shaft. The experience left him partially hanging, but the rope held.

"I guess I put too much weight on that one," he said. "I'll be more careful."

After taking a few more deep breaths, Carl started down the shaft again.

18

Talbot had to admit that he wasn't thrilled about being slid out from a broken window this high above the ground. Even though he understood how he'd be balanced on the long plank they'd showed him—which was supported by ropes run through pulleys mounted to the ceiling—it was still unnerving.

He'd also be dependent on others to pull him back inside once the fighting got rolling, or they simply ran out of rockets for him to fire and grenades for him to throw.

When he got right down to it, he was showing a lot of trust in these people, and that made him uncomfortable. They were his captors, after all.

Then again, he supposed they were trusting him as well. Their forces would be fighting down below, and he could cause a great deal of damage with the weapons they were providing if he had a mind to.

Of course, then they'd drop him off the building.

The five minutes that he'd been told it would take for the enemy to arrive at their location dragged out until it felt more like twenty, but that was because he refused to check his internal chronometer. Waiting for battle always seemed to take forever.

He spent the time examining the rocket launcher that he held on the plank in front of him. The device was a tube that could be extended by grasping both ends and pulling them apart. Small sights within would then pop up, allowing him to aim at the target. It was already extended.

It was going to be a lot like firing the sniper rifle, he suspected. The height from which he'd be firing the weapon would make the sights almost useless. They were designed for a weapon that had to struggle against gravity, and, in this case, it would be working with him. Sort of.

On flat terrain, a rocket would rise in trajectory after it had been fired and then drop back down into the appropriate location to impact the target. Firing from this greater height and at a downward angle, it would probably strike somewhere above where he was aiming. His first shot was going to be a test.

The second thing he'd be testing was how deadly the weapon really was. He had no idea what the lethal radius from the explosion would be, and he needed that information to allocate the weapons he had available. His allies didn't have an inexhaustible number of rockets, so he had to make each one count.

"The enemy is about to come into sight," Richard said from behind him. "It looks like they have scouts out front, so we're going to wait until they're in position before we run you out. Once we're sure they're all in the trap, we'll slide you out, and you can begin firing."

He nodded his agreement without speaking.

Now it didn't seem as if time were dragging at all. The horde warriors weren't dawdling.

As they began filtering into sight, Talbot wondered where they were going. Was there something further inside the city that they wanted to seize? How did they know what was waiting for them? What was their plan to locate and subdue the inhabitants?

Those were all very interesting questions that he'd have to figure out at some later point. Right now, he needed to make certain that they not only didn't get what they wanted but came to an unceremonious end.

"We're going to push you out in five... four... three," Lydia said softly.

Talbot steadied himself and prepared for the motion that he knew was coming. When it came, it was *very* smooth. They'd obviously practiced this technique many times.

He approved since that smoothness meant that he wasn't going to fall off the plank.

As soon as he was stable again, Talbot began scanning the enemy spread out below him. They weren't quite in position just yet, so he waited a couple of extra beats to allow them to get closer. He wanted them to be in place for the other ambushers to have the best effect when they sprang the trap.

A couple of the enemy warriors shouted when they saw his movement, but the crowd below didn't react by freezing. They kept moving. If anything, they sped up a little bit.

Satisfied that the enemy was in as good a position as they were going to get, Talbot rotated the rocket until he could see the enemy through the sights. He depressed the trigger on top of the rocket launcher, and it fired with a loud whoosh.

He closed his eyes tightly for two beats so that he wouldn't get any debris from the rocket motor in them. By the time he opened them again, the rocket had slammed into the ground below him.

It had struck maybe ten meters above where he'd intended. That wasn't too bad. Based on the number of bodies lying around it, the lethal radius was about fifteen meters, but it still hurt others out to about thirty.

He could work with that.

Rather than hand the now-useless rocket back, Talbot let it fall and reached back for the next rocket they'd already extended toward him in a holder on a piece of old pipe.

Even as he did so, he saw another rocket lance down from off to his right and strike in the middle of the crowded area below. A glance that way showed Chloe on a plank just like his, already reaching back for another rocket. She looked focused and was grinning coldly as she killed their enemies.

He approved.

This time he fired toward the back of the enemy column. He opened his eyes just in time to see the rocket strike. His aim was true, and he blew up what looked like a group of officers and their subordinates. That was going to affect the enemy's ability to control their troops.

By this point, a number of the enemy fighters below were firing bows toward his position. Some of them actually managed to strike the plank that he lay upon, but their arrows didn't penetrate the tough synthetic material.

He dropped the second empty tube and reached for the next. Right as he grabbed it, someone below fired off one of the antiarmor rockets they'd used in the big battle to kill his marines inside their powered armor.

The bright projectile missed him and struck the building somewhere far above. Richard and Lydia hauled the plank in just in time for him to avoid being hit by shattered glass and other debris. This was also something they'd obviously planned for.

Once the rain of deadly wreckage ended, they ran him back out again. The man who'd fired the rocket had killed himself—and those around him—with the rocket exhaust. Others a bit farther away writhed in pain from their burns. Talbot hoped any others that might be tempted to use one of those weapons would decide that it wasn't worth the price they'd pay.

Since no one else fired rockets at him, that seemed a safe bet.

One after another, Talbot fired the rockets handed to him into the forces below, targeting the front and rear of the column. He wanted to keep them pinned exactly where they were. If they managed to slide away, the ambush would be less effective.

Based on her targeting, Chloe was following his lead.

"Last rocket," Richard said, extending him the final one. "Hit them dead center."

Talbot obliged, shifting his aim to the packed center of the column. The enemy had congregated far too close to one another while trying to escape death at the rear and front of the column. This rocket would kill many dozens and injure far more.

Without the slightest bit of remorse, he triggered the rocket and sent it on its way. As soon as he assessed the damage that he'd just caused—which was significant—he looked back to see what came next.

They extended a box on another plank that was supported by a second rope and pulley to keep it balanced. Inside the box were dozens of grenades.

He never seen anything so primitive in person, but he was familiar with how they were supposed to work, based on old prespaceflight vids that Kelsey had made him watch. All he had to do was pull the pin and throw the grenade.

The timing of it really didn't matter. Talbot hoped they'd actually reach the ground before they went off, but he was sure that the defenders had already taken that into account.

In quick succession, he pulled the pins from the grenades and lobbed them in long arcs toward where he wanted them to fall. With the combat computer inside his implants calculating how far he could throw and what the wind conditions were, his aim was pretty good. His artificial muscles made throwing them easy, even from a prone position.

Since there were other explosions below, Chloe was again contributing to the mayhem. Her grenades landed closer to the building they were in since she didn't have the augmented muscles he did. Seeing that, he focused on more distant targets.

The grenades landed in clumps of surviving enemies, detonating a second or two after they struck the ground and bounced. Talbot emptied two boxes of grenades before Richard and Lydia pulled him back inside.

Talbot stood and stretched. That had felt good.

He was about to ask them what happened next when there was a loud explosion from down below. He leaned out the opening and saw that the ambushers had set off the mines under the ground and blown the wall they were hiding behind.

As the smoke started clearing, they opened fire on the enemy. Their guns were similar to those used in the old vids that Kelsey had made him watch, too. They might not be as effective as flechettes, but whatever they fired was certainly getting the job done at the ridiculously short range.

With all the death and destruction that he'd already dropped on them, the horde warriors were not in the mental place they needed to be to strike back, and that allowed the defenders to cut them down where they stood.

In less than five minutes, no one in the streets below moved. Most of the enemy were dead, but a number of them had fled. Since they'd scattered in just about every imaginable direction, it was going to be difficult for their commanders to get them back together again.

Unfortunately, Talbot was sure that many of them would run to the remaining column, and word would quickly get out about what had happened here. The defenders could try to reproduce this ambush, but he wasn't going to hold his breath that it would work.

They'd succeeded here, but the first ambush hadn't gone as planned. That group had mauled the city inhabitants. If all of the enemy survivors managed to get back together, this was still going to be a tough fight.

Talbot felt good about what he'd accomplished so far. Not just the fighting and killing, but the building of trust between these people and his own. That would help them get to where they needed to be once they'd kicked the horde out of the city.

* * *

JULIA STARED at the pin in Mertz's hand and felt her jaw drop. "Is that what I think it is?"

"If you think it's a Marine Raider insignia, then you're right," Mertz said. "What I want to know is how it got here."

She stood there with her hands on her hips, trying to imagine a set of circumstances in which someone would've lost something so rare and arcane down at the bottom of an abandoned megacity.

She failed.

"Leader Mordechai did say that the Marine Raiders were here back at the beginning of the Fall, but this pin doesn't look like it's been exposed that long," she finally ventured. "Could it really have been down here that long?"

Jebediah shook his head, eyeing the pin suspiciously. "Unlikely.

Remember that for the first four hundred years, this area was in use. Someone would've found that pin before now if it had been down here since the last Marine Raider was in our city. It had to have been dropped after the power went out.

"I can see a little bit of corrosion, so I don't think it's been here for more than a few years. That means it belonged to the people that stole the fusion plant. Exactly how that's possible, I can't imagine."

"Well, we don't have to solve this mystery right now," Mertz said. "Our immediate objective hasn't changed. We've got to go back down and figure out what to do next. These air bottles are a finite resource that we can't afford to waste."

As they walked down the stairs, Julia tried to figure out how the pin could be connected with the people that had stolen the fusion plant. What was their relation to the Marine Raiders? Were they descendants of some survivors? Or had the Raiders formed some type of organization that had survived all this time?

In the end, she probably wasn't going to figure out the answer anytime soon.

They shut off their air as soon as they made it back to the area with functional life support. The walk down to the bottom of the stairs only took a couple of minutes, and no one said anything. Everyone seemed lost in thought. Like her, they were probably trying to figure out what this meant.

Once they'd reached the lowest level, she gestured at the rooms around them. "I think we need to find a place to sit down and have something to eat. I'm starving."

Before either of the others could respond, there was a loud metallic clang from inside the lift shaft. All three of them turned and stared at it as if it might suddenly come alive.

For a moment, she considered that that might be exactly what had happened. If it had started working again, perhaps that noise was the lift adjusting itself.

"That sounded like something fell onto the lift car," Mertz said. "We should take a look."

Julia pressed the button to open the doors and quickly located the small hatch built into the roof. "Lift me up, and I'll see what happened."

The two men lifted her up, and she opened the hatch. As soon as she had her torso into the darkness beyond, she spotted a short metal bar lying about half a meter from her.

That made her wary. If one had come loose, another could come flying out of the darkness with no warning whatsoever. If so, it could maim or kill her in a heartbeat.

"Is anyone up there?" she shouted.

For a few moments, only the echoes of her shout floated back. Then another voice called down.

"Julia? Are you okay?"

It was Carl Owlet. Damn, but the man was *resourceful*. It seemed as if every time they needed a solution, he was there to offer it.

"The lift stopped working, and the stairs are blocked by a door that I can't open. Other than being stuck down here, we're fine."

"You need to get out of the lift car. I've already broken off a couple of rungs and don't want to hurt you. I've got some equipment with me that I might be able to use to repair the lift, but even if I can't, I'll wager that my cutting tool can get through your door. One way or the other, we'll get you back up.

"Austin and Ralph are on the level where the fusion plant was, so if need be, they can bring more help or maybe use the rope we found to lift us out. Don't worry. The cavalry is here."

Julia dropped back down into the lift, and all three of them exited the car.

She raised an eyebrow at Mertz as soon as they were safely clear. "Is it just me, or does that man have a solution for every problem?"

"He's got an answer even when there *isn't* a problem," Mertz said with a grin. "I've seen him do miraculous things. He's young, but when he gets more seasoning, he's going to be even more formidable. Why do you ask?"

"I was just curious. If I run into someone like Carl later, it would be good to know how he ticks so that I can form an alliance with them."

She couched her language that way because explaining the truth wasn't something that Jebediah needed to hear.

Mertz nodded, seemingly understanding what she was trying to say. "That's sound thinking. If you can find someone like him, you're going to have an ally that will stand with you through thick and thin. One who's more than capable of achieving the goals you set out for him."

Interestingly, it sounded as if Mertz approved. That shocked her a little bit. She'd have expected him to try and wave her off. Instead, he seemed to be giving her the green light to try and form a relationship with her universe's version of Carl.

That gave her a lot to think about. Sadly, she still had a lot of time to work out a plan. They weren't getting out of Frankfort anytime soon.

19

With the experience of the previous fight behind her, Kelsey was in a much better position to effectively attack during the second ambush. The moment the wall came down, she was firing.

The slide on the submachine gun quickly locked back once it had fired every bullet in the magazine. She'd been practicing with those too, so she was faster swapping out the expended magazine for a new one.

The group in front of her was in massive disarray. Someone had been firing rockets into the horde warriors and dropping grenades on them from what Kelsey could see. That had given her and the other ambushers the opportunity they'd needed to completely decimate the forces arrayed against them. In just a few minutes, the battlefield was empty except for the dead and dying.

While the rest of the defenders were gruesomely sorting the dead from the injured and seeing if any of the latter could be saved, Kelsey found the leader of her new group and asked the question that was most prominent on her mind.

"Is my husband okay? His name is Talbot. If possible, I'd like to see him."

The short woman nodded. "He was involved in the ambush, or so I'm told. He fired rockets from the building across from us, so he was never in any real danger once the enemy decided that they couldn't fire rockets back at him. I think we can credit some of our success to his skill. He seems like a great warrior. Much like yourself."

That made Kelsey smile. "Oh, he is. Would it be possible for me to go see him now?"

The woman nodded her assent, and they quickly crossed the street to another building. Finding a clear path through the carnage was impossible, so she just held her breath and accepted that her shoes and pants would be bloody.

From there, they went up several floors and exited into what looked like a staging area for a sniper's nest. If the sniper used rifles, grenades, and rockets.

Talbot was there, along with Chloe Laird and some people she didn't recognize. As soon as he saw her, her husband headed her way, and she greeted him with a grin, her arms wide open.

"I hear you ran into a bit of trouble," he said after he'd squeezed her tight and pushed her back to arm's length. "You seem like you're okay."

She shrugged slightly. "The first ambush didn't account for how ferocious the bastards were. They came right in after us. We hurt them, but not badly enough to break them like you did. Good job, by the way. You really kicked their asses."

"Chloe and I did okay," he admitted with a grin. "That still leaves at least one column that hasn't been bloodied yet. You think they're going to react the same way as the group you ambushed, don't you?"

"If they can," she agreed with a nod. "I'd imagine that a lot of people got away from the two ambushes and will join them, so they'll know what's about to happen. It seems like we've made a good start, but I'm not sure if we can count on it happening again. It looks like you caught them completely unaware and blew the snot out of them. That was decisive."

One of the men standing nearby came up and nodded at her. "Our people executed the third ambush just a few minutes ago. Just as you suspected, it wasn't as effective as this one. Still, they achieve their purpose, and the enemy has begun retreating.

"I think that we're going to have to be satisfied with them going back to the camp they've established just inside Frankfort. They lost one ambush and got hurt in a couple of others, so maybe that's going to make them think twice about trying again today."

"What do we do now?" Talbot asked. "How can we be certain which direction they'll go next, and what do we do when they do it?"

The man shrugged slightly. "We have people watching them. Depending on the direction they head, we'll move forces into place to ambush them again. They haven't run into all of our traps yet, so we've still got a few surprises left.

"The biggest one is that we've got explosives planted underneath certain open areas between buildings. Substantially larger charges than we used here. They didn't hit any this time, but if we play our cards right the next time, we might be able to lure them into a trap they didn't see coming, even if they're wary. If we can, that'll be almost as effective as this attack was."

"How many people are we talking about?" Kelsey asked, giving the man her full attention.

"We know that they've left some reserves to hold their marshaling area, so counting that, they've got at least two thousand people that are still able to fight, probably more. I'd imagine the walking wounded will total another fifteen hundred or so."

Kelsey nodded slowly. "If they regroup, I think Talbot and I might be the best choices to lure them into a trap. It may not seem like it, but we can move *very* quickly when we want to. Given a good opportunity, I think we can draw them into one of the areas you're talking about and get that decisive victory we all need."

Talbot looked as if he wanted to argue, but instead, he shrugged. "What's the plan?"

Kelsey smiled coldly. "We can taunt them with the fact that we're the ones that blew up their castle and leaders. That'll get them all excited. This may be our one chance to decisively engage them in a killing field of our choice. We can't let this pass by."

The people around them looked at her as if she were crazy, and she couldn't blame them. The idea sounded insane.

Hell, it probably was.

It was risky, but they had to thoroughly thrash the horde if they wanted to get out of Frankfort. Not only because they needed the permission of the inhabitants to leave, but because it would be impossible to get away with an effective enemy still fighting all around them.

The horde had slaughtered her crewmates and friends. She wanted revenge, and with this plan, she could get it in a way that it served their purposes.

No matter how they played this, it was going to be dangerous. All kinds of things could still go wrong. Having several thousand enemies baying at one's heels would be hair-raising under the best of circumstances, but that was really the only option if they wanted to end this fight decisively.

"Someone needs to show us where the traps are," she said coldly. "We'll take care of the rest."

* * *

With only a few additional mishaps, Carl managed to get down to the roof of the lift car alive and unharmed. That was something of a relief, considering that he must've snapped a dozen rungs on the way down and knocked yet another one completely free just before he'd reached the lift car.

He certainly hoped that he could get the lift working again because going back up on the ladder was far too dangerous. He untied the rope and left it hanging there. He shouted up the shaft, telling Ralph and Austin to stand by.

Getting through the hatch in the roof of the lift car wasn't a problem, and just a few moments later, he was standing in front of Admiral Mertz, Julia, and Jebediah. To his shock, Julia pulled him into a hug.

"It's *so* good to see you," she said. "We weren't sure that anyone was going to realize that we were gone so soon."

Her hug made him feel a little uncomfortable. He wasn't used to intimate contact with women in general, and he wasn't sure that his wife would approve in any case. In fact, he was pretty sure she wouldn't like it at all.

When Julia let him go, he stepped back self-consciously and smiled as he nodded. "As soon as we realized that you weren't back, we came looking for you. Austin and Ralph will head back up and start gathering a rescue party if they don't hear from us in another hour. Hopefully, we'll join them before then."

Having said that, he reentered the lift and quickly had the control panel open. He plugged his equipment in and ran a brief diagnostic. The problem immediately presented itself.

"It looks like the main control board shorted out. I'm not going to be able to repair this without the right components—which I can salvage from another lift and swap out, given half an hour at some point—so I'm afraid that we're going to have to use the stairs."

Admiral Mertz grunted. "That's not exactly the answer I was looking for, but I guess it doesn't surprise me. Do you have something that can unlock a security door?"

Carl nodded. "I've got something in my toolkit that will help me get through just about any mechanical lock. I've also got a cutter that I can use if I have to."

"Then I suppose we'd best be about it," the admiral said. "I'd rather not waste any more air than we have to."

The climb up only took a few minutes, so Carl was quickly looking at the security door in the stairwell. "It's probably meant to make sure that only maintenance personnel can get down here. This isn't something one can hack, so it's secure in a technological society in a way that an electronic lock isn't. Let's see what I can do."

He opened his toolkit and pulled out a set of lock picks that he'd recreated from a template he'd found in the ship's library aboard *Invincible.* As he'd told the admiral, he very rarely ran into something like this, but when he did, it was nice to have the correct tools for the job.

Thankfully, they didn't weigh very much, so having them in his kit didn't cost him much extra weight.

Sadly, his skill with the picks was relatively basic. He'd only run into a few mechanical locks to practice with. Thankfully, he had some instructional vids stored in his implants that he could access now that they'd been rebooted.

He watched several in quick succession as he fitted the lock picks into the mechanism. In the end, it took him far longer than he liked, but he finally felt the picks catch just the way he wanted and rotated his wrists, turning the lock with a loud click.

"Gotcha!" he exulted as he stood.

That earned him a hearty back slap from Jebediah, which sent him staggering forward. "Excellent work, young man. Now, let's go before we run out of air."

The rest of the climb was uneventful though tiring. By the time they reached the level where the fusion plant had been, they'd used about forty minutes of the time that Austin and Ralph had promised to wait.

The two were pleased to see them, and congratulations were exchanged all around. They pulled the rope up, closed the lift doors, and set course back the way they'd come. They made it back into breathable atmosphere with a healthy margin of air still left in the cache that he'd brought down.

If they were going to be here long, they couldn't count on continually scavenging air bottles to use. He was going to have to tap into the power on the bottom level and get the life-support systems working in the areas that they had to traverse.

Basically, that was the stairwell leading down, the level where the fusion plant had once been, and the second stairwell. Until then, they'd have to harvest more air to be able to get up and down as needed.

More importantly, he had to focus his attention on the maglev train so that they could figure out how to summon it. It might be their ticket out of the city, and he wasn't going to let it slip through his fingers.

"Any word on how the fighting is going?" Admiral Mertz asked.

Carl shook his head. "Nothing so far. I'm hoping that Kelsey and Talbot are okay, but knowing them, they're in the thick of it. I really wish that we'd been able to salvage some operational armor or weapons. Too bad there isn't a stock of weapons left over from when the Marine Raiders were here."

He frowned and turned toward Jebediah. "Didn't someone say that the Raiders went out on a mission and never came back? Surely they didn't take *everything* they had with them. They must've left some equipment behind. I still might be able to salvage something from it that would make a real difference in the fighting."

Jebediah nodded. "We've kept what they left behind secure. I've never been into the room itself, so I can't really tell you much about the contents."

"Could you take me there?"

The large man considered his request for a few moments and then nodded. "I'll let Admiral Mertz and Julia report the situation we found below to my father. While they do, I'll take you to the cache."

Carl wasn't certain that they'd find anything helpful, but it never hurt to try. Sometimes luck was good, sometimes it was bad, but if one didn't check, one never knew.

"Excellent," he said. "Let's get this show on the road."

20

A pair of guards escorted Jared and Julia up into the tower to meet with Leader Mordechai. He wasn't in the wide-open upper floor but down in an interior room about halfway up the tower. Someone had cut away part of an inside wall to give him a view outside the building, but he was still sheltered from any of the weather that was now coming through the shattered windows.

The man himself was seated behind a large desk, doing what looked like *paperwork*. The concept of that seemed almost unimaginable to Jared. This was a post-apocalyptic society. They might've retained some of the knowledge that they'd had from before, but the idea of working with actual paper boggled him.

As soon as they entered the room, Mordechai set aside the pen he'd been using and steepled his fingers as he considered them.

"Where's Jebediah?" he asked, his eyebrow raised.

"He's taken Carl to show him something," Jared said. "He said that he'd be up as soon as he was done with that but that you could accept that he'd verified what we'd told you."

At those words, one of the guards who'd accompanied them on the trip up stepped forward. "I overheard him, Leader Mordechai. That's exactly what Jebediah said."

"Then that's good enough for me," the older man said. "Now comes the mystery of figuring out who took our heritage from us. A theft of that magnitude is unbelievable. The effort that would've been required and the sheer number of people it probably took takes my breath away. The fact that they carried this out right under our noses makes me angry. Do we have any idea how they might've done such a thing?"

Jared reached into his pouch and retrieved the pin he'd found, placing it on the desk. "We found this in the stairwell. It looks like whoever was down there only activated the life-support system for the lowest few levels. This was on the stairs above that safe layer. Do you recognize the emblem?"

The older man picked up and examined the pin, his eyes narrowing. "It looks vaguely familiar, but I can't say that I know how I know it."

"It's the emblem of the Marine Raiders. My sister intends to use something very much like it once she has more of our marines fully transitioned.

"Jebediah said that based on the corrosion, he believed it had only been down there for a few years. Since it appears to be made out of conventional materials, I'm willing to accept that he knows better than I what its durability is. That means that somewhere on the maglev train system, there's a group of people that have some kind of association with the Marine Raiders."

The older man leaned back in his chair and shook his head. "That idea is ludicrous on its face. The Marine Raiders stationed here didn't last more than a few decades after the invasion."

"Could there have been other groups?" Julia asked. "Just because you only know of one doesn't mean that there weren't others. What if their descendants—or some kind of organization formed by them—came here to take the fusion plant?

"Obviously, whoever did this had a lot of technological know-how. Disassembling something as complex as a fusion plant isn't the kind of task that you're going to undertake without knowing how it works. So it's credible that an organization set up by people like that could still be in operation somewhere."

Mordechai sat there for almost a minute without speaking. Then he shrugged.

"The only answers we're going to find are those that we seek ourselves. Since there's a technological society out there somewhere, I think it would behoove both our groups to make some kind of effort in contacting them. The theft is long done, but it may be that my people can leverage the feelings of outrage that we have into some type of concessions from those people.

"For all I know, they may be worthy enough, even if they *are* thieves. It's not as if we've been using that fusion plant for the last hundred years. In any case, the next step must be finding them. At least that will be the case once we've won this fight against the horde."

"Speaking of the fighting, how is it going?" Jared asked. "Are my people okay? Have we managed to drive the horde out of your city?"

The man waggled his hand. "One of the ambushes didn't go so well. A number of our people were killed, and the horde was triumphant there. The second ambush went exceptionally well, and the enemy was decimated.

"I've only just received word that the third ambush fell somewhere in between the other two. We managed to inflict a lot of casualties, but the enemy withdrew in good order. Now all the survivors are retreating toward where they're keeping their reserves. I anticipate that once they regroup, they'll be back.

"Your people are well, though I must warn you that your sister and her husband have volunteered to lure the enemy into another trap. I can't imagine how, but they seem quite determined."

Jared chuckled darkly. "Kelsey's very stubborn. If anyone can make it work, it's her. While they're doing that, we should talk about what we're going to do next. Your son is escorting Carl to take a look at the hardware the Marine Raiders left behind when they vanished.

"It's possible that something will still be usable, even though it won't have power. It would be nice to face a technological society with weapons that might actually make them sit up and take notice."

Mordechai nodded. "While they're doing that, we should discuss what happens next. I've decided to release you, so as of this moment, you are no longer our prisoners but our guests.

"All of your weapons and belongings will be returned to you immediately. When it comes time for you to depart, we'll allow you to do so without any hindrance and give you what aid we can. It is my deepest hope that you will continue to assist us in the matter of the stolen fusion plant so that we can make contact with the thieves as well."

"I'm looking forward to that discussion," Jared said. "Almost as much as I am to lunch because I'm starving."

"Me, too," Julia said. "I'm so hungry that survival rations sound good right now."

Mordechai laughed as he rose from his seat. "Then let's go get something to eat."

* * *

TALBOT RAISED his head slightly and stared out over the area in front of the building they were hiding in. It was positioned much closer to the edge of Frankfort, so the buildings were shorter, and there was more space between them than there had been in the packed interior of the dead megacity.

The horde had taken advantage of that extra space to set up a fortified camp. His implants estimated that there were more than two thousand people inside it. That number was going to rise by at least another thousand as the survivors of the various ambushes trickled in.

He and Kelsey had discussed the matter and decided to wait until as many people as possible were present before they attempted to lure them into the trap. There was no use in leaving a fighting force worthy of the name behind to attack them again. If they could lure them all into an ambush, that would ensure that they achieved the maximum number of casualties.

Satisfied with what he'd seen and confident that none of the sentries had noticed his presence, Talbot stepped farther back into the gloom and found a place to sit next to Kelsey. The room had once been an office of some kind. The abandoned chairs allowed them to sit around a desk that was lit by the little sunlight that filtered in through the doorway.

Based on the ruined elegance of the furnishings, it must've once belonged to someone both wealthy and powerful. Now it smelled of mildew and prolonged neglect.

"I think we're going to have to wait at least another hour for the last of the survivors to make their way back," he said as he sat. "That'll give them a chance to report what happened and really piss the people in charge off. The angrier they are, the more likely they are to come after us."

She nodded and handed him a ration bar. "Then I suggest you eat and drink while you can. We aren't going to have a chance to rest once we start running for our lives. Even with our greater speed, we'll have to stay in sight, or they're going to stop chasing us."

He tore the wrapper off the bar and took a bite. Long practice allowed him to ignore the relatively terrible taste. The ration wasn't meant to be a gourmet meal. Rather, it was packed with nutrients and vitamins that were mandatory in a survival situation.

Still, couldn't someone have tried to make them taste less like sawdust?

"Do you really think that we're doing the right thing here?" he asked. "Getting thousands of people to chase us with murder in their eyes seems to be a pretty chancy thing."

She grinned. "If they catch us, we're screwed. So let that be your motivation to run just a little bit faster."

He grunted. That was the worst motivational speech he'd ever received. His wife really needed to work on that.

"Any word on the expedition to get the fusion plant back online?" he asked.

"I got a call from Carl a few minutes ago. The extended range of his updated implant communicator is handy. We definitely need to see about getting everyone else equipped with one as soon as possible.

"It turns out that somebody's been robbing Frankfort. They got down to the area where the fusion plant should have been, but it was gone. Someone had disassembled the whole thing and carried it off."

The news made him blink. "Seriously? How is that even possible? It's not as if you can disassemble a fusion plant without the technical know-how and have a useful device at the end.

"Even in the Old Empire, it took specialized skills to do that kind of thing. The man or woman on the street couldn't even follow detailed instructions to make that happen. Here and now? Impossible."

"Impossible or not, Carl says that's exactly what they did. Apparently, the theft only took place a couple of years ago, which only adds to the mystery.

"There's apparently a maglev train station on the lowest level of the city. Whoever they were, they used the power serving it and got the life-support system down there back online. They stripped an incredible amount of supplies and equipment from the lowest levels of the city. The ones that are blocked from access because of the bad air.

"I'd be willing to bet they turned on the life-support system all the way up to the level of the fusion plant for that. They got one of the lifts working and used it to transport everything they wanted down to the lowest level and probably took the most valuable things away via the train. Then they shut off life support—except for the lowest levels —and the bad air drifted its way back down, leaving no one the wiser."

Talbot shook his head. "Even hearing you say that, I still find it hard to believe. Still, if we've got an operational train station, that means Carl could probably find us a way to get to these people. Potential allies with technological know-how might be beneficial in our current circumstances."

"I agree. We'll see if Leader Mordechai is on board with that or just stays pissed off that somebody stole all of his stuff. He doesn't seem to be the kind of person to let go of a grudge, if you know what I mean."

The two of them sat chatting for the next half hour, with him making occasional trips to the window to look at the horde camp. By the end of that time, it was apparent that the survivors had begun arriving because the enemy camp was in turmoil.

Kelsey came over when he called her and nodded in satisfaction. "I think we've got enough people down there to be worthwhile. Why don't we go ahead and make a little trip up the street? We'll head back this way as soon as we get their attention. With any luck, we'll make them so angry that the whole lot of them gives chase.

"The nearest area that the defenders have buried explosives is about a kilometer away. It's along one of the main paths into the city, so it's a shame that the horde didn't choose that route when marching in. If they had, the defenders could've blown them up without having to fight."

"If wishes were horses, we'd all be hip deep in horse crap," he said philosophically. "Let's get this over with. I want to take care of these bastards once and for all so that we can get back to saving the Empire."

21

C arl followed Jebediah on a winding trip into the underground tunnels beneath Frankfort. The stash was obviously not centrally located. Thankfully, it didn't seem to be very far underneath the city itself. Otherwise, they'd have had to deal with the bad air again.

Not to say that the air they were breathing was of the highest quality, but it hadn't crossed the threshold of being noxious yet. The carbon dioxide levels were rising by the time they stopped, but it was still within what he'd call tolerable parameters.

Barely.

Rather than doing anything with the lock on the door in front of them, the large man reached up to the ceiling and pushed at a panel there. It rose slightly, and something shiny fell out. The large man grabbed for it but missed. It struck the ground with the distinctive sound of metal.

It was a key, probably like the one that the security door below had once required.

Jebediah picked it up, inserted it into the lock, and twisted. With a loud click, the door unlocked, and the large man pushed it open.

The interior of the room was just as dark as the rest of the megacity, but Carl could tell just from the torches that they carried that there was a significant amount of supplies within the room. The first things that grabbed his attention—commanded it, really—were the four suits of gray Marine Raider armor on stands against the far right-hand wall.

"Holy cow," he said reverently as he stepped into the room, automatically lowering his torch so that it didn't scorch the ceiling. "It looks as if these were put here in an operational state. If so, it may be possible to recharge the power cells and utilize them. That would have a huge impact on combat operations. You really should've said something about these before the fighting started."

"I've never been in this room before," Jebediah said. "I'm sure that my father had a rough idea of what was here, but I suspect that he hasn't been here more than a few times since he was a boy.

"In any case, we wouldn't have trusted you with such a thing before now. Even if we had, there was no power to charge them with nor charging facilities with which to do so."

Carl nodded and moved over to the armor. A quick check showed that the power cells were dead, as expected. He couldn't get any kind of status from the suits at all.

A quick visual inspection told him that, barring any fried electronics or otherwise faulty circuits, the armor looked as if it had been in operational condition when stored.

All of the suits were significantly larger than what would typically fit on Kelsey or Julia. Some of that could be adjusted. He'd done the customization on Kelsey's suit himself, so he was quite familiar with the process.

That didn't mean that it would be easy under the present circumstances. He'd had a ship full of the right equipment and spare parts to make the modifications before. These suits had almost certainly been adjusted for their last users, so there wouldn't be any need for them to have any of the more robust adjustment tools with them.

He'd do what he could.

Carl widened his search to the rest of the room. Placed nearby were cases holding flechette and plasma weapons sized for the armor.

Ammunition for each of them was stored adjacent to the weapons themselves. Each of the power packs was undoubtedly dead, but it should be a reasonably straightforward process to recharge them.

The smaller weapons used batteries inside the magazines themselves for their power. There were a lot of them, and it would take time to fully charge them all. Thankfully, there were a couple of racks made for just that purpose sitting nearby.

The problem was that everything was going to have to be carried down the stairs to the lowest level of the megacity. That would be backbreaking labor and require that Carl had enough air bottles to make it work unless he got the life-support system for the areas he needed to traverse back online. Getting the broken lift working again was also a priority.

If he could do those things, the process would be significantly easier, and it would take one big problem off of his shoulders. It would also allow others to work below without having to be trapped there.

The tricky part was going to be the fact that he couldn't just turn on life support for the entire lower section of the megacity. That might draw enough power to alert the people running it that someone was using their power, which might be enough for them to turn it off on them.

If any of their plans were to work, he had to avoid that outcome at all costs.

He returned his attention to the supplies around him. There were a lot of marine knives, as well as a collection of short swords like Kelsey's. Apparently, these people had had similar ideas to Ned Quincy.

Hell, for all Carl knew, they might literally have gotten the idea from the man. In such a small community, that certainly wasn't a big jump.

If he ever got back to *Persephone*, he'd have to devote some more attention to working on a new home for the AI. Ned's consciousness was currently in stasis inside jury-rigged hardware, but he had some ideas that might allow the strange being to finally have a place to call his own.

Ned had been created inside Kelsey's implants and had lived there his entire life as an artificial intelligence. That was awkward for both of them, so Ned had asked to be removed and archived until such time as a solution was put together.

It was risky. There was no guarantee that Ned would wake up again when his new home was ready. Still, it was a risk that the man had insisted they take.

Carl would do everything he could to make sure the AI survived, but he couldn't do that if they never got off of Terra. Which brought him back around to what he needed to do now.

There were three sets of blades just like Kelsey's, so that was going to make their lives a lot easier when it came to melee fighting. He knew that those who could use the weapons would be thrilled to have them.

He was about to turn away when he spotted another sword stashed behind the others. It wasn't a pair in shoulder harnesses but a single blade. Carl carefully picked up the scabbard and drew it.

The blade was made of the same hull metal as Kelsey's, so it would hold its monomolecular edge forever. Unlike her shorter blades, this one was long and had a gentle, elegant curve. It was very similar to the type of weapon that Clarice Beauchamp favored.

He immediately vowed to see that she got the weapon should they gain access to the cache. It was the least they could do for the woman who'd helped them survive this terrible planet.

Everything else in the room was crated supplies and weapons: handheld plasma grenades, regular explosives, and a wide variety of equipment that might prove useful in a guerrilla war. There were also selections of clothing and unpowered armor that would be useful as well.

Whoever had stocked the cache had done an extremely thorough job. With everything here, the Raiders could've continued fighting for a long time.

He wondered what had happened to them. Obviously, they hadn't taken their powered armor. It had probably been some type of scouting mission, and they'd been ambushed. Even Marine Raiders could be killed if one was willing to spill enough of their own blood to do it.

Having completed his circuit of the room, Carl returned to where Jebediah stood near the door.

"I think a fair bit of this could be useful," the scientist said. "The question is, what will you allow us to use?"

The large man smiled like a shark. "I'm quite certain that we can come to an agreement. You probably won't like the terms for some of the more potent items, but my father will be willing to deal.

"I can tell you now that the most significant thing on his mind— other than throwing the horde out of our city—is getting the fusion plant returned. That may be beyond the scope of what you'd been prepared to offer, but we each have something the other wants. You are perhaps in a better position to negotiate with the thieves, and we have all this equipment that might be critical to the ultimate success of your mission.

"You want it all. I can see that in your eyes. If your admiral is willing to negotiate, you can have it. My father is no fool. He knows that if there's a chance to destroy the artificial intelligences that wrecked the Empire, he must assist in whatever way he can, yet he has to serve our people as well.

"A balance must be struck. My guess? Convince the thieves to return the fusion plant and shielding, restore it to operation, and provide assistance in keeping it running, and you may have everything in this cache."

Carl nodded. "Then let me see if I can negotiate a down payment. If I were to manipulate the life-support system and power that's coming from the maglev system so that it was easy to get people down to those lower levels without having to breathe with air bottles, that would allow you to retrieve everything that was stored there.

"Right now, that's within my power. Everything I need to make that happen is in this room. You just have to give me access to it."

Jebediah nodded at once. "That sounds fair to me, but my father will need to agree. Having seen the vast amount of scavenged equipment already boxed below, I feel quite certain that he will approve of this interim agreement. Come. Let's go find out if I'm right."

* * *

KELSEY AND TALBOT made their way down into the tunnels again. Once there, they set off toward the enemy camp. The key was going to be getting close enough to be seen without being immediately engaged. It was going to be a delicate balancing act of enraging the enemy while not being killed by the rage they'd provoked.

Once they reached an area where she felt comfortable going back up for a good look, they crept up the stairs and peered out from the first floor of the new building. Off in the distance, she could see the edge of the camp and the sentries posted there.

She focused her ocular implants on the sentries and looked them over carefully. They were armed with swords and bows. Kelsey saw no signs of rockets or other advanced weaponry. Specialized groups deeper in the camp might have had them, though.

They might even have one of those EMP weapons, which would be a disaster, but she really doubted it. Those would only be useful against things like powered armor, from the enemy's point of view. They also had to be damned difficult to make. They wouldn't just waste them. They'd save them for some type of last-ditch defense against a large force that had high-technology weapons. Not against a dozen people.

At least that was what she told herself.

Talbot hunched down next to her, looking around the corner of the building. "How do you want to play this?"

"I think we should just step out into the open. They're going to see us right away and send someone to deal with us. That'll give us a chance to get them really riled up before we dodge back out of sight.

"It may take several attempts to draw them out completely. I've never done anything like this before, so I'm not really sure."

"Well, what's the worst that could go wrong?" he asked with a wry smile.

They stepped out of the building together, walked to the center of the open area, and turned toward the sentries. At this point, they were about two hundred meters away from the warriors.

The men on guard saw them and shouted for them to halt.

Kelsey laughed as loudly as she could for her audience. "You expect me to stand here and turn myself in after I blew up your leaders?" she shouted. "You've obviously lost your minds. And now that you've invaded this city, I've killed even more of you. You're powerless to stop me. You can't even *catch* me."

That started several of the men jogging in their direction.

She made a motion to Talbot, and they ducked around the corner of the building and back down into the tunnels again. By the time the guards arrived, she and Talbot were long gone. Their new hideout was in another building a short distance away.

With the maze of tunnels under the megacity, it was going to be hard for the horde to figure out where they'd gone. That would remain true unless the enemy flooded the tunnels, looking for them.

Once they looked back at the enemy camp, she saw that the sentries had returned to their post. It looked like they were arguing. There was a lot of gesticulating and finger pointing.

She allowed them time to summon some officers to deal with the situation. The higher the rage went into their command structure, the better.

They waited about half an hour for the enemy to settle down before she and Talbot confronted the camp from a different direction. This time, the warriors tried to race after them at once, and more people moved into place to back them up.

That was a heartening response. This might work after all. She was pissing them off, and they wanted to make her shut up. They wanted to kill her.

Time to make the pot boil over.

She and Talbot retreated to the building that they'd used as an observation post, grabbed the dozen rockets they'd brought with them, and moved to the next area she'd designated to confront the horde camp. This time, they didn't say anything at all after they'd revealed themselves.

Kelsey fired her rocket while Talbot did the same. The paired explosions blew up a lot of people and set the rest of the crowd that had gathered scattering in different directions.

It turned out one of the people in the crowd had a rocket of his own. He fired it back toward her and her husband. Sadly for him, it must've been difficult to aim because it missed by a wide margin.

Or perhaps it was just of a lower quality than the ones they were using, or he was a terrible shot. With the speed of the weapons, they could hardly have evaded if his aim had been good, but they could certainly make sure he didn't fire any more at them. Talbot fired a rocket that blew the bastard up, along with some of his closest friends.

The two of them raised their aim and began sending rockets into the main camp. The long arcs dropped the warheads into the larger concentrations of people gathered around the tents that the horde warriors had brought with them.

By the time they'd expended their supply of rockets, there was a general movement in the camp toward their position and a lot of shouting. Almost a roar, really.

Yup, they'd seriously pissed them off.

"Let's go," she said, turning to jog away from the disrupted camp.

Retreating from the area was a tricky proposition. They wanted to keep the enemy in sight to troll them but not let them get close enough to where they'd be a threat.

Unfortunately for them, the enemy had other plans.

To her dismay, Kelsey found out that the scouts the city had sent to observe the camp had failed to see about half a dozen horses. Worse, the concealed horsemen had circled around behind Talbot and her and were now blocking their escape.

Now she had to choose between facing the mob behind her and the mounted warriors ahead. That choice wasn't even particularly difficult.

She used the submachine gun she'd brought along to open fire at the horsemen as she charged forward. Several of the riders and their horses went down, but even more of them began pouring into the area ahead. The count was now up to a dozen.

Obviously, the scouts had missed significantly more horses than she'd imagined possible—or, more likely, the horsemen had arrived between the time the scouts had reported, and Kelsey and Talbot had taken up their position near the camp.

Arrows from the pursuers began falling around them, zipping past like angry bees. Kelsey turned on her heel and emptied her weapon at the warriors behind them, trying to make them pull back.

They ignored her fire and rushed forward, ignoring their own casualties. From the number of people that she could see, she might just have succeeded in emptying the camp. That was good if they could get to the ambush site. Not so good if they died right here.

"We're not going to be able to stop them," Talbot said as he switched magazines and continued firing at the horsemen. "What's the plan?"

"We go forward," she said. "Take one of my swords, and when the time is right, just start cutting a hole right through them."

They'd brought a lot of ammunition, but it took a surprisingly short time to empty the last of the magazines. When that happened, they let their guns fall onto their straps, and she drew her swords, handing one to Talbot.

Using their Marine Raider augmentation, they charged into the surviving horsemen, slashing and using their stronger muscles to leap farther than the enemy expected. To add to the chaos, the bowmen behind them didn't even slow their rate of fire, killing and wounding their comrades and horses with wild abandon as they tried to take her and Talbot down.

All she and her husband needed to do was get to the far side of the horsemen and haul ass. If any of the mounted warriors survived, she hoped the chaos would delay their pursuit.

That hope proved to be beyond reach, as the surviving horsemen turned to pursue them as soon as they broke through. Kelsey turned and charged them again, drawing her pistol and firing it with one hand as she prepared to use her sword with the other.

Talbot turned with her, covering her with his pistol. Those were meant to be last-ditch weapons, but she supposed it was all or nothing now.

Then the inevitable happened. An arrow struck Kelsey in the

upper thigh. She grunted in pain and continued firing. Seconds later, the last of the horsemen was down.

The wound was deep and bleeding fast. Her medical nanites would handle that, and her pharmacology unit dumped painkillers into her system to allow her to keep moving. The wound wouldn't stop her, but it would slow her.

Under these circumstances, that would be deadly.

"I'm not going to be able to run with this," she said. "I have to get into the tunnels, and you're going to have to lead them on to the ambush. I'm sorry."

"Bull. Keep covering me."

With that, he tossed her over his shoulder and ran, dodging to try and avoid being peppered with arrows. She used her pistol to engage the enemy, but with all the bouncing around, her aim was crap. Luckily, with that many targets, a miss was difficult to achieve.

In a way, the situation was almost funny. Maybe she'd laugh about it someday.

If she survived.

22

"Holy crap," Julia muttered under her breath as she stared at all the equipment stashed around the room, her eyes wide. "You've hit the freaking jackhole, Carl!"

"Jackpot," he corrected absently as he moved a small crate and started searching another.

"Whatever. Neither one of those words means anything to me."

He turned to stare at her. "Kelsey routinely cleans everyone's clocks at cards and has more than passing familiarity with other forms of gambling. How can you not know what jackpot means?"

She frowned back at him. "Damned if I know. Where could she have learned all that stuff? You know? Never mind. Let's focus on what we have here."

The two of them were inside the room containing the Marine Raider cache, with only a single guard at the door. Not because they were under watch to make sure that they didn't escape but because their hosts wanted to make sure that nothing walked off from the stash without being properly accounted for.

They'd made a preliminary agreement to allow Carl the use of some of the gear to aid him in turning the life-support system in the lowest levels back on. The items that they were taking now were simply on loan to make that happen.

"None of it's powered," Carl said. "It's just been sitting here for five hundred years. Even the most cursory understanding of Imperial tech would tell someone that there's not any juice left.

"That said, if we can get some of this down to the maglev station, it won't be a problem to plug it in and start charging it. The magazines for the flechette pistols, for example, are virtually indestructible. In all the testing that I did with the magazines that we recovered from the battlecruiser *Courageous*, only a couple of them failed to charge. The Old Empire really knew how to build their stuff. We've probably got enough ammunition here for a small war, and if we can find half a dozen magazines that fail, I'll eat them."

"So, what do you want to do first?" she asked, smiling at his joke. "It seems like getting the life-support system down below up and running would be a big help. I know there's still a lot of air bottles scattered around the lower levels of the city, but we've been lucky thus far. Any of them could fail without warning because they were never designed for this kind of neglect. We need to start being more conservative. We're overdue for an accident."

The young scientist nodded. "Agreed. The thing is, I'm going to have to work inside that environment for at least a day. It's going to involve a lot of going from place to place and fixing things. I may even have to move equipment from one location to another. That's going to take a group of people—or someone very strong."

"So, me."

He nodded. "It also means that we need to adjust one of these suits of armor so that I can wear it. The suit reserves are still full, and we can easily swap out with some of the spares that are here in the cache when we run low on air.

"The suit will also provide me with enough strength to do some of the work. It's made to work with your augmented muscles, but it's got enough built-in enhancement to help carry out some of the tasks that need to be done."

He put his hands on his hips and stared at the racked armor. "The only problem is that we're going to have to get them down to the maglev platform so that they can be charged before we can do anything. That means carrying them down while wearing those dinky little air bottles."

"I can carry them down," Julia said. "I'll use up the air reserves faster, but hoisting both sets of armor over my shoulders and hauling them downstairs is going to be within my capability. Barely."

He didn't look convinced. "You might be able to handle all the weight, but that's a lot of bulk. Plus, it's going to be as unwieldy as hell. I think you should probably just take one at a time."

She ignored his suggestion and started unhooking one of the suits of armor. She hefted it for a moment and then tossed it over her shoulder. It *was* unwieldy but nothing that she couldn't handle.

Hell, if push came to shove, she could grab it by one leg and *drag* it down the stairs. It might scuff up the exterior, but this was powered armor. She could beat it with a club, and it would still be operational.

She grabbed a second set of armor off the rack and turned toward him. "I can handle it. How do we adjust one of these to fit me? I'm a little shorter than your average girl. Even you're going to have to shorten some segments to fit your height, mister 'I'm so average.'"

He grinned at that. "And there you were telling me just the other day how above average I was. You're lucky I don't tell my wife that you've been hitting on me."

She froze for just a moment and then grinned back at him. "I like the mouth you've got on you. You really can give as good as you get. And I'm not hitting on you. Your wife is safe, and so are you."

His eyes narrowed slightly, and she could see his lips pressing together a little as he considered her. "If you weren't hitting on me, then I can only imagine that this flirting means you're giving me a test drive to see whether or not you might like my doppelgänger."

Shocked at his unexpected insight, she considered lying, but the man was damned perceptive, and it really didn't matter. Why lie when the truth would serve her just fine?

"That's *exactly* what I'm thinking," she said honestly. "In my universe, Carl Owlet never left Avalon. He's still a graduate student there. Hell, he's probably a PhD by now. Angela has been serving in

Talbot's place as my senior marine officer, so the two of you never met.

"Without the events that drew you together, there isn't going to be a relationship between the two of you. I don't feel like I'm stealing him from Angela, so yes, I'm giving you a test drive.

"I'm not the type to hit on another woman's man. Neither you nor Angela has anything to worry about on that account. But I do want to get to know you better because I think that your doppelgänger and I would be perfect for one another.

"I like you a lot, Carl, and I think I'd like him. You'd have to be the one to tell me if you think he'd feel the same. I suspect your relationship with Kelsey would be somewhat different if you'd never met. Tell me how he'd react to me slowly getting to know him and building a relationship. Could the two of us make something like that work?"

He shrugged. "I've been with Kelsey for so long that I see her more like a crazy sister than a woman, so I'm not sure that you should trust my feelings at this point. You're going to have to make the decision about what makes sense for you to do.

"What I *can* tell you is that he's not going to be comfortable around a princess. You're going to have to do a lot of work to become his friend before you try to become more. It's not exactly like he's got a lot of dating experience, and he's going to be intimidated. Think of him like a wild horse that you have to break to the saddle."

His face reddened when she grinned. "Maybe that wasn't the best analogy."

She laughed. "I think that has a lot of interesting possibilities for me to think about."

Then she sobered. "Someone like you could be the difference between life and death for the New Terran Empire in my universe. And, to be frank, someone like you would make an excellent consort for me.

"I'm not the warrior she is. I need someone like you, a scholar who's brilliant and has wide-ranging interests that appeal to me. I won't know until I meet you there, but yes, I've made the decision that

I'm going to be looking at your doppelgänger as soon as I get back to my universe and sneak onto Avalon.

"By now, it's going to be under AI control. If I can bring back enough information and technology, we can start a guerrilla war and fight our way back. That makes your doppelgänger perfect for me.

"And I really do like you. That's a huge bonus. If I had to forge a relationship for the good of the Empire, I'd do it. If it can bring me a companion that I *want* to spend time with and that I truly like, could I ask for anything more?"

Carl nodded slowly. "I can see it. I think my doppelgänger will find you appealing, but you're going to have to go slow, just like I said."

He considered her intensely for a few moments. "I'm not really supposed to say anything about this, but I think there's something we can do for you that will make a difference back in your universe. Avalon's going to be isolated because of its distance from the Rebel Empire, so even though they've only recently conquered it, the Rebel Empire won't have put as many ships there as they probably should.

"There are ways that we can help you deal with something like that. Technologies that we've built that might help protect Avalon against them. I'll have to talk to Admiral Mertz and Kelsey to be sure, but I think you can do it, particularly if you've got my doppelgänger on your side."

Her heart pounded harder in her chest. She really hoped he was right.

Knowing that she wasn't going to be able to pull any more information out of him until he'd spoken with the others, she hefted both sets of armor while he gathered the equipment that he was going to need. The two of them then headed down toward the lower levels.

* * *

JARED ACCOMPANIED Mordechai back to his office. The few hours they'd spent together over lunch had been very productive, but they hadn't done more than pass ideas back and forth.

The older man wanted his fusion plant back. He didn't know

who'd stolen it, and neither did Jared, but that didn't matter. If Jared wanted the cache of Marine Raider equipment, they were going to have to figure out who'd taken it and get them to return it to Frankfort.

Jared *wanted* the Marine Raider equipment. Just the powered armor alone would be sufficient to get Kelsey, Julia, and Talbot fully combat capable. They'd once again be a force worthy of taking out almost any obstruction they came across.

The other weapons and supplies would make their job of getting off this planet easier, too. It wouldn't help them get back to *Persephone*, but that was a problem for another day.

Mordechai leaned back in his chair and gave Jared a long, considering look. "Your man says that he can get life support restored so that we can access the equipment and supplies on the lowest levels. I'm more than willing to trade some of the Marine Raider equipment for that accomplishment.

"As I've already passed along to the guard I've placed outside the room, I'm allowing him the use of the armor and whatever supplies he needs to complete his work. Once it's done, I'll make that trade permanent and give you some other equipment that will assist you in your mission of finding those that stole our fusion plant and making them return it.

"Once you've managed to convince them to do so, and the fusion plant is set up and operational, then all of the equipment and supplies inside the cache are yours. That's the deal that I'm willing to offer."

Jared knew he wasn't going to get a better offer.

"I accept. We'll do everything within our power to bring your fusion plant back and get it operational for you. I'm not sure we can convince them to provide maintenance, but if not, we can do what we can to train your people, though our time is short."

He didn't know how he'd convince the thieves to return the fusion plant, but they'd overcome difficult situations before. So long as he could find these others and learn more about them, there was a possibility that they could come to an arrangement.

If not, he might just have to steal the fusion plant back.

"Have you heard from Kelsey and Talbot?" he asked, changing the subject.

The older man nodded. "They managed to draw the enemy into chasing them. My scouts report that there has been some skirmishing along the way and that she was injured, but our people in the buildings fired enough shots into their pursuers to keep them back far enough for them to flee.

"At this moment, they're headed toward the trap. For the life of me, I can't imagine what she did to get all of those people chasing her. It seems like your sister has a gift for arousing the anger of her enemies."

Jared was worried about Kelsey's injury, but he knew how tough she was. Not only was she a Marine Raider—with all of the enhancements and augmentation that afforded her—but she was mentally tough. If she was still moving, then she wasn't very badly hurt.

At least that's what he told himself.

"How far away from the trap are they?"

"They'll be there within half an hour. It really depends on how direct a course they take. If the enemy forces them into diverting, then they might have to take a longer route. If the enemy starts slowing down, she's going to circle back and draw them into pursuit again.

"Even while they're doing that, our people are moving around the outskirts of the enemy so that they can surround them once they find themselves in our trap. No matter what happens, they're going to be too deep inside Frankfort to escape.

"They might have the numbers to beat us in a straight-up fight, but we have sufficient weaponry to make sure that we win in this environment. Killing many of them in this trap will save my people from unneeded injury or death. For that, I am indebted to you."

"What will you do once you beat them here?" Jared asked curiously. "They've got a lot of horsemen outside the city, and those can still be a problem."

The older man nodded. "Can we conquer their city? No. Can we set the rest of it on fire and drive them farther away? Yes. We'll use rockets and burn them out."

Even though doing something like that was hard to stomach, the tactician inside Jared understood why it needed to be done.

Changing subjects, Jared leaned forward and put his elbows on the arms of his chair. "Once Carl gets the life-support systems on the lowest levels operational, what comes next?"

"I think that depends on you," the old man said. "Are you prepared to begin your exploration farther up the tunnels? If you can summon the train that the thieves used, perhaps you can use it to find them.

"As for us, my people and I will move the supplies they've gathered below to somewhere less accessible should they come back. At any point, those who turned the power on can turn it back off again, so I don't want to lose this opportunity to recover what is ours."

"I hope you realize that you and these people might still be able to come to some type of agreement," Jared said. "They have enough technical know-how to completely disassemble and remove a fusion plant. They could help you rebuild this city.

"They also seem to be the type that can help salvage other parts of your city for reuse. If they've done this in other places, then they certainly have the experience. We won't really know until we get a chance to see who we're dealing with, but there's a potential partnership there if you can get past the fact that they stole from you.

"What I urge you to remember is that they may not have known there were still decent people in this city. They might have come the way they did to avoid the horde. If that's who they thought controlled Frankfort, it wasn't meant to be an insult to you or your people."

He licked his lips slightly. "Forgive me for saying so, but you and your people seem like the kind that might hold grudges. In this case, if you're looking for a true allegiance that might offer benefit to your people, perhaps you should allow them to prove themselves to you."

The other man chuckled. "We're not as bad as you seem to think we are, Admiral. Once you've made contact and we have an opportunity to speak with them, I feel confident that some type of arrangement will eventually be worked out.

"The only thing that I'm insisting you accomplish before that happens is to get them to return our fusion plant and shielding to us, restore it to the condition that it was in before they took it, and make it operational."

He held up a hand before Jared could respond. "I know that we don't have the skill to operate such a high-technology device. That's where the negotiation with the others will come in. I believe that we can come to an arrangement in which they provide the technological know-how to maintain the fusion plant and teach us to do so in exchange for services we can offer.

"Rest assured that I will not allow my pique at the way they've treated us to harm the long-term prospects of my people. Focus on these first steps, Admiral Mertz. If you're going to get to the Imperial Palace, you must find these people. I suggest that you hope that they're not as bad as you thought we were when we first met."

Jared repressed a shudder at that. "Let's hope not. We've already had enough things go wrong on this mission. Just once, I'd like to have something go right."

Mordechai gave him a lopsided smile. "Exactly how likely is that?"

"Damned unlikely," he muttered darkly. "Almost impossible, really."

Even as the other man chuckled, Jared wished he'd been joking. With their luck, they were still at least one big fight away from getting to the Imperial Palace. He could feel it deep in his bones.

23

Talbot raced forward with Kelsey over his shoulder, sprinting around corners and dodging to the other side of open areas to keep the enemy from getting a lock on them as they fled. He'd already spent the last twenty minutes running toward the trap and had been grateful that a couple of snipers along the way had fired shots that kept the screaming mass of horde warriors from *quite* catching up with them.

Not that he thought they'd be able to manage that for much longer. Once the enemy made a concerted effort to catch up, he'd have to put on a dash of speed, using his augmentation to open up the distance, and then the jig would be up.

Once they knew that he could've gotten away any time, they'd know this was a trap. The only thing making this trick possible was their unthinking rage. If they ever started using their brains, they'd quickly regroup and retreat to their camp.

They might even leave the city, and that would deny the locals the opportunity to end this conflict for the next couple of decades.

Using the map overlay function built into his implants, he knew they were only a couple of turns and one good dash away from the trap. He'd been unable to see that anything was buried under the ground when the locals had shown them the area, but considering how well they'd hidden the doors in their tunnels and their ambush sites behind solid walls, he had no doubt that the bombs were there.

As he rounded the final corner and entered the straightaway toward where the trap lay, a woman shouted down at him from one of the buildings. "Horsemen are circling around to stop you! Hurry up!"

He didn't bother responding, because the time had come to run. If they got pinned in the area with the bombs, the defenders probably wouldn't hesitate to trigger the explosives, even if he and Kelsey were right in the middle of them.

His only hope at this point was to get Kelsey past the area where the bombs were hidden and hope that the horde warriors kept coming. If they did, he could probably evade the horsemen.

That was a good plan—or at least he thought so, right up until the horsemen came around the corner just past the area where the explosives were planted. There must've been fifty of them, and there was no way that he and Kelsey were getting past them.

They couldn't retreat with all of the foot soldiers closing in behind them, but they weren't cut off completely just yet. If they really had to, they could run into one of the buildings and make their way into the tunnels.

If they did that, though, it wouldn't draw everybody possible into the kill zone. Talbot had to draw this out as long as he possibly could before they ran. If he didn't execute this flawlessly, they were completely and utterly screwed.

"So, you think you've got us?" he shouted at the horsemen. "You think this is all we have? We'll keep killing you until we drop."

Those were brave words that he hoped drew a lot of people toward them. Most people would've just stood off at bow range and opened fire.

A cruel enemy, on the other hand, would want to surround them so tightly that they couldn't help but see the fate that awaited them. Perhaps they'd even want to capture them alive so that they could be fed into the torture machine that the horde favored.

Personally, that was what he expected. The horde would lose people just to have the opportunity to torture him and Kelsey.

He turned slowly in place, his pistol in hand. Kelsey had hers ready as well, but he doubted they had more than a couple of magazines left between them. When compared to the number of people slowly filling the area, it wasn't going to be enough.

Not even close.

It was getting crowded between the buildings, with the enemy jockeying for position and packing themselves in tightly. No matter how this turned out, the explosives were going to take a deadly toll on the horde.

A large man, dressed in black armor, dismounted and took off his helmet. Talbot recognized him as the man that Julia had spoken to inside the horde city. He'd pegged the fellow as an officer of some kind.

Now that handsome face was contorted with rage. "You've killed the king, his family, and all the high nobles. We're going to take you back to the city and make you regret that. You're going to live for weeks as we take your bodies apart one piece at a time.

"Just when you think death is inescapable, we'll find a way to keep you alive for just a little bit longer. The agonies that you'll suffer will be unspeakable, and I'll savor each and every scream I tear from your throats."

Talbot simply grinned at the man. "Hard pass."

Without waiting for a response, he spun Kelsey off of his shoulder and hurled her through the shattered windows of the building beside them, easily getting her light form onto the third floor.

Even as the enemy charged toward him, Talbot took two quick steps forward, crouched, and levered his powerful muscles to leap after her. He almost didn't make it, but his hands just managed to grab the ledge outside where the window had once been on the same floor where Kelsey had landed.

She was there a second later, grabbing him by the wrists and yanking him into the building. What looked like a storm of arrows flew through the air where they'd just been, and his side ached with the impact of hitting the floor.

The two of them hobbled for the stairwell in the center of the building. If they didn't beat the horde down into the ground, the enemy would cut them off inside the building, and they'd die. Worse, the explosives that were about to go off might kill them too.

They barely made it fifteen meters into the building before the world went insane. The blast was unlike anything he'd ever felt before. It picked him up and slammed him through an interior wall.

Then it felt as if the building were coming apart. Talbot could hear the groaning of steel and other materials as they bent, and it sounded as if the upper floors were coming down.

Even as he was thinking that they were screwed and struggling to get to his feet, Kelsey put an arm around his waist and picked him up off the floor, obviously still favoring her injured leg but not letting it slow her down.

"Hang on!" she shouted.

Even as the building shook and parts of it started to fall, she raced to the far side of the building and jumped through the shattered window.

The impact was brutal, and the pain in his side exploded. It didn't feel like broken ribs, though. It felt worse.

Even as she dragged him to his feet, the building behind them began crumbling.

With a wall of debris racing up behind them, they ran into the building ahead of them and barely made it inside before a wash of debris slammed against the side of the building and brought the ceiling down on their heads.

Surprised that he wasn't dead, Talbot blinked and shifted the debris. It wasn't the building that had collapsed on them, only the panels set into the ceiling of this floor.

They staggered to their feet again and made their way deeper into the building until they found a stairwell that went down into the tunnels. Only once they were there did they even begin to start to feel safe.

"Let me take a look at that," Kelsey said as she turned to look at the broken-off arrows in his side.

He blinked at them stupidly, not even remembering having been shot. When had that happened? Maybe when he'd jumped for the first building? He didn't remember getting hit, but his adrenaline had been through the roof. Now he could tell that the painkillers in his pharmacology unit were keeping the agony at bay.

"We've got to keep going. Lily can take a look at me as soon as we get back, but we can't stay here. If the building comes down, it could still kill us. We'll run into some of the scouts in this area soon. They'll help us get to where we need to be."

Reluctantly Kelsey nodded her agreement, picked him up, and set off. They wouldn't be able to find out how effective the ambush had been until later, but he was pretty sure that they'd put paid to the majority of the invaders.

This fight was over.

* * *

CARL WAS glad that Julia was doing the heavy lifting by the time they'd reached the base of the final set of stairs. He couldn't imagine having had to carry both sets of armor down like she'd done. Even just his tools and the charging equipment had been almost too much.

Once they reached the platform at the maglev train station, he quickly found access to the power conduits. With the equipment that he'd brought, he knew that he'd be able to make a decent estimate of how much power was currently flowing and then guess at how much they could utilize for the life-support systems without alerting those on the other end.

Recharging the armor, weapon magazines, and power packs wasn't going to be that much of a draw. Nowhere in the league of keeping life support running for the area they'd need to allow unfettered access to this level.

As soon as he had the charging station spliced into the power circuits, he connected the cables to the armor where Julia had set both sets against the wall. He smiled in satisfaction when the power started to flow, and he was finally able to begin running self-diagnostics on them.

The batteries seemed intact and would probably hold a charge. Nothing negative leapt out about the armor in general, either. The suits appeared to be in decent condition. Carl crossed his fingers and hoped that continued to be the case as they drew more power.

He laid out the rest of his tools and began removing the parts of the armor that weren't required to be connected to the charger. Adjusting a suit for Julia was going to be difficult. She had the same slight frame as Kelsey did—obviously—and the only way that he'd been able to manage that the first time was because he'd had a lot more equipment at hand to customize things.

He'd make it work. It wouldn't be a perfect fit, but she'd be able to use the armor.

The work was somewhat mind numbing. When Carl looked up about half an hour later, he found himself alone. Julia must be scouting the area, he decided.

Now that they'd gotten access to the cache and he'd had an opportunity to charge some of the magazines, they were no longer unarmed. He swapped out the magazines that had now fully charged and inserted one of them into a flechette pistol, which he put into a hip holster. Another powerpack went into the stunner on his off side, situated in a cross-draw holster like Kelsey favored.

Completing the initial work on Julia's armor took about an hour. Making modifications to the set that he intended for his own use took maybe twenty minutes. Yay for being almost regular sized for a Marine Raider.

By the time he'd finished, the armor's power cells were at about sixty percent.

"How's it looking?" Julia asked from beside him.

He jumped a little and scowled at her. "Do you have to sneak around like that?"

She gave him an apologetic smile. "Sorry. I thought you'd heard me coming. I've been wandering around the platform, looking to see what I could find. It seems as if whoever was here cleaned everything out pretty thoroughly.

"I did find the operations center, though. It has a big map of what looks like the maglev tunnel network. Want to take a look?"

"Sure," he said as he stood. "This needs to finish charging anyway. Take a flechette pistol and stunner. Better safe than sorry."

Once she'd armed herself, she quickly led him through a door set into the wall behind one of the decorative columns. He hadn't seen it, and that was probably by design. On the maintenance level, they'd want to keep people from wandering where they weren't supposed to be.

Behind the door was a control room that wouldn't have been out of place aboard a warship. Lots of consoles, and as she'd said, a large map on the front wall. It only took a single glance to recognize that it had to be a map of the layout for the maglev train network, as she'd guessed.

He gave it his full attention, centering himself in the open area in front of it with his hands on his hips. Several incoming maglev lines fed into Frankfort.

There was a switching station maybe ten kilometers away that allowed for a single set of tunnels to feed into multiple outlets. The tunnels were bidirectional, with spare slots for the trains to use when workers were maintaining them.

Some of the incoming lines fed into the areas just under the city, but others would be for maintenance use, like the one down here. Others would be situated in the middle levels for the delivery of supplies and equipment. The uppermost levels would've been for passenger travel.

Since Frankfort was at the center of the map, that made it easy for him to see what lay in the direction of the Imperial Palace. The answer was, unfortunately, nothing.

There was a line leading directly to Imperial City, but the megalopolis had been utterly destroyed by the kinetic strikes a century ago. There was no telling how far away the maglev tunnels would be damaged, either.

The map was obviously meant to have lights where trains were located, but there were no brightly lit dots indicating active trains. Carl had no idea if that part of the system was broken or there really was no traffic. That would take some digging into the system to determine.

Interestingly, there was a substation short of Imperial City that looked like it might be a spur that had once served the Imperial

Palace. There was no train line designated from there, but it didn't take a genius to figure out that there would be security concerns with having that data widely available.

The existence of a spur line was something of an assumption, but it had to be a valid one. They wouldn't cart all the supplies and people that needed to go to the Imperial Palace over land or through the air. Not only would there be too much traffic, but the security people would also want to control access, and a maglev spur would be perfect for that.

He gestured toward the wall as he turned to Julia. "It looks like we're going to be able to take one of the tunnels and get fairly close to the Imperial Palace. If I'm not mistaken, there's a spur station that will lead down a secure line directly to the palace."

"Okay," she said, eyeing the map. "So how are we going to figure out where the people who stole the fusion plant went? They could've come from just about anywhere, based on this map. We're supposed to be tracking them down, but we don't want to run into them without at least knowing a little more about who we're dealing with."

"I'll be able to figure that out in relatively short order. Once I'm plugged into the control system, I'll be able to see which train visited last and maybe even where it came from and went to. Since the power is on, that probably means the command-and-control network is active, so I might be able to call it directly back to us.

"If it comes from the direction we need to go, we'll have to deal with the thieves immediately. If it's coming from somewhere else, the admiral may decide that it's best to just avoid conflict for right now. This problem isn't one that we can afford to get bogged down in."

Julia shrugged, turning to look at the rest of the dim room. "That sounds good to me. I think I've seen as much fighting as I can stomach for the moment. How long is it going to be before the armor is fully charged?"

"It was at sixty percent when we came here, so it's probably over seventy percent now. Let's go find out."

Together, they made their way back to where he'd left the armor charging. He was pleased to note that both batteries were at seventy-five percent. That would be more than enough to get them suited up and complete the testing process. He could leave the cables plugged in to continue charging the armor while he did the final work of fitting Julia's set.

Reassembling Julia's armor only took a couple of minutes. He'd already shortened the arms and legs as much as he could, so he only had a few final adjustments left to make. It wouldn't be completely comfortable, but at least she'd be able to use it.

He plugged his testing equipment into her armor and was pleased to see that it had no major malfunctions. There were a couple of small parts and control circuits that needed replacement, but he had the spares available and would be able to quickly get them swapped out.

After ten minutes of doing exactly that, he pronounced her armor ready.

"I'll head back to the platform while you get yourself ready," he said as he started to turn away.

"That's not going to work," she said with a shake of her head. "I'm going to need someone to hold the armor while I get into it since we have no racks."

Carl blinked, unsure if that was the best idea. "I'm not sure I can do that without compromising your dignity. If I've got to position the armor, that means I have to see what I'm doing."

Sadly, they hadn't found any skinsuits in the Marine Raider cache and hadn't been willing to spend the time to open every single crate to locate them. The armor was meant to mold around a person wearing a skinsuit, but it would work almost as well on bare skin. Clothing would hinder the operation of the armor, cause chafing, and prohibit the use of the built-in plumbing.

"Your virtue is safe with me," she said dryly. "While I doubt that I'll ever be as comfortable stripping down in front of the universe in general as Kelsey, we're adults. You've seen her naked before, so you're not going to see anything you haven't quite literally seen before."

That was easy to say, but Carl knew it wasn't going to be that easy in practice. She might look exactly like Kelsey, but Julia was a different person. He felt embarrassed as she began stripping down, even though she'd turned her back. He averted his eyes as much as possible and held the armor up to block most of her form.

The armor wasn't light, so he wasn't going to be that adept at turning his head while moving the parts of it where they needed to be for her. He'd be draping it over her rather than allowing her to slip inside it.

Julia kept her back to him, and he only had to look at her once she started backing up. He aligned the armor and made sure it slipped over her slim form. He had to hold it still as she worked to get her plumbing connections in place and sealed up.

That made him feel really self-conscious. He could only imagine how awkward she felt.

"How does it feel?" he asked, relieved when the process was over and she was inside the armor a few minutes later.

"Kind of weird," she admitted. "I'm used to wearing a skinsuit. I'm sure that feeling will fade. Are you okay? You look a little red. The armor wasn't too heavy, was it?"

Carl flushed a little brighter as she smirked at him, showing that she knew it wasn't the weight of the armor that had gotten to him. "At least I'll get my revenge. If you'll hold up the other set of armor, I'll get myself ready."

He turned his back to her and quickly stripped off his clothes. He was feeling pretty good about not burning with embarrassment right up until she spoke.

"You've got a cute butt."

"That's harassment," he said with as much dignity as he could manage. "My face is up here."

She laughed. "Relax. I wasn't staring at your butt. Not really. Barely at all."

Carl sighed and backed up to where she held the armor out for him. He quickly attached the plumbing and slid his arms into the sleeves. Once he had the upper torso secure, he got the legs sealed up and verified that all the latches were secure.

He turned to face Julia and squatted, moving his body around as much as he could so that the armor would settle. It actually felt reasonably comfortable.

Mirroring his motions, Julia did the same. "It feels a little rough in places, but I think this will work. What do we do now?"

"Let's check the charge levels."

Both sets of armor were at more than ninety percent now. If he was being persnickety, he'd wait until they were fully charged, but this was definitely good enough. He disconnected the power cables and secured them nearby with the charging equipment.

"We'll go up floor by floor, and as I find the life-support system that feeds the stairwells, I'll get it turned on and do what checking and replacement of parts that I can," he said. "It should still be in pretty good shape, considering that they had this all operational just a couple of years ago. I'm guessing that it's going to take us probably two or three hours to get everything we need online.

"Once we get back up to the middle levels, I'll strip parts from another lift, and we can get this one working again. That'll add another half hour but make accessing this level much easier."

"So we'll allow three hours for the process," she agreed as she started back toward the stairs. "I suppose we'd best get started. The sooner we get this done, the sooner we can be on our way."

That was something that Carl could get behind. He grabbed the rest of his gear and quickly fell in behind her.

24

Kelsey was *really* worried by the time she got Talbot to Lily. Marine Raiders were tough, but the arrows in his side were proving a challenge for his medical nanites to deal with, probably because they were stuck in something important.

Not that getting him there was easy with a broken-off arrow in her thigh. Thankfully, she'd quickly run into some of the defenders that had helped get them both to where Lily had set up shop.

Doctor Stone had been dealing with several injured people when they'd arrived, with Talbot barely conscious. The other woman immediately directed them to lay her husband down on an area of the floor where she could get at him.

She examined the arrows and the flesh they were broken off in with her scanner. "These are going to have to come out right now. Once I get them out, I can use the portable regenerator to give him a leg up, but he's in a bad way. Once the injury occurred, he really should've stopped moving. He's cut himself up pretty good."

"It wasn't as if we had the option of stopping," Kelsey said somewhat dryly. "Is he in any real danger?"

"If you'd waited another fifteen or twenty minutes to get here, it would've been chancier. His medical nanites are going to be able to boost his blood regeneration, but even with modern drugs, it's going to take time. I'll try to round up some donors, but I'm not certain how well that's going to be received by people here."

"Do you need any help?"

Lily shook her head. "Everyone gathered here knows a little bit about medicine and can assist me in doing the work. Jared stuck his head in a couple of minutes ago and said that he'd like to see you once you got back. Apparently, there's some good news that he wants to discuss with you."

That was nice to hear. It had been a long time since they'd had any good news.

Then Lily noticed the blood on her leg. "Is that yours?"

Before she could respond, Lily ran the scanner over her leg. "That needs to come out. Lay down over there and let one of my assistants get it so that you don't hurt yourself any more."

The woman who was waiting for her had an ugly looking set of pliers and a long, sharp knife. Thankfully, Kelsey could flood her system with painkillers.

That didn't make the extraction pain free, but it made it bearable. Thankfully, the arrow came out with a minimum of cutting to free the head. Once that was done, the woman sewed the wound closed, slapped a bandage over it, and moved on to the next patient.

That worked for her.

Kelsey rose and walked over to where Lily was just finishing with Talbot. The pain was manageable, and she could walk. That was a win in her book.

She knelt down beside Talbot and put her hand on his shoulder. His eyes fluttered open, and he looked up at her blearily.

"Lily says you're going to be fine, slacker," she said soothingly. "I've got to go see Jared. I'll be back to check on you soon as I can. Don't die on me."

The corners of his lips turned up slightly. "I promise I won't. Go find out what's going on. I'll be better by the time you get back. And find me something to eat. I'm starving."

Still worried about her husband, Kelsey headed out. She tagged up with one of the guards assigned to keep an eye on her, and he quickly escorted her to the air handler room, where it seemed that Leader Mordechai and some of his top people had gathered.

Kelsey walked into the room and stopped dead. Julia and Carl were there. More importantly, they were wearing Marine Raider powered armor, with their helmets off.

"What the *hell?*" she asked as she walked around the two of them. "Where did you find these?"

"It's a long story," Jared said as he gestured toward one of the seats. "Park it, and we'll get everybody caught up on the details."

He frowned at her. Rather, he frowned at Talbot's blood on her chest from where she'd hauled him out of the fight and at her leg.

"Is any of that your blood?"

"Some," she admitted. "I'm good now. Most of it is Talbot's, and Lilly says he's going to be okay. Eventually."

Never taking her eyes off her doppelgänger and her young friend, Kelsey sat. She'd thought she wouldn't see this kind of thing again until they got off Terra. She was utterly floored.

When they finished bringing her up to speed, she raised her hand slightly. "What about the attack? Did we drive the horde back, or are we still going to have to deal with some of them?"

Mordechai smiled widely. "The trap that you led them into was more successful than we'd imagined possible. There were survivors, of course, but not many. None of those escaped the city. The invasion is over.

"Considering that they must've lost between four and five thousand of their warriors in this incursion, I seriously doubt that they'll be back anytime soon. Their forces outside the city didn't suffer any losses other than the ones incurred when you destroyed their treasure room and palace and the fight for domination that caused, but they'd never had as many mounted warriors as foot soldiers. Considering how warlike they are in general, I don't believe they'll be back up to their normal fighting strength for at least a full generation or two.

"Since they had to execute so many of their surviving leaders to settle the rulership question, whoever runs them now is going to be consolidating power for some time. He'll have his mind on other things than trying to come after us."

The older man leaned back in his chair and considered Kelsey. "I've heard great things about how well you fought. Both you and your husband exhibited capabilities that I never would've expected possible. It appears my understanding of what a Marine Raider could do was incomplete and understated. Well done."

"There is something else that I need to tell you," Jared said solemnly. "When we were going up and down the stairs, I found this."

He opened the pouch at his belt and handed her a small metal pin. She took it from him and then almost dropped it as soon as she saw what was on its face: the emblem of the Marine Raiders.

She stared at him. "How is that possible? Has it been down there for five hundred years?"

"Doubtful. I think that whoever stole the fusion plant was wearing it, based on its condition. Maybe those people are descendants of Marine Raiders. Maybe their group was trained by the Raiders back in the day or perhaps simply inspired by them.

"Whoever they are, they still have technology and a connection to the Marine Raiders. We're going to have to find out who they are because, if we can get off this planet, they're probably going to play some part in getting us there."

Kelsey sat back and turned her mind inward, ignoring the rest of them for a minute. The news was shocking. She wasn't sure which of the possibilities could be the truth. Hell, they could *all* be true. Or it was something so strange that none of them could possibly guess the connection.

Coming back to herself, she focused on Carl. "Is there any way to use the maglev system to determine where these people came from and where they took the fusion plant?"

He shook his head. "The system was never designed to give a location for a train that's not currently in service, so our best bet is going to be reactivating it and then seeing where it comes from."

She gave him a raised eyebrow. "That's going to tell them that we're onto them. Is that what we really want to do?"

"Do we have a choice?" Jared asked. "Unless we want to walk a thousand kilometers through an unknown tunnel system with potentially toxic air, we're going to need that train. We might as well get it into our heads that we're going to be talking with them.

"We'll go in as prepared as we can, but we have to be ready to fight a technologically advanced group if things go badly. We'll do our best to make friends, but there's only so much we can do to cajole them into doing what we want."

Kelsey sighed. One more group that they might have to fight their way through to get what humanity needed. It felt like they'd either been on their way to Terra or down on the surface of this damned planet forever. She just wanted to be back in space and on her way to a new location with a new mission. This one felt like it would never end.

She turned her attention to Carl. "How soon are we going to be ready to do this?"

The young scientist smiled slightly. "I can go downstairs and call the train right now if that's what you want."

"I think we should rest up after the fight," Jared said. "We can gather all the equipment that we'll need, but tomorrow morning is soon enough."

Kelsey nodded. "A good night's sleep would do us all some good. If our history is anything to go by, we might not be getting any rest tomorrow."

She could hardly believe that they were almost ready to leave Frankfort and try to get to the Imperial Palace. Yes, they'd have to go through another group of people to get there, but this was just the kind of break that they'd been desperately needing since they'd arrived on Terra.

They had to make this work. They just had to.

* * *

JARED WAS UP EARLY the next morning and made his way down to the lowest level of the city. The air smelled significantly better on the journey than it had the last time, and he hadn't needed any air bottles.

Once there, he took a brief tour of the maglev control center and was impressed that so much of it still seemed operational. Carl was already going through what he could of the system. He'd plugged some of his gear into one of the consoles and now had the controls up and was trying to figure out how they worked.

Jared sat down next to him. "What have you found?"

"About what you'd expect," the young man said. "The system has had failures here and there, but it has enough redundancy that it can still do what we need it to. I've gotten the serial number of the train. It's been inactive for seven months.

"None of the other trains that used to use this system have been online for at least a century, so this one has to belong to the people that we're looking for. I can't tell you where it is, because it's not active at the moment, though.

"The system was never designed to pinpoint the location of an inactive train. Sadly, it can't even tell me the location where it last received a signal from it. Like I said, the original designers didn't think that was necessary. I mean, who steals a train?

"What I *can* do is send a signal to reactivate it and then summon it here. Once it starts moving, I'll be able to determine its location and where it's coming from immediately, because it's going to show up on the big board there.

"So long as it's on automatic control, I should be able to determine a lot of things about it. If there's anyone on board, they can cut me off pretty fast if they've got the knowledge to do it."

Carl quirked an eyebrow at him. "Did Kelsey ever make you watch any of those *Star Trek* vids? Particularly *The Wrath of Khan*?"

Jared shook his head slightly. "She's made me watch a lot of things, but I don't remember anything by that name. What's its significance?"

"In that vid, they have a situation where bad people stole one of their ships, so the good guys utilized their knowledge of its systems to lower its defenses remotely at a critical moment during a fight because nobody had bothered to change the codes their Fleet used.

"It's nothing like what we do with our ships since we don't allow other vessels to control them, but it's a lot like what happens with the maglev train system here. I'm utilizing the controls built into the system meant to redirect traffic. Those trains are designed to obey commands from authorized control systems unless that feature is turned off.

"I'll wager that since these folks seem to be the only ones using the system, they've never bothered changing the codes. If I'm right, their train will drive out right from under their noses before they can stop it. Once it's in motion, Ralph will hack it and change the control code to prevent them from calling it back."

"That sounds awfully complicated," Jared said with a scowl. "Once you gain control of the train, can you determine if anyone is on board?"

The young scientist shrugged slightly. "I can access the vid feeds from inside the control area on the train. If someone shows up there, I'll see them. I'm not going to be able to look into the passenger areas or where they keep cargo.

"The other feeds can be accessed from inside the train, but there was never any need for a general controller to be able to examine that information."

Carl leaned back in his seat, obviously thinking about it. "I suppose it's still possible, though. Once Ralph hacks the train, he can probably get access to the internal vid feeds. I'm not going to be able to say one way or the other until he gives it a shot."

"If we can get access to those interior vids, I want to make that happen."

"When are we planning to kick this off?" Carl asked.

He checked his internal chronometer. "They should have the last of the equipment that we'll be taking with us down here in about an hour. I think that would be an excellent time to make this happen.

"I spoke to Leader Mordechai this morning, and he said that he'd send troops with us if we wanted. While extra bodies might be good, I'm not sure that mixing the people that were our captors yesterday with the thieves that stole from them a few years ago is a great plan. I'd rather keep this first meeting as straightforward as we possibly can."

Carl chuckled at that. "You won't get any argument from me. What about Talbot? Is he going to be ready to travel?"

"Travel, yes. Fight, no. Lily says that he needs to rest a couple days before he tries to exert himself. I'm not going to argue with her.

"We're going to take all four sets of armor, which is why you had the other two brought down and charged them up this morning. Since we only have two Marine Raiders—counting Julia—you're going to be using the set that you've already fitted for yourself.

"The last one is going to Lieutenant Laird. As a trained marine, she's going to have an idea of what needs to happen if things break bad. She hasn't used Raider armor, but she has used the standard marine version. That'll give her a leg up."

"I'll get them fitted as soon as possible," Carl agreed. "Add another hour to your time estimate to cover it."

The scientist turned in his seat to face Jared. "Are you worried about this trip, sir? These people have technology, and they might be bad guys. If that's the case, they might overwhelm us, and we'll be screwed again."

"Sometimes you just have to do the best you can," Jared said as he clapped the other man on the shoulder and stood. "I'm going back upstairs to say our goodbyes. Be ready to start Operation Choo-Choo in two hours. We're probably only going to get one try at this, so I'd rather not have it all come down around our ears."

"Operation Choo-Choo?" Carl asked, amused. "That has to be a Kelsey thing."

"Got it in one. Now, back to work."

Jared smirked a little as he headed toward the door. Of course Kelsey had come up with the name. He had only the vaguest idea of how it connected to the maglev train, but she'd been insistent.

His expression grew more pensive once he was away from everyone else. He was less confident than he'd tried to sound. It was all too likely that they'd meet this next group and end up in another fight. One they might not be able to win.

They'd have to proceed as cautiously as they could and hope for the best because if they screwed this up, that was it for humanity. The human race might not die today, but it *would* die. And that was something he couldn't allow to happen.

25

J ulia set the large pack next to the pile that she and Kelsey had already hauled to the maglev platform. Even with the lift now working, it had taken the two of them more than an hour to carry down the bags that Carl had packed for them.

Lieutenant Laird had stayed in the cache room and continued packing what their former captors would allow them to take while they moved it. Thank God they didn't have to carry everything down stairs the whole way.

Now that they'd repositioned everything on the platform, the rest of the folks going with them began sorting the contents so that everyone would have what they needed.

Carl had also come out of the control room and begun fitting armor to Chloe Laird, now that she'd arrived, and started fine-tuning Kelsey's armor.

Once she was done, Julia edged over to her. "Do you think we're going to make it?"

She had to ask because it seemed hard to imagine that they were going to get off this planet with the override. They'd been through so much and lost so many people that she was feeling really cynical about their chances at this point.

Kelsey gave her a sideways glance. "Don't fall into the trap of thinking that we're going to fail. We've got to have a positive outlook, even when things look darkest. That's how we triumph again and again, because we don't take no for an answer."

Julia considered that for a few seconds and then shrugged. "I guess that's one of the differences between us. I've failed so many times that I've just stopped believing that I can win. We're so far behind the eight ball—both here and back in my universe—that victory seems unimaginable at this point. The AIs hold all the cards."

Kelsey put her hands on Julia's shoulders. "You've got to remember that they don't know about you. They don't know about the people that we're training or the ships that we found for you.

"The knowledge of how things work here is going to give you a leg up there. By the time we're done getting the override and fighting the master AI at Twilight River, you'll know what you have to do.

"And you know that we'll help you do it. Maybe not us personally, because I doubt my father—our father—will allow Jared or myself to go to your universe, but we can send plenty of ships packed with advisors and helpers to guide you.

"Admittedly, it's going to be a challenge, but you can't go through life expecting everything to fail. At some point, if all you do is look forward to failure, you're going to give up. When that happens, victory is forever beyond your grasp. Don't fall into that trap. Imagine victory and then make it happen."

"You make it all sound so simple," Julia grumbled. "I know that it's not, and that's what makes me lose hope. We have so many balls in the air. All it takes is dropping one for the enemy to win. So many people that I love have already died. It's hard to believe I can redeem them."

Before Kelsey could respond, Carl waved the two of them over. Julia followed in her doppelgänger's footsteps.

"Kelsey, the armor is ready for you to put on and run through a test routine," Carl said. "It's not completely customized for you, but it's the best I can do with the generic equipment I've got on hand. If we ever get back to *Persephone*, I can have it completely customized inside an hour. The same goes for you, Julia. That's not going to be a problem."

"I'm sad that I had to leave my original armor here," Julia said with a shake of her head. "The black armor, I mean. It's odd how the color matters to me. I have no idea why it's different here, either. One of those little mysteries that we'll never know the answer to."

"It just goes to prove that when you're looking at the multiverse as a theory, there are going to be inexplicable differences between even the most similar realities," Carl said, visibly dropping into lecture mode. "Honestly, it wouldn't surprise me if there were universes out there that are exactly like either one of ours, with only things like the names of ships being different. Or perhaps even different people aboard, assigned to different positions. The combinations are literally infinite.

"I wouldn't get hung up on the details if I were you. When we get back to the ship, I can change the color for you. That's not really that complicated an issue. It'll take a little experimentation, but I can work it out in a couple of hours."

She nodded, but she wasn't sure that was what she really wanted. The black armor belonged to a different person. Even in the short time that she'd been in this universe, Julia had changed. Even thinking of herself by her assumed name was feeling more natural.

Honestly, it was like getting a fresh start. She could leave her mistakes and failures behind by merely changing her name. Julia would do better than Kelsey had in her universe.

Of that, she would make sure.

Julia nodded distractedly and looked around the platform. It seemed as if almost everyone was there and packing their gear. They'd only brought along things that they thought they could carry, as they knew that they might have to hike at some point.

There was only so much equipment that they could take that would help them in the long run, too. The immediate goal had to be getting from point A to point B and dealing with the people that they were going to negotiate with if that was even happening first.

The train would be great—if it actually arrived—but wasn't going to get them to the Imperial Palace. That was going to take some hiking, whether it be aboveground, where they'd have to potentially fight other people, or through the tunnels, where they needed supplies to allow them to see, breathe, and eat.

Weirdly, that made her think about the horses that they'd been forced to leave tethered outside the horde city. They'd left the reins in such a way that the horses could tug them loose, but she was confident that the horde had recaptured them by now.

Thankfully, those murderous bastards were actually the kind of people that cared for their animals. Still, she missed the ability to ride. What an odd, introspective thing it was to think about how horse riding brought her pleasure at a time like this.

While she was thinking about that, Mertz exited the control room and began waving for them to gather around.

"Everyone, it's time to get the last of your gear packed. Now that Carl has the armor fitted to our fighters, he's going to call the train. I'm not sure how long it's going to take to get here, so you need to begin getting yourselves in order. It might bring hostile guests right to our doorstep, and we'll want to give them a warm welcome."

Julia laughed at his joke as Kelsey stripped down and began putting her armor on. As usual, the woman paid no attention to who was standing around her, not even bothering to shield her privates by discreetly turning her body. It was as if public nudity no longer even registered for her.

That was another thing about the other woman that she'd never be able to comprehend. Her body consciousness wouldn't allow her to be so cavalier about strutting around naked in front of strangers. Or worse, platonic friends.

Just taking her clothes off in front of Carl earlier had pushed the limits of what she could imagine herself doing. Thankfully, he'd been a gentleman about the entire affair.

She really was going to have to have a conversation with Angela if they got to *Persephone*. She needed to reassure the woman and get her help understanding Carl as deeply as she could before the time came to seduce him in her universe.

The use of the word "seduce" made her pause. Her original intention had only been to lure the man in so that she could begin forming a partnership with him, but seduction had popped so easily into her mind.

There was definitely an attraction building in her mind, and that was something else she'd have to talk about with Angela. She needed to make sure the other woman knew that this version of Carl was off limits, and she knew it.

While Kelsey was getting ready, Julia went back into the control room. Carl was now sitting at one of the consoles, separated from the others, and working diligently with a virtual keyboard. She sat down next to him, causing him to glance over with a raised eyebrow.

"I want to apologize," she said quietly.

He frowned and gave her his full attention. "For what?"

"You're a married man, and I should have been more discreet when we fitted my armor. Maybe lying down on the floor and finding a way to wiggle into it. It was inappropriate to put a married man in the position where he had to look at another woman without her clothes on. It was disrespectful to you and to your wife."

He shook his head with a slight smile. "You did what needed doing, and I'm not disturbed by it. I can also assure you that Angela won't be bothered by it either. She's been a marine for a long time, and now she's a Marine Raider. That's just the way it is for them."

Julia let the air she'd been holding out slowly. "That's good to hear. I really didn't want Angela to beat me up. She's intimidating enough as a marine in my universe. As a Marine Raider, I can't imagine how scary she'd be."

Carl chuckled. "I doubt very seriously that she'd beat you up. If she were mad, she'd be much more likely to yell at you. Trust me when I say that it's going to be okay."

He went back to work, making sure that it was apparent to her that the matter was settled, so far as he was concerned. Without saying a word, she rose, stepped over to the nearest wall, and leaned against it.

She was lucky. He was a kind man who would make an excellent consort for her. She really hoped that she could get back home and meet him.

By the time she'd finished thinking that through, Mertz had

walked over to Carl. "Do you really think you're going to be able to summon the train without any trouble? If so, it's time."

"Let's find out," Carl said.

* * *

CARL TOOK a deep breath and sent out the reactivation signal. Since he had the serial number for the train controller, that made it a simple matter to ping the entire network for it.

Almost immediately, a response came back that the train was in a powered-down configuration and had begun reactivating. The controller gave him an estimate of five minutes before it would be prepared to leave its current location.

That was actually pretty fast. It meant that all the systems on the train were operational. That five minutes would give the controller time to check all the propulsion and braking systems before the train began moving. If the people that had been using it were able to shut off that sequence in the next few minutes, they'd stop it from leaving their station.

Of course, they might also just choose to put people on board to confront whoever was stealing their train. If so, there were going to be people arriving on the platform that were pretty upset that they'd been taken for a ride.

Just as the counter on the timer struck five minutes, Carl saw a red dot appear on the main board. Unsurprisingly, it was flashing at what he suspected was the spur leading to the Imperial Palace.

Of course it was. Why wouldn't it be directly where they were going? It seemed perfectly fitting that the people who'd stolen the fusion plant from Frankfort had also holed up in the one place that they absolutely needed to be.

And if history was anything to go by, they wouldn't be friendly either.

What was mildly confusing to him was the fact that the blinking red dot wasn't moving. All it did was remain in one place and flash. He wasn't sure what that meant. If he'd read the files correctly, it should be green and moving.

He checked the readouts and brought up the camera inside the control area of the train itself. There was no one there, which was a relief. It meant that no one with the ability to control the train had gotten there in time to make a difference.

The controls indicated the train was in motion. That probably meant that the flashing red light indicated that it was on the spur and thus not able to be seen on the main map. A couple of minutes later, the dot turned to a solid green and began moving toward Frankfort.

"I've got it on the screen and moving," he said somewhat needlessly. Everyone else in the room had undoubtedly noticed it. "Ralph, can you see about hacking into its systems and linking into the vid system? The admiral wants to know if we've got passengers."

"On it," Ralph said as he began typing furiously on his virtual keyboard. "It doesn't look like this system is too complicated, and I've already managed to insert a couple of feelers that should give me a good idea what I'm looking at shortly."

Five seconds later, the young man grinned. "I'm in. One of my feelers found a back door that someone had designed into the system that I was able to activate. I'm bringing up the cameras in a rotating format. It'll be on the screen to our right."

As the images began flashing up onto the indicated screen, Carl's heart sank. Not only was the train occupied, but its passengers were also armed. They might not have gotten anyone capable of controlling the train aboard during that five-minute window, but there'd been armed fighters ready to move. That meant that there was going to be a confrontation as soon as the train arrived.

"Can you freeze some of those images and maybe enlarge them?" Kelsey asked. She stood next to the console in her new Raider armor, her helmet nestled into the crook of her arm.

Ralph shook his head. "I can freeze the feed, but enlarging the image will just reduce the resolution to the point where you can't see what you're looking for. That kind of nonsense is just a vid show trick. The real world doesn't work that way."

"Then do it," she said. "I might not be able to see all the details, but if what I'm looking for is there, I'll see it."

As soon as Ralph froze one of the images on the screen, she

stepped closer to the big screen and stared up at the fighter. "Is it just me, or do they look like they have pins similar to the one that Jared found in the stairwell? It's right there on the lapel. And that sure looks like a uniform, doesn't it?"

Carl rose from his console and joined her in examining the man standing there. He was young and had the kind of close-cut hair that one might associate with the military. He looked just like the other dozen or so that had been standing in the same car.

"Ralph, you're the one running the vid feed," he said. "How many cars are we talking about and how many people? Do you see anyone that looks different than this guy?"

"They've got people in four of the cars," the young hacker said. "Roughly a dozen per car, so somewhere around fifty people. The men all look like him and are wearing that uniform, whatever it is. There are maybe a third that are female. The uniform is the same, but they have longer hair.

"They've got flechette rifles strapped over their shoulders, and I see flechette pistols in holsters on their hips. If we get into a fight with these people, we're going to have to be really careful, or we'll end up destroying the train."

Admiral Mertz joined them and peered up at the frozen image. "I think you're right, Kelsey. That sure does look like the same kind of pin, even though I can't make out the details at this resolution. The fact that there are so many of them, dressed in the same way, indicates this is probably an organization that the Raiders founded hundreds of years ago. Or maybe they inspired it. We'll have to find out when they get here."

He turned to face his sister. "Do you think you can use that mystique to your advantage when they arrive? If we can browbeat them, I'd much rather do that than fight. Ralph's right. If we start shooting, the train is going to be the first casualty."

Kelsey shrugged. "I can try. The only thing that I can't control is how they're going to respond. Maybe if they see some of us in armor, they'll realize that we're Marine Raiders. They won't know who has augmentation and who doesn't, so everyone needs to be armored up.

"Everyone that isn't in the control room needs to set up some of the weapons that we brought down to form a crossfire that we can use against them if they decide they're going to be hostile.

"I'd prefer stunners on wide beam. If I could be sure we'd get them all, I'd say ambush them. As it is, we'll probably have to talk first —if they'll let us—but I'll be damned if I give them a chance to kill one of us."

Admiral Mertz nodded and turned toward him. "Carl, how long until they arrive?"

He quickly walked back over to his console and brought up the data. "Judging by their current speed, it looks like they'll be here in about twenty-five minutes. If we're going to be in a fight, why don't we use some of the weapons that we've brought down to rig up a booby trap for them?"

Kelsey stepped over to him, her expression interested. "You've intrigued me, O designer of deadly weapons. What do you have in mind?"

"We've got all those explosives. We know *exactly* where the train is going to stop. Why don't we set up mines facing the cars where we know the enemy is going to be? Rather than hide them, we make them obvious.

"That way, when the doors open and they come out, they'll already be in the field of fire of weapons that they can't stop or control. We can tell them that we don't intend to set the mines off unless they start fighting, and maybe that'll calm things down until we can figure out what we're going to do."

Kelsey put on an impressed expression. "That's brilliant. We can stash people with rifles and stunners behind some of the columns to help cover them as well. If they realize that they're in a death trap, they might hesitate long enough for us to at least talk them down."

Without another word, Kelsey headed out, presumably to begin setting up the explosives.

"Good work, Carl," Admiral Mertz said. "Now, let's get everything locked down here. We don't want them shooting this place up and causing any of the systems here to do anything that they shouldn't."

"Yes, sir. I'll have everything ready."

Now all they had to do was wait until the thieves arrived. Then they'd find out whether or not they could stop them from fighting or if there was going to be a shootout that destroyed the train they so desperately needed to get to the Imperial Palace.

The Imperial Palace that, it seemed, was already occupied.

26

T he next twenty minutes gave Kelsey an opportunity to work with Lieutenant Laird while setting up the explosives that they'd brought with them. Basically, these were antipersonnel mines that were designed around shaped charges that shot steel balls into the targets while leaving the area behind them *relatively* safe.

And even though the idea left her uncomfortable, she also assisted in planting explosive charges down under where the train would settle. Those were to destroy the train if the fighting became too difficult, and they had to end it quickly.

It would also mean that they'd be unable to use the train to get to the Imperial Palace, so she intended to avoid that outcome if at all possible.

If they could get past this first confrontation, she might be able to deescalate the situation and keep the other side from making any irreversible decisions. Once the killing started, she and her people would be forced to fight their way through to the Imperial Palace and capture it.

It would be far better if they could do this with words rather than weapons.

All of the noncombatants—plus Talbot—were in the control room. There was absolutely no need for them to be in danger. The walls were thin, but the control consoles would provide some cover if things went bad.

Jared, Sean, and several of the others with the skills to use flechette rifles were hidden behind some of the columns, ready to provide cover if needed. The only ones left visible on the platform were herself, Lieutenant Laird, Carl, and Julia.

Only she and Julia could use their armor effectively, but Chloe was a trained fighter and had used standard marine armor before. She'd do fine, Kelsey was sure.

Carl, on the other hand, was just there for show. He had orders that if the people on the train started shooting, he was to get his skinny little butt back into the control room and form the final line of defense in case she and the rest couldn't hold.

She resisted the urge to pace. Even though her nanites were working on her leg wound, it still ached and gave her occasional jolts of pain to remind her that she'd been hurt. Nothing that would stop her from doing what she needed to, but enough to make her aware of the injury.

Right on schedule, the maglev train pulled into the station and slowed to a halt just like Carl had programmed it to do. As soon as it settled to the ground, the doors slid open, and men and women began pouring out, their rifles up.

The train wasn't that big, all things considered. It consisted of an engine and four cars. The latter looked more like they were made for cargo because Kelsey couldn't see any seats inside. That made sense, considering that these people were using the train to strip nearby areas of equipment and supplies.

All told, Carl's count of fifty was pretty accurate. Her implants totaled the hostiles at fifty-one.

Each of the soldiers held an Imperial-made flechette rifle and had a flechette pistol in a holster on their belt. While Kelsey couldn't see behind their backs, there was a good chance that they carried stunners there. It was interesting that they'd decided to lead with lethal weaponry. Interesting and telling.

The people she'd positioned behind the columns would lead with stunners on wide beam, likely taking out most of the people on the platform if hostilities broke out. It spoke to how they'd rather not kill unless they had no choice.

The flechette rifles were a danger, but only if those people knew how to use them. Other than Kelsey, everyone had their helmets locked down, and their armor would be sufficient to stop a lot of the flechettes from penetrating.

Kelsey had her helmet off because she wanted to make the point that this didn't have to end like that. As the soldiers came out, their attention focused on her, probably because she was different.

"I'm sure you're all wondering why I've called you here," she said in a dry tone. "Before anyone gets too excited, let me suggest that you lower your weapons. If you start shooting, we're going to have to take you all down, and I'd prefer not to do that."

One of the women stepped forward, not lowering her weapon in the slightest. "Identify yourself. Why have you stolen our train?"

"Don't you think that's a little judgmental?" Kelsey asked, tilting her head slightly to the side. "After all, you used that train to steal a fusion plant from this city. Not only that, but I'm also sure that you took a lot of other things that were quite valuable as well.

"So, rather than call each other names, why don't we start with deescalating the situation before you make any more accusations?"

Before the other woman could speak, Kelsey gestured toward the antipersonnel mines arrayed in front of them. "Those mines will kill everyone on that side of the platform if you decide to open fire. Inside our armor, it's not going to hurt us at all. I really do suggest that you take this slowly because if you make a mistake right now, I'm going to be the only one left to regret it."

The woman eyed the antipersonnel mines and obviously considered ordering her people back into the train. Her thoughts seemed to pass across her face, and then, instead, she made a gesture for them to lower their weapons.

They didn't disarm themselves, but that was fine with Kelsey. She really didn't expect them to. All she wanted was for them to avoid making a lethal mistake.

"Who are you, and how do you know any of this?" the woman asked. "And how are you making the holy armor work?"

Kelsey blinked at that last. Holy armor? That seemed kind of... weird.

"My name is Kelsey Bandar, and I'm a Marine Raider."

The woman's expression went from cautious and suspicious to downright hostile. Her weapon came back up, and so did all the rest.

"Liar. Tell us the truth, or we'll kill you right now."

"Doesn't the fact that I'm working the armor count for something? What kind of proof would satisfy you?"

Before the other woman could speak, Julia stepped forward. Without waiting for the woman to say anything, her doppelgänger headed toward the front of the train and jumped down from the platform.

Then she bent low and lifted the front end of the train. That had to be a considerable strain on her and her armor, but she managed it.

"Does this count?" Julia asked through the speakers on the exterior of her armor. She then lowered the train back down and stared at the soldiers through her blank metal faceplate.

The troops arrayed on the platform stared at Julia, their weapons slowly sinking back down, and their faces struck with a mixture of shock and awe. The woman in command of these troops was seemingly unsure of how to respond.

Once Julia had jumped back up on the platform, making the feat look graceful in spite of her relative inexperience with the armor, the woman in charge of the troops swallowed visibly and gently laid her rifle on the ground.

"Everyone lay down your arms," she said.

All of the troops on the platform set their rifles down, unholstered their pistols, and set them on the ground as well. They then produced the stunners that Kelsey had suspected were there and set them next to the rest.

Once they'd done so, they stepped away from the weapons, even as the woman advanced on Kelsey.

"We deserve an explanation. Who are you really, and how are you related to the holy one?"

Kelsey shrugged slightly and then realized that the gesture wouldn't be visible through her armor. "I'm not sure who the holy one is, so you're going to have to explain it to me. What I said earlier was true. I'm a Marine Raider. I've come to gather what we need to free the Empire.

"The people of this city are angry that you stole their fusion plant, and we've agreed to discuss the matter with your leaders. We'd prefer to do so peacefully. How do we make that happen?"

The woman studied Kelsey for a long moment. "Just seeing you in that armor means that I need to bring you back to our base. Once I do, you can speak with our leaders, and they will make that decision.

"If you truly are a Marine Raider, then I don't believe you're going to have much difficulty in negotiating a solution. But you're going to have to explain everything to the god."

Kelsey frowned. "God? I still don't understand."

The woman smiled coolly. "It's quite simple. The god is a *real* Marine Raider, and I look forward to hearing how he responds to your tall tale."

* * *

JULIA WATCHED the exchange between Kelsey and the others with interest. When the conversation reached the point where the woman stated that their "god" was a Marine Raider, she laughed out loud. Thankfully, she'd shut off her external speakers, and no one could hear her.

That was ridiculous. Other than Kelsey and the people she'd begun enhancing, there were no Marine Raiders left in this Empire. They'd all died out long ago. These people were lying, even if she didn't understand what they had to gain by doing so.

The most likely explanation was that someone had tricked them. Though, Julia had to admit, whoever it was had gotten the train working and also managed to guide them through the process of disassembling the fusion plant safely. It had to be someone with a lot more knowledge than she'd expected anyone on Terra to have.

None of the Marine Raiders that had been on Terra back then

could have possibly lived this long, and the ability to create them had fallen into the hands of the computers long ago.

There was obviously some kind of trickery underway. That meant the meeting with these people was going to be dangerous. After all, anyone with actual Marine Raider augmentation was a threat to the lie this person was telling.

She wondered how Kelsey was going to handle that. Was the woman going to realize that they were in danger when the trick was exposed? Her doppelgänger was really smart, and she was a lot more worldly than Julia, so she really hoped that was the case.

If the thoughts that were running through Julia's head had occurred to Kelsey, she wasn't letting it show on her face. She was busy asking the woman questions about their god and being deflected.

All the woman would say was that it wasn't her place to discuss the god. That if Kelsey wanted more information, she'd need to speak to her leaders.

The one positive aspect of this was that she'd said that she'd escort them there. It looked like the prospect of fighting it out here on the platform was over.

Kelsey stepped back from the soldiers and over to Julia. "What do you think we should do? They're basically inviting us back to their place, but it could be a trap."

"If it's not a trap, it's some kind of hoax," Julia said bluntly. "We both know that Marine Raiders don't live that long. Whoever they're referring to as their god is pulling the wool over their eyes."

She frowned. "And I don't even know where that saying came from, but it had to be something you said because it makes no sense."

Kelsey chuckled. "When you watch a lot of old vids, you pick up all kinds of obscure turns of phrase. I suggest that we only take a few of us when we go see them. That way, only some of us are at risk if the hammer comes down.

"If they really wanted to stop us from bringing the train here, they could've killed the power back at the Imperial Palace, and it would've stopped. They had plenty of time to do that, but they left it running. That means that whoever's in charge wants these people to come back and report. We've got to use that to our advantage."

She turned to face Julia more directly. "I'm going to suggest to Jared that only the four of us that can use the armor go. That way, they're not going to have an opportunity to take hostages without getting into a *real* fight. We'll leave the others here so that they can arrange a rescue if things go badly."

"And how are they going to get there?" Julia asked. "If these people aren't happy at seeing us and kill the power to the train, the Imperial Palace is still a thousand kilometers away. Not to mention that our potential rescuers won't have any armor to bring to the fight. This seems like a bad idea, Kelsey."

"Life isn't without risks," her doppelgänger said philosophically. "As my husband would tell you, I'm prone to taking more risks than the average person. If you want to stay here and reinforce the rescue team, I'll go along with that. I still think you should come with us, but the call is yours."

Julia sighed in exasperation. "How is it that you're so headstrong, and I'm not? I thought we were supposed to be the same person until a couple of years ago. Could you explain to me exactly how you're *so* different?"

"Just lucky, I guess," Kelsey said with a grin. "That doesn't change the question. Do you want to stay here or go with me?"

Julia slowly counted down from ten in her head to get the exasperation out of her voice. "I'll go with you, of course. If they're going to jump somebody, we've got to kick their asses."

Kelsey clapped her on the shoulder. "Now you're talking like a Marine Raider. Here's what we're going to do. We're going to step back into the other room and let Jared know what we're doing, and then we're going to let these people escort us to see their leaders.

"If the power gets cut, they're going to have to come and get us. Personally, I don't see that happening. These don't seem like the kind that shoot first and ask questions later like the horde.

"They're looking for answers and want to hear what we have to say. They may not give us what we want, but I believe that we can come to some type of arrangement if we work hard enough.

"More importantly, we have to come to some kind of understanding, or we won't get access to the Imperial Palace. We'll have to go through them one way or the other, and I'd much rather do that without shooting."

On that, Julia agreed. They didn't have the numbers to fight a large group because they'd lose, even with their access to Marine Raider armor and modern weapons.

Losing Scott was bad enough. Losing the rest would be unthinkable.

While Chloe and Carl kept an eye on their prisoners—or perhaps guests—she followed Kelsey in to speak with Mertz. The man listened to his sister's plan and then shook his head.

"If we separate ourselves, the chances of us being overwhelmed individually are too high. We've initiated contact, and now it's time for us to go see who the man behind the curtain is. Get everyone together, and we'll load them onto the train."

Julia sighed and hoped that they could carry this off. That they weren't jumping from the frying pan into the fire. Whatever that meant.

27

J ared eyed the soldiers in the train compartment behind them once the train had reversed course and headed back into the tunnel. The fact that the soldiers seemed willing to allow their higher-ups to deal with the problem didn't mean that they were safe to be around. No, it was far better to keep to themselves for the moment.

All of them were in good shape and ready for trouble except for Talbot. He lay on a small mattress that they'd salvaged from somewhere. He was still pale, and Lily didn't want him moving on his own for a day. They'd found a stretcher to move him in, which did nothing to improve the gruff man's temper.

He'd thought hard about leaving Talbot behind, but the Marine Raider had insisted that he needed to go. In the end, Jared had decided that he was right. They couldn't afford to leave anyone behind. Whatever happened now, it was going to happen to all of them.

One of the things he'd noticed right away was that none of the captured soldiers had implants. That made sense. Implant technology was something that the AIs had heavily restricted. These people might be technologically superior to the residents of Frankfort, but they had to deal with only having the equipment they had on hand.

By the time the AIs had suppressed Terra, they'd controlled all of the implant facilities on the planet and had undoubtedly yanked all of the equipment as soon as they were ready to start dropping kinetic strikes. Or simply made certain that none of it survived intact.

As the train went through the dark tunnel, occasionally passing through a pool of light cast by a functional illumination panel, he wondered what they were going to find when they reached the Imperial Palace. The story of there being a Marine Raider was incredible, if true.

He wasn't as cynical as Julia, so he wasn't discounting the idea out of hand. After all, what did they really know about the technology that went into creating the Marine Raiders? The specialized medical nanites they'd used were more advanced than those used by Fleet, but even the latter could significantly extend someone's life. Was it really so unbelievable that there might be a survivor of the original Marine Raider cadre here on Terra?

Still, he'd need to see proof of that to believe it.

If he was right, the soldiers were descendants of the original Marine Raiders left here on Terra or those closely associated with them. Someone had kept the power on at the Imperial Palace, and they still had access to technology.

The minutes dragged by slowly and seemed to go even slower the farther they traveled. Eventually, the maglev train reached the spur and curved into another tunnel. As Jared was looking out the window, he could see the one they'd departed from. It led toward Imperial City, which was nothing more than a water-filled crater now.

The thought of all that death horrified him. It also steeled his determination to overcome whatever situation they found at the Imperial Palace and get what they needed to destroy the AIs once and for all.

He couldn't believe how close they were to their destination. They'd been trying to get to the Imperial Palace for so long that he'd started thinking they'd never make it.

If the original plan had worked out, they'd have landed there with two pinnaces full of personnel. That would've almost certainly drawn a hostile response.

Even so, he'd had all the marines and their powered armor. They could've dealt with the problem, as he was willing to bet anything that these people no longer had access to something like that.

After another ten minutes, the train pulled into a station. Arrayed along the platform were about the same number of troops that he and his people had captured, their weapons pointed at the train. None were in powered armor, confirming his guess.

Obviously, there'd been some communication with his prisoners, and the defenders were ready to receive them. That was fine. He'd have expected nothing less.

"No matter what they say, we're not going to disarm," he said as he watched their prisoners leaving the other cars and streaming behind their armed comrades. That got a nod of agreement from the rest. They were done surrendering.

Taking the lead, Jared stepped out onto the platform. He'd considered carrying a flechette rifle but had decided against it. In the end, he'd settled for a flechette pistol on his hip and a stunner on his off side, in the style that Kelsey favored, a fashion that was fast becoming standard for both the marines and Fleet personnel on excursions.

If they ever made it back to Avalon, he'd recommend that Grand Admiral Yeats make that official.

Jared was dressed in a marine camouflage uniform that they'd recovered from the cache, as were the rest of his group that didn't have powered armor. He wore unpowered armor—as did they, except for Talbot.

Behind him, the four in Raider armor arrayed themselves. They were armed to the teeth with weapons suitable for use in the armor. If there was a fight, they'd end it decisively. His personal plan was to dive back into the train if shooting started.

"Halt and put down your weapons!" someone in the group of soldiers on the platform shouted at them.

Jared raised his hands slightly. "My name is Jared Mertz, and I'm an admiral with Fleet. Not the Fleet that crushed the Empire on behalf of the artificial intelligences but part of a group of survivors that managed to escape the original rebellion.

"We won't put our arms down. We've come to negotiate with the leaders here for the return of the fusion plant that you took from the city of Frankfort."

An older man, his hair more gray than black, pushed his way through the defenders. He eyed Jared and the four in powered armor critically. "You have a lot of nerve coming into our domain this way. You stole our train and assaulted our people."

"You stole the fusion plant from the city of Frankfort," Jared countered. "Do we really want to start arguing about who stole what? I'd have thought you'd be more interested in talking about the Marine Raiders at my back."

Jared gestured toward the four behind him. "We've heard that you also have a Marine Raider here. Perhaps ours should speak with yours and figure out between themselves what needs to happen."

The man started to say something but stopped and put a hand to his ear. Jared could see that there was an earbud, so he was in communication with someone else. Another indication of higher technology.

The man frowned deeply and said something under his voice. It looked as if he was arguing with whoever had spoken. Whoever that was, they seemed insistent. The man dropped his hand and glared at Jared.

"The god wishes to speak with one of your people. I have chosen that one." The man gestured toward Talbot, who had just been carried out on a stretcher.

"He's wounded. Pick someone else."

"I will not. The god gives you his word as a Marine Raider that your warrior will be returned to you unharmed and before any decision or action is taken."

Jared considered the unexpected twist of fate. There was a risk in letting them take Talbot, but it might be worth taking.

"I don't like them taking him off alone," Kelsey said through her outer speakers as she stepped up beside him. "I should go with them."

"The god insists that he come alone," the man in front of them said. "Is his word not good enough for you?"

The soldiers arrayed in front of them all stiffened slightly, and their weapons rose a little. A negative answer wouldn't be well received.

Jared held up a hand toward Kelsey. "Let's see how this plays out."

* * *

TALBOT WONDERED what he was going to find when the soldiers carrying his stretcher delivered him to his destination. Like the rest of them, he had no idea who was really pulling the strings behind the scenes here in the Imperial Palace.

Four of the soldiers carried his stretcher while another four walked around them with their flechette rifles at the ready. They'd taken his weapons, and he hadn't fussed. They were taking him to see somebody important to them, and he got their security concerns.

He had no idea how the maglev train platform was positioned inside the Imperial Palace, but the soldiers took him into an operational lift and descended several levels. He was grateful because going down stairs with him on a stretcher might've ended badly.

Lily had done as much as she could for him with the portable regenerator, but he was still weak. Even with his augmentation, the arrows had penetrated vital organs, and he was wary of tearing the wounds open again. Whatever happened next, he was going to do his best to keep the situation as drama free as he possibly could unless they gave him no choice.

When they exited the lift, the soldiers carried him along a wide corridor and stopped before two large doors that didn't look like they belonged there. They were made of carved wood, showing battle scenes.

In a way, they reminded him of some of the carvings that he'd seen in the horde city, though these seemed to involve people with advanced weaponry. He made sure to record them with his implants for later study.

Flanking the doors were two guards in white uniforms that were reminiscent of the white uniforms worn by the Imperial Guard back on Avalon. The two groups exchanged words before the men in white opened the large doors and allowed the men carrying Talbot to go inside. They stopped the other soldiers, though.

As soon as the men carrying his stretcher entered the room, Talbot felt his eyes adjusting. The illumination levels in this space were low. If he hadn't had ocular augmentation, he wasn't certain that he would've been able to see very far into the gloom. There were six more guards in white inside, arrayed against the walls, each with a flechette rifle in their hands.

In many ways, the large room was similar to the Imperial throne room back on Avalon. It was wide but also very long. With his enhanced sight, he could see that there were tapestries hung along the walls that showed battle scenes similar to those carved into the doors, though the gloom obscured the fine details.

Talbot turned his attention to where the men were carrying him. There was a long couch set up on a dais ahead of them. On it, a man lounged.

A horribly disfigured man.

As Talbot was brought closer, he could see that the man's face was terribly scarred, and he was missing his right eye. His salt-and-pepper hair and beard were crisscrossed with gray streaks that probably indicated scarring underneath.

The man lay on his side with his left arm resting across his midsection. His right arm was missing. There were no legs at the end of the couch, either. It looked as if the man were a triple amputee, and even the single limb that he had left was twisted, and the hand only had two fingers and a thumb.

The man gestured for the people carrying Talbot to set him down nearby. There were pillows scattered about, and the soldiers used them to prop Talbot up so that he could see the man on the couch.

Without speaking, the man gestured, and the soldiers retreated toward the doors. He waited until they'd exited the room completely before he spoke.

"When they told me that a group with people claiming to have

Marine Raiders had arrived, I found that difficult to believe," the man said slowly, his voice sounding dry and unused.

Talbot gave the man a lopsided grin. "When I heard that you were a Marine Raider and a god, I found that hard to believe."

The corners of the man's mouth quirked upward slightly. "That unwarranted title is something of a cosmic joke since I'm incapable of doing much of anything for myself. I'm no god, but I *am* a Marine Raider. Can those people in powered armor prove they are?"

"Yep." Talbot reached out and grabbed one of the metal poles that were part of the stretcher that they'd carried him in on. He clenched his fist. With a loud groan, it bent and snapped off. He dropped it to the floor with a metallic clang.

For several seconds, there was nothing but silence in the room. Then the man blinked and shook his head. "That is *not* what I expected to see."

Talbot started to respond, but his implants pinged with an incoming communication request. Shocked, he accepted.

The man's expression became almost slack-jawed as he stared at Talbot. "Dear God, you have implants. Could it really be true?"

Of course I do, Talbot sent back through the implant connection. *I'm a Marine Raider.*

"I've got the full package," Talbot said aloud, terminating the implant connection. "Augmented muscles with graphene coating on the bones and reinforced joints, augmentation in my eyes, ears, nose, artificial muscles, and a full pharmacology unit. Like I said, I'm a Marine Raider. So, who are you?"

The man's smile became wry. "An anomaly. Before I answer that question, I want to hear you say that you don't serve the AIs."

Talbot shook his head. "We don't. In fact, we came here to get something to fight them with. Something that can kill the master AI."

The other man's eyes narrowed. "You're talking about Operation Imperium."

"I don't know what Operation Imperium is," Talbot said, shrugging one shoulder. "Our people were settled on a planet far from the center of the Empire. During the fighting, the rebels used EMP weapons, and we lost our technology, but we managed to keep them from actually putting people on the planet itself.

"We lost all knowledge of what had gone on here at Terra over the next five hundred years. We've been learning bits and pieces once we started exploring again. For the moment, the AIs don't know that we exist, though I suspect at this point they're starting to get a clue. What I do know is that the master AI is at Twilight River, and we've come for something in the vaults that can shut it down."

The man nodded. "Like I said, Operation Imperium. You're looking for the override."

Talbot blinked in shock. "You've heard of it?"

"Just like I know that Emperor Marcus sent Crown Prince Lucian to Avalon. Rather, Emperor Lucien, since he made him co-emperor before he led the AI's forces away from Terra. Avalon is the planet you're speaking about, right?"

Not sure how to interpret this turn of events, Talbot nodded wordlessly.

"Then I think we both have parts of the puzzle," the man said. "I wasn't joking when I said that I was an anomaly. Emperor Marcus ordered strike teams of Marine Raiders and regular marines to stay on Terra and fight a guerrilla war once invasion became imminent. This is going to be very difficult for you to believe, but I was one of those Marine Raiders."

Talbot felt his eyes narrow. "That's bull. Nobody lives that long."

The man's mouth quirked into a sardonic smile. "I've often wished that were true. I'm just too stubborn to commit suicide. My pharmacology unit has been out of pain medication for centuries now. At times, the agony is indescribable.

"Marine Raider nanites were brand new—less than twenty years —when I became a Raider. Before then, they had the same ones issued to the Fleet. No one had done any truly long-term studies on them at that point. Though, to be fair, I suppose long term is a tricky subject when talking about life spans in the Empire.

"It turns out that they do provide something at least approximating immortality. I don't think I've physically aged more than a decade in the last five centuries. Maybe less. I'm so chewed up that it's hard to tell."

Talbot struggled to understand what the man had said. That couldn't be true. The idea of someone living that long was ludicrous.

Nodding at his expression, the man continued. "I'm going to have some words with the ruling council. These people are all descendants of our original support teams. We made sure that we had plenty of technology hidden with them, and I've used it to keep them educated once the hammer came down about a hundred years ago.

"We've only been inside the Imperial Palace for about sixty years. It seemed like a good place to move to. Small and easy to defend, and very well shielded. Now, I think I really want to hear the story of how you became a Marine Raider."

Talbot chuckled darkly. "That's a *very* long story, and I'm not the right one to tell it. You're going to want to speak to my wife. She's a descendent of Lucian, and her father is the reigning emperor of what we call the New Terran Empire."

The man on the couch blinked, his eyes wide as he sat up as much as he could. "You brought the heir to the throne on a mission like this? Are you mad?"

That made Talbot laugh. "You'd need to meet her to understand. We don't *tell* her to do anything. She does what she wants, and we just try to keep up.

"I'm not going to tell her story for her, but she received Marine Raider augmentation before any of us. She certainly didn't come by her implants through any normal process, and quite frankly, she's wildly unsuited to be a Marine Raider just based on her size, but she's got the spirit. Oh, God, does she have the spirit."

The man considered him again, this time for almost a minute, without speaking. Then he reached over with his remaining hand and picked up what looked like a handheld radio.

"Bring more of them to me. Particularly the leadership of their group. Some of them can remain in the corridor with their weapons. Again, they are not to be attacked or harmed."

Without allowing time for anyone to respond, the man turned the radio off.

"You asked who I am. My name is Jake Peters, and I was in tactical command of the guerrilla forces in this area when Terra first came under attack. My rank, though I haven't needed to use it for a damned long time, was major. As I stated, I was a Marine Raider.

"I don't suppose that you have a doctor with you. I could really use a shot of pain medication."

28

K elsey stared at the man on the couch, stunned. She was completely and utterly gobsmacked. She'd sat cross-legged on the floor, listening as he'd told his story. Hearing what had happened from someone who'd actually been there was surreal.

Reginald Bell, the single man they'd ever found who'd survived all that time, had done so only with the help of a stasis unit, a technology that wasn't rated for anything like the three centuries that it had kept him alive.

The former Fleet officer had been an ensign—a probationary tactical officer on the battlecruiser *Courageous*—during the rebellion. A man in his early twenties when he'd gotten his Fleet implants.

The ancient man lived almost two hundred and eighty years outside the stasis unit, which was an incredible achievement. It was undoubtedly also an outlier on the curve but showed what was at least possible with Fleet-grade medical nanites.

Jake Peters had lived through nearly twice that number of years, and though a physical wreck, he obviously still had many years yet to live.

Was he immortal? She sincerely doubted it, but there was an old quote she'd come across in her reading by an author named Arthur C.

Clarke: "Any sufficiently advanced technology is indistinguishable from magic."

This certainly sounded like magic to her.

Jake Peters and his comrades had struggled over the years, but one by one, they'd been killed. To the best of his knowledge, none of the others had been alive twenty-five years after Terra fell.

He'd been gravely injured early in the fight, and though he'd been able to get civilian-grade artificial limbs through people that were associated with the resistance, he wasn't combat capable anymore. He'd had to retire to directing the fight from the shadows.

At some point over the intervening five hundred years, he'd somehow transitioned from being their leader to their god. He couldn't quite pin down when it had happened, but nothing he said seemed to change their minds.

Kelsey could see how that was possible. When someone didn't age, when they stayed the same as you grew old and died, generation after generation, at some point, you were going to decide that they were more than human.

Since the AIs had smashed Terra a hundred years ago, his civilian limbs had failed one by one until he'd been left crippled again. The lack of advanced medicine and the lack of people trained in its use left him trapped once again inside a scarred and pained body.

Jared, who'd been sitting next to her, nodded when the man finished. "That's a hard story. I'm sorry for all the pain and suffering that you've been through. It's downright amazing that you're still alive.

"We've met one other person who was born before the Fall. He was an ensign in Fleet and ended up in a stasis chamber as an old man. He wasn't awake for all that time, but at least he'd seen the Empire at its height before the rebellion."

"I suppose I'm not surprised," the scarred man said. "When you've got as many people as the Empire used to have, a few were going to figure out how to extend their lives that long. What terrifies me is that no one knew how effective the Marine Raider nanites were going to be.

"They were just advertised as a step up from what Fleet used.

Well, maybe two steps. Like I said, they'd been in use in the Marine Raider community for a couple of decades when the rebellion started. There hadn't been time to do a truly long-term study, and people were only beginning to suspect how effective they might be.

"Even so, I'd have to say their guesses were wildly wrong. No one even dreamed that they'd grant someone a lifetime that lasted half a millennium. At this point, I'm terrified that other Raiders were captured during the rebellion, their implants overridden, and they've been alive this entire time. I can't imagine anything that horrible."

Considering that the AIs had disabled the medical nanites in the shock troops they'd forcibly upgraded, Kelsey suspected that the AIs *had* gotten their electronic hands on some and knew just how long-lived they might be. Based on that, it was likely that none of those people were still alive now.

The man took a deep breath and looked over at Kelsey. "I understand that you came into your augmentation through a nonstandard path. Your husband wouldn't give me any of the details. He said it was your story, and if you don't mind, I think I'd like to hear it."

Before she could say anything, Jared rose to his feet, making her look at him askance. He nodded to the man and turned to her.

"Before she starts, I should make a complete introduction. Major Peters, allow me to present my sister, Crown Princess Kelsey Bandar, heir to the Imperial Throne of the New Terran Empire. She's also Colonel Bandar of the Marine Raiders. Since she was the first and the most skilled of those upgraded, she gets to be in charge of them."

He turned to Julia. "This is her younger twin, Julia. She's also been upgraded, though her training is far from complete."

"Highnesses," the man said, inclining his head. "Forgive me for saying so, but it's a far step from having the equipment to being a Marine Raider."

"I *did* have training, Major," Kelsey said, rising to her feet. "It was a bizarre form of training, and one that I don't really expect you to believe offhand, but I'll lay it out for you anyway. Did my husband tell you which ship I came here in?"

Peters shook his head. "That never came up."

Kelsey nodded. "Until very recently, I was in command of the Marine Raider strike ship *Persephone*. We recovered her after the Fall. Her crew was dead, of course, but her commanding officer had taken the unusual step of leaving a message for those that came after him.

"You knew him, and I know that for a fact. His name was Ned Quincy, and even though I didn't know your last name, I knew *you* the moment I laid eyes on you because I've seen a memory of the two of you together.

"You weren't wearing rank tabs, so I didn't know your rank either. You were on some planet together, unloading and transferring gear between pinnaces. Ned called you Jake."

The man on the couch blinked. And then he blinked again before sitting up a little straighter. "How the hell could that even be possible?"

Kelsey tapped the side of her head. "He made a bunch of memory recordings of him doing all kinds of things. I'm not sure if he ever told anyone about it, but he had one of his tech people put some type of library program into his implants to coordinate the use of all those memory engrams of him doing various things.

"Ned said that he started doing it at the beginning of the rebellion to document everything that he and his people went through, so it's possible he told you about it."

"He did," Jake said slowly. "You talk about him as if he were still alive."

"Ned Quincy's body died, but his personality survived. When I pulled all those memory engrams into my own implants, a more advanced computer system worked on the library program he'd used to enhance its capabilities, and that somehow created a small-scale artificial intelligence that had his memories and personality.

"No one really understands how that's possible, and we have no way of replicating it without potentially making two Ned Quincys, which would be wrong. He's no longer inside my implants, but he lived there for over a year. He taught me everything I know about the Marine Raiders. Everything that he'd recorded, anyway.

"If he didn't know something, he studied it and made me learn it, too. All of that was integrated into my training, and he put me through what he called hell week as he tested me on *everything*. I doubt I got more than an hour of sleep a day, but I passed.

"So while I don't have the experience someone like you has, I *am* a Marine Raider. My husband has done the same thing, as has the person in command of *Persephone*, Major Angela Ellis. One by one, we're bringing the Marine Raider organization back to life.

"My sister isn't there yet, and I won't go into how she got her implants, but she's making progress."

If Kelsey had had her druthers, she'd have left Julia out of this, but people had seen her doppelgänger in Raider armor. She still wore her armor, minus her helmet. Better safe than sorry.

Carl, Chloe, and Julia were out in the hall, still fully armored up and armed. If something went wrong, they'd come busting in, weapons blazing.

Jake's expression remained blank. "That's an interesting story. I don't suppose you have any way of proving it."

She smiled slightly. "You know that Ned was a master of the Art, don't you?"

"He was one of the best," the man readily admitted. "He almost took the Raider competition one year. I've never personally met anyone better at that kind of thing."

"Then maybe I can demonstrate a little of what he taught me. You should be able to see his influence in my style. Will your guards object if I retrieve my swords?"

The white-uniformed guards—some kind of nod to either a priesthood, the old Imperial Guard, or perhaps both—had insisted that everyone in the room be disarmed before they entered the presence of their god.

Jake made a gesture, and an unhappy man in white went outside to retrieve her swords.

Once he'd returned with them, Kelsey strapped them on and stepped into a clear area a bit distant from the couch. They'd turned the lighting up so that everyone could clearly see one another, and there was no need to make the guards think she was about to slice and dice their god.

She went through a number of the fighting katas that she'd

learned, using all of her Marine Raider augmentation and skill. Then she put some of her own work into it and proceeded to show how she could be a ferocious attacker or defender.

Once she'd finished and sheathed the swords, Jake nodded slowly. "It's hard to argue with the evidence of my own eye. I'll grant you that only someone very skilled in the Art and comfortable with their implants and augmentation could do that. I can also see something that reminds me of Ned.

"That said, I still find what you're telling me hard to believe. I knew Ned and commanded another strike ship back then. We were contemporaries. I can't imagine how you could even know that, but I'm willing to at least consider the possibility. Where is he now?"

"He's in computer storage aboard *Persephone*. One of our scientists extracted him from my implants. Now they're in the process of building an artificial body that will fool the program into believing that he's still inside Marine Raider implants.

"It's going to take a while to even understand the basics of what they need to do. Eventually, though, Ned is going to wake up again. He will live again."

Jake shook his head. "That's really hard to take just on someone's word."

"Let me give you some more evidence," Kelsey said. "I'm going to send you some files."

She initiated a connection to his implants and then sent him a lot of images and video files that she'd recorded aboard *Persephone*. Ones that were taken inside the bridge and other portions of the ship that wouldn't be known to anyone who hadn't been there. She also sent him the recording of the meeting between the man and Ned that she'd referenced.

He sighed and rubbed his face with his remaining hand. "I can't argue with any of that. That's me, and I remember the meeting well enough, though I hadn't recorded it. The layout of the planet and the uniform I was wearing are indisputable.

"There's also no way that you could've known the layout of *Persephone*. I've been aboard her, and that's exactly how she's laid out. I can even see some of the same scars and blemishes on the bulkheads of the bridge. They were there when I visited, so you must've been aboard that ship.

"If I grant that, I suppose I have to give you the rest of your story, as difficult as it is to believe."

He shook his head and chuckled. "I suppose it isn't any more preposterous than me being over five centuries old, so we'll just have to accept what the other is saying. You are a Marine Raider, and Ned—or some semblance of him—is still alive somewhere."

Kelsey stripped off the sheathed swords and handed them back to the guard. He quickly scurried away. She supposed he really didn't have any idea how dangerous she was with just her hands.

"Now that I'm unarmed again, there's something else that I'd like to discuss with you. In private."

Jake nodded and gestured for the guards to move back to the walls. They'd still be able to see everything that was going on but be unable to hear any normally pitched conversation.

Once they were out of earshot, Kelsey continued. "We need your help. We've come here for something that can beat the artificial intelligences."

"The override," Peters said with a nod. "I'm aware that it's down in the vault because that was part of my briefing. I have no way of getting in there, but I suppose you do. I can't claim that I have complete control over events that take place here in the Imperial Palace, but I'll do what I can to smooth that path for you.

"The leadership of the group that I once formed to support us has taken on a life of its own. They give me a lot of leeway in what I can order them to do, but I've run into some things that they've refused. They're decent people, but be cautious around them."

"Thank you," she said, smiling in gratitude. "We appreciate the help, though I'm still not sure how we're going to get off this planet and back to *Persephone*. Even if we manage that, we've still got to get out of the Terra system somehow."

"The Marine Raiders left a lot of caches of equipment and supplies," he said. "I know where you can find a couple of stealthed Marine Raider pinnaces."

That made her grin. "It just so happens that both Jared and I know how to fly. Maybe everything isn't lost after all. Why didn't you use one to get away from here?"

He shrugged. "Where would I go? The AIs had conquered the entire Empire. What use was it trying to get to another world?

"If they caught me, I'd have suffered an eternity of being a slave in my own body. I fought them and lost. Maybe you can win—and I'm more than willing to help you do it—but my time is past.

"When we moved to the Imperial Palace, we still had some older folk that could fly the pinnaces. They're stashed in the underground hangar, so you can probably get access to them. No promises on their condition, though."

"We'll make it work. Thank you."

"Don't thank me yet," he said in a low voice. "The leadership council isn't going to tolerate strangers like you here in the Imperial Palace for very long. At some point very soon, they're going to decide that it's time for you to go. You need to act fast if you intend to get what you need before then."

She smiled coldly. "Leave that to us."

29

An hour later, Carl was in the medical center that had once been reserved for the Imperial Family. It looked like it was still in pretty decent shape and seemed to have been well stocked.

The Imperial Palace had been abandoned before Terra had fallen, so no one had used this facility in more than five centuries. It looked as if the Rebel Empire had sent people to search it—as well as the rest of the Imperial Palace—to make certain that no one was hiding here, but they'd left it abandoned.

Doctor Stone was going through the medical gear piece by piece, and if anything needed to be repaired, he was right on hand to do the work. Like the room itself, most of it was in good shape, but he'd found the tools and replacement parts he needed if he had to do any serious work.

It was very similar to the repairs he'd had to do on the derelict battlecruiser *Courageous*. The Empire built to last, but everything had its limits.

Once everything was ready, they'd brought Kelsey, Talbot, and the crippled Raider into the room. Talbot went into one of the spare beds while everyone else focused their attention on Major Peters.

The man's guardians were not happy that he was leaving what they saw as his temple, but he'd made a fuss, and they'd allowed it. Now they stood next to the door, glowering at everyone with disapproving eyes.

Doctor Stone got the man up onto the exam table with Kelsey's assistance. Once she'd run the scanner across him several times, she pursed her lips.

"It looks like your physical injuries are relatively benign as far as such things go, though considering the amount of scarring and the loss of your limbs, I understand why it might not feel that way.

"The good news is that we'll be able to attach Marine Raider–grade artificial limbs if we ever get our hands on any. That wasn't a certainty, even though you'd been fitted for artificial limbs before. The ones I'm talking about are capable of delivering the same kind of strength that your augmented muscles used.

"The bad news is that we don't have anything like that here. In fact, there are no artificial limbs at all. I'm sure you already knew that because that would've been one of the first things you'd checked, but we looked again just to be sure."

Peters nodded slightly. "When we first arrived, I had them tear this place apart looking for any without luck."

Stone nodded. "Now that we've gotten that out of the way, we can get to something that's of more immediate importance to you. I'm going to tap into Kelsey's pharmacology unit and transfer half of her pain medication to you. You need that much more than she does right now."

Carl could see the man visibly relax. "That would be amazing, Doctor. This constant pain has been dragging on my soul."

"Between Kelsey and Talbot, we can bring you up to full on all your meds," she said. "Anything that they're low on afterward, we'll make up from our stocks on *Persephone*."

She lowered her voice, likely to make sure the guards didn't hear her. Carl could barely hear her.

"If we can talk you into going to *Persephone* with us, we've everything necessary to bring a Raider back to full capability, even after a major injury. I urge you to consider that option."

Peters pursed his lips, his eyes sliding toward the guards. "I'll have to think about it. I've been here so long that I'm not sure if I can leave. At this point, I doubt that these people would let me, even if I insisted."

"That's a problem for later then," Doctor Stone said loudly enough that the guards, who were becoming a bit concerned about the conversation that they couldn't overhear, visibly relaxed. "Kelsey, if you'd go ahead and lie down on your stomach on the adjacent exam table, I'll extract the drugs from your pharmacology unit and transfer them directly across to Major Peters. This would be easier from the front, but I can manage with just opening the back of your torso armor."

The process of moving the drugs from Kelsey to the crippled Marine Raider took about twenty minutes. When they were done, the man sighed and relaxed even further. "Man, you don't know how good this feels. I've dreamed of being pain free for *so* long."

"I've got a few more things to check, but you can go, Kelsey," Doctor Stone said. "And thank you for your help, Carl. I can get Talbot over here and hooked up without any assistance."

With them both being dismissed, Kelsey drew Carl out of the room and took them to another room, where Admiral Mertz was waiting. Two of the soldiers trailed along behind them, making sure that their hosts knew where they were at any time.

"We're going down to the vault," she said once they were inside the room and out of earshot of any of their watchers. "Everybody is busy keeping an eye on Peters, so it gives us a chance to slip away without a whole lot of attention being paid to us. We need to get the override before our hosts decide to kick us out."

"What are we going to do about the spies keeping an eye on us?" Carl asked.

Admiral Mertz smiled wickedly. "We're going to let them keep doing it. If my plan works the way I expect it to, they're not even going to be aware of what we're up to. While there's probably more than one way into the vaults, the information I got from the Imperial Scepter talks about a secret passage. We'll use that to give our watchdogs the slip.

"Since they're happier keeping an eye on us as a group, we'll all go to the Imperial Residence together. Once we get inside, we can use the secret passage while Clarice keeps up a conversation that makes the guards think that we're all inside. You'll note that they don't feel the need to keep an eye on us directly but are happy to guard the doors where we congregate. We'll use that to our advantage."

"Actually, we need to make another stop first," Kelsey said. "It's on the way."

She led them back toward the room where Major Peters had been kept. The guards fell in behind them as they walked.

To Carl's surprise, she went past that room and led them to an even more ornate set of doors, which were propped open. It was much larger than the place where Major Peters had been, and even though the doors were open, it smelled of disuse. The walls were covered in faded and threadbare tapestries, and a dais at the end held a golden throne.

The Imperial Throne.

Carl was awestruck. This was the place where Kelsey's ancestors had ruled over the Terran Empire for more than ten thousand years. He couldn't imagine how much history had taken place in this very room.

Kelsey led them to the back of the room, where she ducked behind the throne and through another doorway set in the rear wall. The guards remained in the main room, seemingly disinterested in following them.

The suite looked as if it had been used when dressing for state ceremonies. The racks were filled with the remains of formalwear. After five hundred years, everything was in terrible condition, but it didn't seem to have been disturbed.

Kelsey looked around for a few moments and then ducked through another door into what was obviously a private office. Carl immediately spotted a stand that looked like it was made for the Imperial Scepter.

Obviously thinking the same thing, Kelsey dug into her bag and pulled out the scepter, fitting it once more into the place that had been made for it.

"I bet that no one ever thought this thing would come back home," she said softly. "Life is strange sometimes."

She returned the scepter to her bag before circling the office and stopping at another stand, which held the remaining pieces of the Imperial Regalia. The Imperial Crown sat on a faded velvet pad, and underneath it was a thick, unadorned golden chain with heavy links.

"I bet my father would love to have these, and since we may never come this way again, I figured it was the right time to pick them up. I'd hoped they'd been left undisturbed. Sometimes the gods smile."

Carl considered that. She wasn't nearly as mortal as most. If Major Peters was anything to go by, she might live for a thousand years or more. Though, with all the fighting and other crazy stuff she did, that seemed unlikely.

Then another thought struck him. They'd given Kelsey's father Marine Raider medical nanites. He might be an older man, but he wasn't *that* old. He might still rule the New Terran Empire for a long, *long* time. How would that change society? Or would he choose to step down before then?

Once word got back to Avalon, it was going to set off a firestorm. Perhaps he should speak with everyone about keeping that little detail quiet for the time being.

As he'd pondered the implications of that, Kelsey had secured the regalia in her bag. Now she was looking at perhaps a dozen books on one of the shelves of a nearby bookshelf. He managed to see that the pages were filled with handwritten words when she opened one.

If he had to guess, those were probably Emperor Marcus's journals—historical treasures of incalculable value.

She closed the book and started stuffing them all into her bag. They'd fill it, and it would be damned heavy, but she was strong enough to handle it.

With that out of the way, the group returned to the throne room and continued on toward the Imperial Residence via another corridor accessed from the side of the chamber nearest the throne. Their bored escorts fell in behind them.

The hall was lined with oil paintings that depicted the emperors that had once ruled over the Terran Empire. Closest to the throne room was Emperor Marcus himself. It seemed as they went back toward the residence, they were going backward in time.

Carl made sure to pause at each long enough to get a high-resolution image through his implants. There were plaques below each painting that gave their names and the dates that they'd reigned.

He took particular interest in the first emperor as they arrived at the doors to the Imperial Residence. The plaque listed his name as Andrew Bandar, gave his regnal name as Andrew the First, and listed him as an admiral in the Fleet of the Terran Republic.

Carl knew little about the man. He'd overthrown the corrupt Terran Republic and formed the Terran Empire. There was probably one hell of a story there, but it was mostly lost in the sands of time.

He was a handsome man, young for his rank. Oddly, he bore a striking resemblance to Admiral Mertz. The two men could have been brothers if not separated by millennia.

While he'd been considering the painting, the rest had opened the doors to the residence and were moving inside. He hurried to join them before the guards could catch up.

Kelsey closed the doors in their faces, and everyone waited to see if they demanded entry. They didn't. It seemed they were content to wait outside. That was good. Otherwise, they'd have had to come up with another plan or do something irrevocable.

The common area in the Imperial Residence was a wonder. First, it was huge. Not as big as the throne room but far more palatial than anything he could ever imagine living in.

The deep carpet on the floor had likely once been white, though it was now so coated with dirt and dust that it was a dingy gray. Finely carved chairs, tables, and other pieces of ornate furniture sat scattered around the vast room.

What really took his breath away, though, was the extravagant centerpiece: a stone fountain almost ten meters across. It was filled with virulent green algae and smelled *awful*.

Above it was what had once been a waterfall. Natural stones piled one upon another going up three meters. Off to the right side, built of similar stones, a table projected directly out of the fountain. It was probably five meters long and bracketed by benches made of the same stone.

Kelsey turned toward them. "The table has the means of activating the secret entrance, which is under the fountain. It's going to require Jared's DNA to activate, but there's some kind of switch that needs to be turned on. Carl, can you find where this needs to happen and make sure that it's working?"

With a nod, Carl slid under the table. At the end directly opposite the fountain, there was a reader plate recessed into the underside of the table. He plugged a cable into it and brought up his diagnostic equipment on his tablet.

The reader had power but was switched off. It wanted verification of authority to reactivate.

"It needs your authentication, Kelsey," he said. "You can use your implants to connect with it, but you'll have to use my tablet as a bridge. Someone wanted to make absolutely sure that no one could get access to the hardware by accident. It has no implant-capable connectivity."

Moments later, his tablet showed the reader was active, so he unplugged his tablet and slid out from under the table.

"It should work now," he said as he put away his equipment. "Your DNA should activate it, Admiral."

Admiral Mertz placed his hand on the reader, and nothing happened.

30

It took Jared holding his hand on the reader for five seconds before anything happened. Probably to prevent an inadvertent touch from activating it. His first indication of success was when there was a soft grinding sound from inside the fountain, and the water began draining away.

Relieved more than he could say, he watched the ugly green water mostly disappear before the stone bottom of the fountain sank into the floor. Once it had gone down about a hundred centimeters, it split into sections and retracted underneath the floor, revealing a set of stairs twisting tightly in a circle as they descended into the darkness.

It was very reminiscent of the stairs under the horde treasure building, and that gave him unexpected chills.

It looked as if the water had been intended to go into a reservoir of some kind, but the algae had clogged things up, and a fair amount of it showered onto the steps. They were now slick and treacherous looking. Everyone would have to be very careful when they went down them.

Jared turned to Clarice Beauchamp. "Keep up a running conversation with yourself. If the guards stick their heads in, make sure they can see you, and keep talking like we're in one of the other rooms. That might be enough."

"And if it's not?"

"Then you might have to use your new sword."

He'd taken her aside and given her the long blade from the Marine Raider cache before they'd left Frankfort. It wasn't worth what helping them had cost her, but it was what they had to give. Her people wouldn't accept high technology, but no matter how deadly and miraculous the sword was, it was just metal.

The warrior nodded and clasped her hand around the weapon's hilt. "They will not pass while I still live. You have my word. Good luck, Admiral."

Kelsey led the way down the stairs, moving slowly and keeping her hand on the rail. Her augmented vision would allow her to see what was in front of her more easily than he could.

That turned out to be unnecessary, as lights in the chamber below came on as soon as she started down. It turned out that the stairs only went down a dozen meters before they opened into a wide chamber directly underneath the common room in the Imperial Residence.

Once he'd made his way down, he saw that this room only had one exit, the short corridor that led directly to a lift. Jared walked over and pressed the call button. Moments later, the doors opened and revealed a lift car that could hold all of them. Barely.

Once they'd packed themselves inside, someone pressed the only button on the panel, the doors closed, and the lift descended. The trip took longer than he'd expected, but the doors opened again without any trouble.

Kelsey stepped out of the lift and into another short corridor that ended in what looked like a dead end, though there was a button prominently placed on the wall beside it. With a shrug, she pressed it, and the dead-end wall slid aside, revealing a larger corridor that led to the left and right.

He stuck his head out and saw that there was no button on the other side. In fact, it looked like this was a concealed door that no one would know was here.

"How do we keep it from closing?" he asked.

"I got a signal from the controller when I pressed the button," his sister said. "It wanted my authentication codes, and in return, it gave me permission to remotely control it from the other side. We're good on that front.

"The problem I see is that there was nothing on the map about this. Basically, it only told us to go to the Imperial Residence and use the secret passage. Which direction do we go?"

"Let's split up and go in opposite directions," he suggested. "We'll only go a hundred meters and then come back. Be watchful for any security devices. These are the Imperial Vaults, and there's no telling what's down here."

Jared found what he thought was the entrance to the vaults less than fifty meters down the right-hand side of the corridor, on the opposite wall from the secret lift. The large metal doors looked as if they would be sufficient to stop any kind of attack. There was a palm reader next to them.

A quick shout brought the rest of the team to his location, and Kelsey examined the reader for a moment before she quickly gestured for him to put his hand on it.

He did so, and it immediately prompted him to input an authentication code that he didn't have. Thankfully, he knew someone who did.

"It needs your codes, Kelsey."

She frowned. "I'm not getting any kind of prompt, so it must've just sent it to you because you were touching the reader. Let's try together."

Kelsey pulled off her gauntlet and placed a finger against the reader as he put his hand on it again. Once again, he was rejected, but for a different reason. Now it was complaining that there were too many sources of DNA.

"How can I touch the reader to get the signal without giving it my DNA?" Kelsey asked in a peeved tone. "I can't give you the codes, because my implants won't let me export them for obvious security reasons. What do we do?"

"Stick your hand out," Carl said. "I think I have something that might help."

The scientist dug into his tool bag and pulled out a small canister. He held it close to Kelsey's hand and sprayed a moderately thick gel into her palm. He then started rubbing it in.

"Give it a few seconds to dry," he said. "It'll act as a sealer and keep any DNA from coming across from your hand to the reader. Just to be safe, you might want to rub a finger across the admiral's skin before you use it so that it has his DNA."

Jared nodded. "We'll also be careful that it only looks like we're putting one hand onto the scanner. I'll keep my pinky a little bit up at the tip, and you can stick the end of yours just under it. Maybe if we do that, we can fool it."

"Let's hope this works," Kelsey said as they positioned their hands just above the reader and put them down together.

"I can sense it demanding the code," Kelsey said. "Sending it now."

A few moments later, the huge doors began retracting into the walls. The group around them erupted in cheers even as Jared stared. The doors were *significantly* thicker than he'd expected.

At a guess, they were about three meters thick and looked like they were made of hull metal. They were thicker than the armor on his superdreadnought.

Basically, if the entire vault was sheathed like this, it was invulnerable to anything short of orbital bombardment. It would even take a nuke placed right next to it and probably protect the vault's contents.

Thankfully, they'd made it inside.

"Let's see if we can find the override," he said. "Don't touch anything. I hate to be a worrywart, but it would be just like some paranoid security type to leave something tempting to set off a trap for the unwary. We don't want to be locked inside, because no one will be coming to rescue us."

"That's perhaps an exaggeration," Kelsey said. "I've interfaced with the palace systems and reenabled the communication systems. We can interface with them via our implants—even down here—and have them connect us with Talbot or Lily. I'm confident he could figure something out."

"Did you see that door?" he demanded. "I'm not willing to take chances, so everyone keep your hands to yourselves."

With that, he stepped into the vault, and the overhead lights came on.

* * *

JULIA STEPPED into the Imperial Vaults and was immediately overwhelmed by the scale of the place. As large as the Imperial throne room had been, this place was *far* more substantial.

And unlike the room above, this one was hardly empty. In fact, it looked like a warehouse. It was full of crates, all piled up to the ceiling a dozen meters overhead.

The air was dead, smelling of dust and age. No one had been here in a very long time.

"How are we going to find the override?" she asked grimly. "Are we going to have to start busting things open?"

The wreckage they'd made in the horde's treasure chamber was fresh in her mind. And as tightly packed as these crates were, she didn't think she'd have much luck knocking any stacks over.

Kelsey shook her head. "Emperor Marcus sent Lucian a full inventory of this place. He also told him exactly where we had to go to find the override. All we have to do is walk to the back of the room and pick it up."

That sounded suspiciously easy. Nothing they'd done thus far had been that simple, so she'd believe it when she saw it.

"What's in the rest of these crates?" she asked as they started into the stacks. "And why keep it all down here in an impenetrable vault?"

Kelsey shrugged. "I'd imagine this vault has been down here since they built the Imperial Palace. Whichever emperor was in charge at that point must've decided that this would be where the important stuff went. It's filled with gifts and offerings from various parts of the Empire, usually presented on the emperor's birthday.

"That kind of thing went on pretty much the entire time the Terran Empire existed. What we're looking at here is about ten thousand years' worth of gifts from any number of worlds to the reigning emperor of the day.

"That means that this room is filled with objects of incalculable cultural value, and probably every precious metal and stone known to humanity. Unimaginable works of art. But we're only interested in one thing though: the override."

They continued on in silence while Julia looked at the immense stacks of crates all around them and imagined the kinds of things that would be inside them. It was mind-boggling. All of this should be on display in a massive museum, not buried under a dead palace on a wrecked world.

If she were successful in overthrowing the AIs in her universe, she'd make certain to start building one. Humanity deserved to see its heritage.

Partway back, she discovered that not everything was in crates. Off to her left-hand side was a statue that had to be at least three meters tall. It was made of pale, polished stone and looked hand carved. It was exquisite.

She had no idea who the woman was supposed to be, but what little clothes she wore seemed unspeakably ancient. Why men felt the need to have art in which women were scantily dressed, partly—or fully—naked, or in provocative poses, she just didn't understand. It was one of the mysteries of life.

Just because she wanted to know who the woman was, she captured an image of the statue so that she could look it up later. If any records existed outside the list of contents that Mertz had, that was. She hoped so, as she'd rather find out on her own than ask him.

When they finally reached the rear of the massive room, Kelsey led them to a small crate. "This is the one in the picture that Emperor Marcus sent. He didn't say anything about any security protocol. Honestly, I don't know why anyone would bother. It's at the rear of a huge room in a small crate with no markings at all. Even diligent searchers would pass it right by."

"We should still be careful," Mertz said. "The last thing we want to do is to try and open it the wrong way and have it destroy the contents. That would be an utter disaster."

Carl stepped forward and ran a scanner across the exterior of the crate. "It's got no electronics in the box itself and no locking mechanism. Basically, it's just wood and conventional packing materials around something technological that's unpowered. We can open it up."

Kelsey reached forward and gently tugged the lid until it popped free. Nestled among packing materials was what looked like a small computer drive. It had some type of port where it could be plugged into another system, but it was totally unremarkable.

And utterly irreplaceable.

"So, this is the override that stops the master AI," she said slowly. "It looks so... normal."

"It *is* pretty normal," Carl said as he gingerly plucked the device out of the crate. "It's literally a basic drive meant to plug into the AI hardware and shut down the system or override anything that the controller wants. The only thing that makes it unique is the encrypted code that's bound to this one specific set of hardware.

"We won't be able to transfer the code to any other drive. It has to be this one. I'll have to take it apart and replace the power supply, but that should be simple enough."

"Why didn't they make more of them?" she demanded. "That might've helped humanity stop those monsters."

"They didn't realize that they needed them," he answered with a shrug. "No one in their right minds would have believed that an AI that didn't even have manipulators would be able to take over human beings to use as its toys. That's horror novel stuff.

"If the Singularity hadn't meddled, nothing like this could have occurred. Their agents had to have physically assisted the AI for those initial conversions. Only then would the AI have had a way to do more."

Mertz took the override from Carl and put it into his pocket. "Kelsey, you've got the inventory. Is there anything else here that we should take with us?"

Julia's doppelgänger shook her head. "Technically, *everything* here should be saved, but none of it's useful for our purposes now. We can come back once this is all over and take it to Avalon."

"Or move the seat of power here," Mertz said. "When the Rebel Empire falls, it might be best if we just relocate the government here. Terra is more centrally located for the Empire as a whole. Once we start rebuilding, it's not going to be convenient for the rulers of the Empire to be out on the rim like Avalon is."

Kelsey snorted. "I can't imagine my father would be happy about moving."

"He has time to get used to the idea. With those modified Marine Raider medical nanites in his system, he's going to be the emperor for a *very* long time."

Her doppelgänger shook her head. "It's a good thing that I'm not looking to inherit the throne anytime soon. Come on. I want to do something to the security system before we leave."

When they arrived back at the main doors, Kelsey stopped at a terminal just inside them. "Jared, press your palm here just like we did outside."

A few seconds later, she smiled. "Okay, Julia, press your palm to the door. I've got this gunk on my hands, so you'll be working with me to register our DNA. I'm adding us all to the security system. If something happens, I want to make sure that someone else can get back into this place."

Julia did so, and the system prompted her to set an access code. She used the one she had as the heir, and the system accepted it. She knew from checking that her authentication codes were exactly the same as Kelsey's, so they were both covered.

She made a mental note that she'd have to get samples of Mertz's DNA before she went home. With the right coating on her hand, she could fool the system just like Kelsey had. She wouldn't need to keep her Mertz alive once she caught him.

It took a couple of minutes for everyone to add their DNA to the security system. Once the process was done, Kelsey gestured back toward the concealed lift.

"It's time to get things in motion. We've gotten what we came for, and it's time to get off this planet. That means we have to get the FTL com online so that we can contact *Persephone*. Carl, that's your job.

"Once we know what's happening in the rest of the system, we can decide if we're going to take a shot at the AI in orbit. If we can get to it, we will. If we can't, we're going to have to just sneak away without being noticed.

"I don't like leaving Terra under the control of these murderous AIs, but it's not exactly like we have a battle fleet on hand to take it away." She paused and then smiled. "Actually, I suppose we do. We just don't know where it is right now."

Mertz nodded. "Let's get back to *Persephone*. We'll get in contact with Marcus using the same trick that you used to signal us. There's no guarantee that he's going to recognize the attempted communication, but we have to try.

"We'll hope that he's a lot faster on the uptake than I was. If so, we'll arrange to meet them somewhere mutually convenient. Our next stop has to be Twilight River. It's time to end this war and free humanity."

With that, they started toward the secret door leading to the lift. The endgame was upon them.

31

Talbot had been asleep for over an hour when Lily woke him up. She'd been able to use the large regenerator at the Imperial Palace to fully heal his damaged organs, but he'd been exhausted by the time she'd finished.

He levered himself up from the bed he was resting on. "Thanks, Lilly."

She clapped a hand on his shoulder. "No problem, big man. That's my job. Try not to get banged up so much next time. Especially if I don't have anything to fix you with."

"I'll sure as hell try. Any word on the trip downstairs?"

He felt comfortable asking because there were no guards in the room with them. They were probably standing out in the hall, making sure that he and Lily didn't wander off. Peters was gone, so they'd undoubtedly taken him back to his hall.

"Kelsey called to let me know that everything went as planned. It seems that she's accessed the palace systems and reenabled them for our use. We're ready to exit stage left."

He frowned slightly. "What does *that* mean?"

Lily shrugged. "Ask your wife. Since we're ready to go, they think you need to have a conversation with Major Peters. We need to know for sure whether or not he's going to come with us.

"Everyone else is either providing a distraction for the guards by doing otherwise mundane tasks or is with Carl as he works on making contact with *Persephone*. The admiral said to tell you that he'd prefer if Peters came with us."

Talbot wasn't sure he could convince the man, though doing something to fully repair the horrific damage to his body might well do the trick. The only way to find out for sure was to try.

"I'm on it," he said as he stood.

Once he had his shoes on, he made his way out of the medical center, picking up an escort at the door, and headed toward the large room where they kept Peters. The man's guards in their white uniforms stopped him outside that room.

"What is your business with the god?" a short woman with dark hair asked imperiously.

"I want to continue the discussion that we started earlier," Talbot said, unperturbed. "There's nothing to be worried about. I'll be happy to leave my weapons here with you."

The woman seemed somewhat suspicious, but she allowed Talbot inside once he'd divested himself of his weapons.

Peters sat up a little bit straighter on his couch as Talbot approached, waving the guards out of earshot. "You're looking better."

"I'm feeling better," Talbot said as he sat on the edge of the dais. Even though he was fully healed, parts of him still felt a little tender.

"Did your friends pick up your package?" Peters asked.

Talbot nodded. "Without a hitch."

"So, what's your plan now?"

"I'd rather talk about *your* plans," Talbot countered. "We've got facilities board *Persephone* to mitigate all the damage that's been done to you. Do you want to be mobile again? Do you want to be able to use your Marine Raider augmentation at full power again?"

Peters considered Talbot for a few moments and then shrugged. "I'm not certain that my preferences really matter. Like I said, I'm not exactly in control of my own fate. I'm a figurehead.

"They tolerate me giving orders about some things, but then they go ahead and do what they want most of the time. The leadership council makes the decisions, and I'm sure that they won't allow me to leave, no matter what I say."

"But do you want to?" Talbot asked softly. "It just so happens that we're experts at breaking people out of places and getting around recalcitrant guards. If you want to leave, all you have to do is say the word."

The man sagged a little. "I don't want to see these people harmed, but I'll admit that I'm tired of being stuck here. The drugs you gave me will only last a decade or so. I don't know if I can go back to life with that kind of pain."

"It sounds as if you've already made up your mind, but you just haven't convinced yourself of that yet. You want to leave."

"I suppose I do. The question is, how are you to make that happen?"

Talbot rose to his feet and stepped over to the couch. Making sure that the suddenly hyperalert guards couldn't see his right side, he extracted the stunner he'd pocketed there and dropped it next to the crippled man's remaining hand. Peters promptly made it vanish under the blanket.

The guards really should've been a little less trusting of someone who came alone and volunteered to give up his weapons. Talbot stepped back without undue haste, creating enough space that the guards stopped advancing.

"You let us worry about the exit strategy," Talbot said. "I promise that we won't use any more force than necessary. If we can manage to get out with just stunners, that's what we'll do.

"But one way or the other, we'll get you out alive. If they want to use deadly force to stop you from leaving, then you're going to have to accept that we might have to use deadly force in response."

"I hope it doesn't come to that," Peters said with a sigh. "For all their flaws, these are decent people doing decent work."

"Speaking of decent work, we need to make sure that the fusion plant they took, as well as the shielding that would keep it from being detectable from orbit, is sent back to Frankfort. The people there would make excellent allies for your people.

"Terra is our past, but it's their future. You should let them build it back up together. To start the process, they'll have to return what was taken and get it set up so that it's operational. Can you convince them to do that?"

Peters shrugged slightly. "Possibly. I don't think it's actually being used. They're somewhat like packrats. They'll make a stink about it, but if I push things, they'll probably do it, especially if I make the point that these others would make decent allies. We don't have many of those since they insist on being hidden. I should probably start the process now.

"In any case, you've still got to check over the pinnaces to make sure that they're operational. It's been a long time since they've been up in the air, much less space. And if I were you, I wouldn't dawdle."

"I'll focus on that while you work your end," Talbot said. "We won't make any irrevocable decisions until we hear that you got your end in motion. The palace systems will allow you to connect with us via your implants. Let us know if something comes up and be ready to go at a moment's notice."

With that, Talbot made his way out and reclaimed his weapons. He sure hoped that Carl and the rest would be able to get the pinnaces operational. If they didn't get at least one working, they were stuck on Terra. All of their sacrifices would've been for nothing.

* * *

CARL LOOKED over the parts on his makeshift worktable and selected a few components that he knew he was going to need before even opening the FTL com. The device was extremely simple, as far as that sort of thing went, but it definitely needed the right parts to work correctly.

Thankfully, the bins here at the Imperial Palace were well shielded and had everything he could possibly need. He wished he could take it all with him because the stash would've proved damned useful.

Sadly, that wasn't to be.

Working slowly and carefully, he completely disassembled the FTL com, tested every component, and replaced any that failed or were questionable. It took almost an hour to get everything put back together again, but it passed its self-check when he connected it to a power supply and some jury-rigged speakers.

With more than a hint of trepidation, he initiated an audio call request to *Persephone*. Long seconds passed, and then a voice channel opened.

Since they were in the same system, it could be used at full speed rather than the Morse code setting that they'd had to use for longer-range communication. He could even have video if he'd bothered to attach the necessary peripherals, but he hadn't bothered. For this, voice was sufficient.

He cleared his throat. "*Persephone*, this is Carl Owlet calling. Are you receiving?"

"Carl, it's good to hear your voice," Fiona said a moment later. "We were all very worried about you after the AI destroyed your pinnaces. I'm assuming the fact you're speaking with me now means that you were not anywhere close to the target zone. Is everyone okay?"

It still amazed him how a computer could show such palpable emotion. Not a facsimile of feelings but actual emotions. The concern in Fiona's voice wasn't fake. The Old Empire scientists who'd created the AIs had made electronic life.

Well, and created the doom of humanity, of course.

He sighed. "We weren't there, but things haven't gone well. We were ambushed by armed locals, and only about a dozen of us are left. Admiral Mertz, Princess Kelsey, her doppelgänger, and most of the senior staff are still alive, but we've lost everyone else. I need to talk to Angela."

"I'm so sorry to hear that," the AI said with genuine sorrow. "I'm transferring your call now. We've also had some interesting experiences, and I'm sure that she will want to tell you what we've learned."

A few moments later, Major Angela Ellis, commander of *Persephone* and his wife, came onto the line.

"Are you okay?" she asked, her voice anxious. "Is everyone else okay?"

"I'm okay. There was an EMP that took out not only our equipment but our implants. It rendered us unconscious and left us at the mercy of people that wanted to kill us. Thankfully, Julia escaped and was able to help the survivors get away. Only the senior people are left."

"Oh, God," Angela asked, her voice a mixture of anguish and confusion. "Who's Julia?"

"Sorry. Julia is Kelsey's doppelgänger. Kelsey decided that it was too confusing having names like Kelsey One and Kelsey Two, so she made the other one rename herself Julia. If I understand correctly, that's the name of one of their cousins."

"Huh. I suppose that makes perfect sense. Where are you?"

"We're at the Imperial Palace, and we've recovered the override. We even have a line on a couple of Marine Raider pinnaces that may be flyable.

"If they're not, I'm not sure what we're going to do. That's really the only shot we have of getting back into space. What's the situation up there?"

"Let's just say that when the AI discovered that you were still alive, things got very busy up here. A lot of the ships that were scattered throughout the system made their way to Terra orbit.

"They're particularly tight around the orbital that we think the AI is on. If you had any ideas about sneaking onto it and attacking the AI, I suggest you forget that plan immediately."

Carl had pretty much expected that, so it was a relief not to have to worry about taking a dozen people to attack an AI on its own station. Still, that left the problem of getting off the planet.

"What about the rest of the system?" he asked. "Have you been able to get into contact with Marcus?"

"As a matter of fact, we have. They're having some difficulty getting to Terra from the direction they were forced to go, but they haven't been discovered yet. They've also had some command drama in the admiral's absence, but it seems like they have everything in order now.

"We've also found a far flip point that we can use to get out of the Terra system, but because of all the traffic in the system, we've done little more than make sure we can get through it. We're being *very* careful not to be detected."

"That's excellent news," Carl said with a smile. "Now all we have to do is get off Terra and slip through the net they've thrown around the planet."

"When do you think you'll have a status on your pinnaces?" his wife asked. "We can get *Persephone* into a decent position to pick you up and then slide back out of the area without being detected, but it really all depends on you."

"We should have information on that shortly. I've got a decent repository of parts here that I can use to repair any damage to the pinnaces' systems, but until I actually go through everything, I'm not going to know. Admiral Mertz is going to be in contact with you before we make the attempt, but I just wanted to hear your voice. I've missed you."

"I've missed you, too," she said softly. "I can't tell you how worried I've been. I'm so sorry that we lost so many friends and shipmates, but I'm ecstatic that you're still alive. Come home to me. I need to hold you in my arms and know that you're safe."

He smiled at the thought. "I'll be up as soon as I can. I've got to go now, but somebody will contact you shortly. I love you."

"I love you, too. Now go kick some ass."

He turned the FTL com off and leaned back in his chair, rubbing his face. Now all he had to do was get a couple of ancient Marine Raider pinnaces functioning again so that they could slip past every computer-controlled warship in the damned system, board *Persephone*, and sneak out of the heavily occupied system.

What could possibly go wrong?

32

Once Talbot convinced Peters to order the group holding him to give the fusion plant back to Frankfort, it didn't take long at all for them to summon Jared.

As he was escorted into the room, he noted that the group trended older. All of those arrayed against him wore stern expressions, as if they didn't want to talk to him at all. Maybe they didn't. Maybe they just wanted him and his people gone so that they could go back to their regular lives.

They were undoubtedly displeased that Jake Peters had given them the order. The major had indicated they were like pack rats, taking whatever they found and putting it securely away, just in case they might need it later.

Considering the world that they found themselves in, Jared couldn't blame them. That still didn't mean that he could let this slide. He'd made a deal with Leader Mordechai, and he intended to keep it.

Even knowing everything that he did, he was still amazed that they'd managed to disassemble and move the fusion plant at all. A task like that required skills and equipment that had to be in very short supply.

Yes, they had computers with full libraries at their beck and call, but some skills couldn't be mastered without actually doing them. Had they failed with fusion plants in other cities in order to build those skills? That was a bit frightening.

The woman at the center of the table leaned forward and glared at Jared. She hadn't bothered giving him her name, so that had to be a good clue about how this conversation was going to go.

"What you demand is unacceptable."

Jared shrugged. If she wanted to get right to the point, he'd accommodate her.

"What either of us wants is irrelevant, isn't it?" he asked in a tone that sounded more than a bit indifferent to his ear. "Didn't your god give you an order? How can you defy him? He *is* your god, right?"

"Of course he's our god," a man down the table to the left snapped. "Keep your unbeliever mouth shut."

The woman held up her hand and shot a disapproving look at the man who'd spoken. Then she returned her glare to Jared.

"The god does not direct our day-to-day operations. Everything we do is in service to him, but *we* make the final decisions."

Jared nodded slowly. "So you're frauds. You claim to serve your god, but you really serve yourselves. I guess I shouldn't be surprised. Tell me, how do you think your followers will feel if that information gets out?

"And before you decide that you need to do something drastic to prevent that, my people are already discussing what your god has said to anyone that will listen. This news will not be suppressed. You can either choose to obey your god and lose one of the spare fusion plants you've scavenged, or you can be found out for what you truly are."

He was taking a real risk by taking a hard line like this, but if he didn't, he was pretty sure they'd either stonewall or attack his group.

"You have no business telling us what we should or should not do or manipulating our followers," the woman said harshly. "You will gather your people and depart at once."

"Not until you redeem your god's word. Either you do that, or we're going to be a thorn in your side. If you want us gone with a minimum of fuss, you're going to have to give back that little bit of equipment that you took from Frankfort. Once you've done so, we'll leave at once."

His ultimatum led to an argument among the leadership council. Eventually, the woman made a gesture and ended the discussion.

"Very well. We will return it to the city from which it came. You may send some of your people to verify that it has arrived, been installed, and turned back on. Then, once the train returns here, you will leave. If you do not, you will be killed. Is that clear enough for you?"

"Yes," Jared said as he turned on his heel. "I think our business is completed."

With that, he walked out of the room without waiting for either their permission or acknowledgment. He'd made no friends, but he didn't have time to be coy. They needed to finalize their planning to get out of the Imperial Palace. They'd be buried in guards within minutes unless he missed his guess.

Jared found everyone gathered in the Imperial Residence. He walked into the main room, past the two guards even as he heard more booted feet coming up the corridor. That would be the extra guards he'd expected.

"I've gotten the FTL com working," Carl said as he closed the door. "*Persephone* is out there and ready to receive us. Angela has even managed to make contact with Marcus.

"The good news is that they're still safe. They said Terra's orbit is filled with enemy ships, and the orbital that the AI is on is now guarded even more closely than before. There's absolutely no way that we're going to be able to do anything to it."

Jared nodded. He'd expected something like that.

"Then it looks as if our goal is to just get off this planet and escape from the Terra system without being captured or killed," he said. "With the regular flip points so well guarded, that probably means we're going to have to find an undiscovered multi-flip point or far flip point."

"I should've mentioned that they found a far flip point," Carl said. "They've already tested it and said that it will get us out of the system."

"That's great news," Kelsey almost gushed. "We've got what we came for, and now we can finally get out of here."

"We do have one problem," Talbot said. "Jake Peters. We're going to have to figure out how to get him out without all of these cultists freaking out."

"I'm afraid that the people running this place aren't going to be cooperative," Jared said with a grunt. "They've agreed to send the fusion plant and shielding back to Frankfort, as well as reassemble it, so we'll have redeemed our word there. Honestly, it's in their own best interest, and I hope that they'll eventually see that.

"We need to send some of our number on the maglev train to make sure it really gets there and that they turn it on. Then we can go there ourselves and gather the cache. I understand that *Persephone* is well stocked, but we don't know what we're going to need in the future. That's a lot of Marine Raider equipment that we just can't afford to leave behind.

"Also, it's good to make certain that people follow through on their deals. When we come back—and we *will* come back eventually—we'll have established a baseline of cooperation with the people of Frankfort. They'll remember that we kept our word and know that we'll be good partners in reestablishing Terra."

He turned his attention to Kelsey. "We're going to have to figure out an extraction plan for Major Peters. We're going to have to breach those doors and get him out.

"Carl, your team needs to go over the pinnaces and make sure that they're ready to go. If we can't get one of them working, then we're not going to be able to get off this planet. I hate to put the pressure on you, but do whatever you have to do."

"We'll make it work," Carl said with a nod.

"I'll leave the details of the extraction to Talbot," Kelsey said. "I'll go with Carl and help them by preflighting the pinnaces. I'm the only one—other than yourself—that's trained as a pilot, so I'll need to make absolutely certain that one of them is functional by the time we're ready to go.

"A lot of what happens next really depends on the timing. We're going to have to put our best people where they need to be. Chloe can help Talbot. If they can't come up with a decent extraction plan, I'll eat one of the pinnaces."

Jared chuckled. "I'll bet. Okay, people, it's crunch time. We've gotten what we came for, and now it's time to get out of here. Let's go out there and make it happen."

* * *

KELSEY FOLLOWED CARL, Austin, and Ralph down to the level where all the vehicles were once kept underneath the Imperial Palace. As Jared had guessed, they'd picked up extra guards. Four disapproving young men armed with flechette rifles and pistols followed them.

The conspicuous absence of stunners was telling.

She had no idea how they were going to react once they realized that she and her friends intended to take the pinnaces. Probably not calmly.

When they arrived at the correct level, they found various atmospheric craft parked in neat lines in the hangar. All were covered by dust. Hulking over everything at the far end was a pair of Marine Raider pinnaces.

One of the young men raised a hand and stepped forward as they started to enter the hangar. "Halt. You're not authorized to examine our equipment any longer."

It seemed that the time for tiptoeing around the looming confrontation was over. She'd hoped that they wouldn't have to start trouble before the train had even left, but needs must.

"Carl, start giving the pinnaces a good check while I deal with our friends," she said softly. Then she turned to face the four men.

"I'm afraid that we really can't do that."

Without waiting for a response, she yanked her stunner from her off side and took them all down with a wide-beam shot even as they were starting to bring their weapons to bear on her. They'd been expecting an argument, not an attack. That momentary hesitation had cost them.

They all dropped like puppets with their strings cut. They'd be out for at least an hour.

"The clock is running, boys," Kelsey said, raising her voice. "Hustle."

She went to each of the unconscious guards and dragged them into the hangar and out of sight. If someone came looking to see what was going on down here, she didn't want them seeing that they'd already attacked their guards. That would just start the fighting early.

The next group, when it came, still wouldn't be expecting outright violence. She'd probably be able to handle them as well.

It was going to be the third group that was problematic.

Carl manipulated the controls to the ramp on one of the pinnaces, and it lowered smoothly to the floor. "Looks like the power still on. That's a good sign."

Instead of going up the ramp, he ducked underneath the pinnace. Moments later, he was back and nodding. "It's got a power cable running from the power grid. That's going to help."

Kelsey reached out with her implants even as the three men were going inside. Since the pinnace was online, that allowed her to do some remote checking.

It wasn't fully online, of course, but its automated systems responded to her link request and granted her access once she'd presented her codes. She brought the computer up and began running a self-diagnostic on the flight control systems.

To her utter shock, almost all of them passed. There were a couple of systems that were down, but they were running off their backups. She'd want to have Carl do a little bit of work on a couple of things, but if push came to shove, they'd be able to take off in it right now.

She turned her attention to the second one and repeated the process. Once again, the majority of its systems were functional, and those that weren't had backups. Somebody had been maintaining them. Maybe not for the last few decades, but they hadn't been abandoned for much longer than that.

Kelsey accessed the palace systems and send a message to Lily for her to send Clarice Beauchamp down to the hangar. She included directions to get there.

A few minutes later, the woman arrived with a pair of irritated guards at her heels. Without waiting for them to say anything, Kelsey used her stunner on narrow beam and took them down.

The warrior had her sword out and was looking for foes as soon as the bodies hit the floor. When she saw that nothing needed her immediate attention, she sheathed her new weapon and walked up to Kelsey.

"What's going on?" the warrior asked.

"They're about to throw us out. The pinnaces are functional, so we're going to break Major Peters out. They're about to send the fusion plant back to Frankfort, and I want you to go with it.

"By this time, I'm sure the people at Frankfort have guards on the platform to make sure that no one tries to sneak in and take anything else. What I'd like you to do is make certain that Leader Mordechai knows that we're going to be joining them very shortly. I'm sure they've got all kinds of weapons, and I'd rather not be shot down."

The woman nodded. "I'll go down to the train station and oversee the movement of the fusion plant. I look forward to seeing you again in Frankfort."

Kelsey extended her hand, and the two women locked forearms. "Me too. Thanks for everything."

Once the woman had departed, Kelsey returned to keeping watch while Carl and his boys made certain that the pinnaces were functional. The clock was definitely running, and she sincerely hoped that the train departed before everything came apart.

Her next call was to Jared. "Operation Johnny Bravo is in progress. I'm sending Clarice on the train, and we'll join her in Frankfort once we get out of here. Retrieving Major Peters is going to be the most challenging aspect of this, I suspect. It's a good thing that Talbot is on that."

"I'll make sure that everything on our end is in motion," her brother said. "Try not to kill anybody. Mertz out."

Kelsey turned and yelled up the nearest ramp. "Carl, I've tapped into the system and see a couple of things that I'd like you to work on. Remember that nothing you do can take any of the major systems offline, because we might have to leave on a moment's notice. Understood?"

"Copy that," he yelled back. "Send the information to my implants, and we'll get started. I'll send Austin over to the other pinnace. If we can get them both ready, great. If one of them fails, at least we'll have a backup. Ralph will take care of bypassing the lockouts on the hangar doors."

With everything in motion, Kelsey set herself into a good place to ambush anyone coming through the main doors. As soon as the people running this place figured out what was going on, they'd swarm them, and the fight would be on.

Her goal was to make certain that nobody figured out what they were doing in the hangar. The next steps of the operation were up to Jared and Talbot. If they got their jobs done, then the team would be gone within the next hour.

Things might be tight, and they might have to fight their way out, but she swore to herself that once they'd defeated the AIs, she'd be back. This place was her family's legacy going back ten thousand years, and she'd be damned if she'd leave it in the hands of jerks like this.

33

When Julia heard that they were about to send the fusion plant and shielding back to Frankfort with only Clarice Beauchamp to escort it, she approached Mertz. "I think you're making a mistake. Things might go badly here. You should send all the noncombatants back to the city."

Rather than arguing, he was silent for a few moments and then nodded. "You're probably right. Hoping that everybody can get to the pinnaces and out of here without being caught up in a fight is unrealistic.

"Right now, the people in charge don't know that we're planning to steal the pinnaces. They also don't know that we're going to take Major Peters with us. Either of those two things is going to start a fight that could get someone killed."

He grimaced slightly. "Actually, the fighting has *already* started. The guards with Kelsey, Carl, and the others down in the hangar tried to stop them from looking at the pinnaces, so she stunned them. The clock is ticking now.

"Take all the noncombatants with you and join Clarice on the train. Once you get to Frankfort, wait for us. With you going along in armor, there's very little chance that the soldiers these people send will be able to overcome you. They're unlikely to even try.

"I know this is going to introduce some complications into their relationship, but there's nothing we can do about that. Honestly, I still think that the people in the city will come out ahead. While they have technology, they're not exactly numerous."

He inclined his head toward her. "Good thinking, by the way."

Taking the compliment with an unexpected smile, Julia excused herself and gathered all the noncombatants except for Carl, Ralph, and Austin. Since they were working on the pinnaces, Kelsey would keep them safe.

By the time she'd gotten them to the maglev platform, the soldiers from the group holding the Imperial Palace had almost finished loading the fusion plant and its shielding. She wondered how Beauchamp was supposed to know that everything they needed was there.

The answer turned out to be Olivia West. She was overseeing the loading and apparently in communication with Carl via the systems inside the Imperial Palace to discuss what was supposed to be there. According to her, it looked like everything had been crated and labeled for future use, so it was a simple matter to go down a manifest in his mind to tell that everything they needed was there.

That might not mean much if some small, critical part were missing, but there was only so much that they could do. They wouldn't know if it was all functional until Carl got to Frankfort.

"I talked with Mertz, and he said that all the noncombatants are coming back on the train with us," she told Olivia. "They're going to meet us at Frankfort."

The other woman scowled. "Does that number include him? I realize that he's a pilot, but he's basically a noncombatant when you come to ground fighting. One of our leaders needs to go back on this train."

"They have two pinnaces and two pilots," Julia disagreed. "I understand that's putting all of our eggs in one basket—yet another Kelsey saying that I don't fully understand—but in this case, it's necessary."

She held up a hand when the other woman started to object. "We're on an *extremely* tight schedule, and arguing with him about this is only going to disrupt him at a critical juncture. Kelsey has already taken… steps that are going to cause us problems if we don't hurry."

Olivia sighed. "Great. We'll just have to hope for the best."

Twenty minutes later, the fusion plant and its shielding were loaded onto the train, and all the noncombatants had boarded, with Julia following behind the last of the soldiers. Since she was locked inside her armor and heavily armed, she doubted they were going to try anything, but she stayed on the lookout for trouble.

She linked her implants into the train and monitored all the cars as they left the station. Carl was in communication with her and verified that they'd made the turn heading for Frankfort.

I'm about to kill communications between the train and the palace, he told her. *I've already rigged the system so that they'll think it's still operational, but any attempt by the palace to call them is going to fail.*

And what if the people on the train try to call them?

Hopefully, with such a short trip, they won't try. Worst case, they'll attempt to send a message once they've arrived at the station to let the palace know that they've arrived. I've set up the com system here to forward incoming requests to me. I'll do my best to make sure they don't realize anything is going on, but you're going to have to keep your eyes open.

Thanks, Carl. Good luck.

You too, Julia.

After about ten minutes, she allowed herself to relax slightly. It seemed as if the scheme was going off just like they'd planned. That didn't stop her from keeping a close eye on everyone around her. If they made a move, she was going to be ready.

To her relief, they pulled into the station at Frankfort without anyone the wiser. She noted that the platform was filled with guards from the city. Standing at their center was Jebediah.

Everyone there had their primitive weapons raised when the doors opened, but she stepped out and changed her helmet to show her face through the holographic projectors.

"It's okay," she said. "We've got the fusion plant, and these people are here to make sure that it's installed."

Jebediah gestured toward his people, and they relaxed slightly, though she noted that they didn't really lower their weapons. They were worried about the people from the Imperial Palace, just like she was.

"So, who are they?" he asked her once the guards began unloading the crates. "And are you Julia or Kelsey?"

"Julia. And these are potential allies. Ones that we're going to piss off before this is done. Those of us that aren't here are in the process of stealing a couple of Marine Raider pinnaces that they had stashed at the Imperial Palace.

"That's what's going to get us to orbit. They're going to be seriously pissed about that. Admiral Mertz said to tell you that he's sorry."

Jebediah chuckled. "It seems like poetic justice to me. Don't worry. My father is an able negotiator. He'll blame you for everything, you won't be here to deny it, and we'll eventually find some common ground with these people.

"Once they finish unloading the equipment, I'll have someone take you up to the room where it once sat. We can oversee the installation together and await the arrival of your friends. I'll see that word is dispatched to our sentries above ground to make certain that no one thinks their arrival is that of an enemy.

"We'll also make certain that we don't let them in where the intruders can see them. No need to make them wonder how they suddenly and unexpectedly appeared."

He stood silent for a few minutes as the people from the Imperial Palace finished unloading the crates and started moving them laboriously to the lift. Some residents of Frankfort helped speed the process while others kept guard.

When the two of them finally stood alone on the platform, Jebediah turned to face her. "Will you or your people ever return? And by that, I mean once you've dealt with the computers."

She removed her helmet and shook out her damp hair. "Almost certainly. I don't know how long it will be, but I feel confident that my sister and Admiral Mertz will evict these people from the Imperial

Palace. That's going to cause more problems, I'm sure, but it's our birthright."

Jebediah laughed again. "While we're willing to ally ourselves with these people, they represent the past, not the future. When the time comes, if you can take the Imperial Palace, do so with our blessing. Many places in the world could use advanced people like these. They will adapt.

"Now, let's go upstairs and watch this wondrous process. I can't wait to see our city once more providing for itself."

She walked beside the man as they headed toward the lift. Her thoughts weren't on the fusion plant, though. She was worried about Kelsey and the rest.

They had the hardest job at this point, and everything rested on them being able to get away cleanly. Julia hoped they had a little bit of luck on their side because if they didn't, things were going to get really, really ugly.

* * *

TALBOT LED CHLOE toward the room where the others kept Jake Peters. Four guards were walking behind them now, and he was beginning to suspect that gaining access to the Marine Raider was going to be difficult.

Nevertheless, they were going to get him out right now, or someone was going to bleed. Kelsey had already said that the pinnaces were ready to go, so all he had to do was get Peters, get to the hangar, and they'd be on their way.

There were several more guards outside the entryway to the area where Peters was kept, and they didn't look happy to see Talbot. One of them stepped forward and raised a hand. "The god has declined to see you. Leave."

"I think I'd like to hear that from the god," Talbot said easily.

He sent an implant message to Peters that the man immediately accepted.

We're being denied entrance.

They've doubled the guard inside, so I think they know something is going on.

We'll be inside in just a minute. We'll handle the guards outside. You take care of the ones in there.

He killed the connection, drew his stunner, and fired from his hip on wide beam. That took down all the guards in front of him but wasn't sufficient to penetrate the door. Behind him, Chloe whirled in place at the same time, taking out the guards trailing them. Moments later, they were the only ones awake in the hall.

It took them a couple of moments to figure out how to open the doors, and by the time they'd done so, they saw that Peters had taken care of his own guards with the stunner that Talbot had slipped him earlier.

The former Marine Raider looked down at the weapon and grinned lopsidedly at Talbot. "It's been a long time since I fought anybody and even longer since I've held an Imperial weapon in my hand. It kind of felt good."

"Keep watch while Chloe and I get everybody inside," he said. "As soon as we're done, we're getting the hell out of here."

The two of them quickly dragged all the guards inside the room and dumped them beside the main door. Then, with Chloe leading the way in her armor, he hefted Peters over his shoulder, and they headed toward the hangar.

They were definitely committed now. They either had to get to the hangar, or they'd never escape.

His hopes of avoiding trouble ended when a trio of guards came around the corner ahead of them and saw him carrying Peters. Two of them immediately charged while the last one ducked back out of sight, already screaming.

Chloe stunned the first two even as they were raising their weapons to fire, and then the three of them rushed down the stairs that they'd been headed toward.

They ran into a couple guards when they exited on the hangar level. Since they'd had their weapons out, it looked as if they'd run out of patience for Kelsey, too.

Talbot locked the door controls once they were inside the hangar. The locals would probably get through soon enough, but the doors were thick. That would hopefully delay them long enough to get the pinnaces out of the Imperial Palace and clear of its defenses.

He doubted very seriously that they'd fire any of the weapons designed to shoot aircraft down. That would garner the attention of the AI in orbit. Unless they were suicidal, as soon as the pinnaces were clear, they were safe.

Since the ramps to both pinnaces were lowered, and he could see that they were both under power, he just picked the closest one and raced inside it, gesturing for Chloe to get into the other.

It took him half a minute to secure Peters in one of the harnesses and race to the flight deck. Kelsey was seated in the pilot's seat, and it looked like she was in the final stages of getting ready to take off.

He dropped into the copilot's seat and strapped himself in. "Where's everybody else?"

"Jared's in the other pinnace. Carl, Austin, and Ralph are working to override the lock on the bay doors. Whoever was here last sealed it down pretty good. If they can't get the manual locks undone, we're screwed."

"Then let's hope they figure it out."

Looking through the viewports at the front of the pinnace, he saw the three working at a panel beside the large, blast-proof doors. They were hunched over and talking back and forth while Carl did something inside the panel.

Through the ramp that was still open, Talbot heard what sounded like a loud thumping somewhere behind them. The locals were trying to get into the hangar.

"I should probably take care of that," he said, starting to undo his restraints.

"Stay where you are," Kelsey said. "I think Carl just did it."

He looked forward and saw that Carl had turned and raised both of his thumbs toward the ceiling. The three of them raced back toward the pinnaces.

"I've used my codes to override the lockout," Kelsey said. "That should get the doors moving. Carl and the rest are headed for Jared's pinnace. Raise the ramp."

He did so remotely, and moments later, the large hatch at the end of the room began slowly rising. As soon as the ramp status went green, Kelsey lifted the pinnace off the deck and began edging toward the opening.

As soon as she could, Kelsey added a little bit more thrust and went under the door. Talbot saw that the exit led into a tunnel that was probably heavily shielded because no one really wanted their enemies to know what was going on underneath their homes.

A minute later, he saw another hatch in front of them that had already opened, and beyond that was sunlight fading into dusk. Kelsey brought them through the opening, and they rose into the air as she applied power and sent them racing over the darkening forest below them.

"Jared's out of the tunnel," she said. "I just sent the signal to lock the exit down again. As soon as we were through the first blast door, I closed it behind us. They won't be chasing us. Unless they're stupid, we're done here."

"Are you going to be able to use it to get back in?" he asked. "When we come back, we're going to need a way to get inside that facility. Being able to fly in right under their noses would be useful."

She shrugged. "We can hope, but we probably shouldn't count on it. There are other ways in, and they can't lock me out of the computer systems. I can undo any security measure they enact by fiat. But that's a problem for another day."

He settled back into his seat as she took the pinnace low over the ground, ducking in between hills and keeping them from rising too high. She wouldn't want to give the AI a chance to notice them. With their suspicions up, they'd be looking. Even with Marine Raider stealth technology, they didn't really want to take too many chances.

They had the override. Now all they had to do was get it safely past the AIs. And, of course, escape the Terra system itself.

He didn't try to fool himself. That was going to be tricky. Even with pinnaces like these, they couldn't just waltz right past the ships up there. They'd have to trust to luck to give them a break when the time came.

One way or the other, they were almost done on Terra.

34

Carl watched through the scanners as the pinnaces slowly glided over the ruined megacity of Frankfort. Kelsey and the admiral had landed shortly after escaping the Imperial Palace and waited for the moon to set and leave everything in complete darkness. They hadn't wanted to tempt fate by landing in the city while it was still possible someone would see them.

With the stealth material that the pinnaces were made out of, they should be safe from detection by the AI or the ships in orbit. If not, they'd hardly have time to know, because a kinetic strike would take them out before they had more than a few seconds' warning.

Since they didn't want to have the pinnaces visible from orbit after they landed, they'd needed a place large enough to get them under cover. They'd chosen a building that had once been some kind of sports arena.

They had no idea what the interior conditions would be like, but the plan was to fly through the partially collapsed roof and into the interior, gliding into an area that wouldn't be visible from above. They'd just have to hope that there wasn't another collapse while they were there.

Kelsey and the admiral brought their pinnaces in slowly and

carefully, aligning them with the section of collapsed roof until they were just a few meters above the debris on the floor before gliding over to a relatively clear area near one of the remaining interior walls. There, they set down and deactivated everything once they'd dropped the ramps.

He led his people and Lieutenant Laird down the ramp, covering the area with one of the flechette rifles. There was no sign of movement, but the shadows seemed to twitch in every direction he looked.

Over at the other pinnace, Talbot came down the ramp holding the crippled Marine Raider with Kelsey right behind him. Carl heard Admiral Mertz joining him as well.

Carl couldn't believe that they'd retrieved the override and actually escaped the Imperial Palace. That was a *huge* victory.

"How are we going to find a way to an area that we're familiar with?" Carl asked as they gathered.

"The city has some major trunks laid out in a grid pattern," Kelsey said. "It won't be hard to get underground and find one of those. Then it's just a matter of letting them know that we're here without triggering some type of hostile response."

"We used to have a team stationed here in Frankfort," Peters said. "They lasted about twenty years. I suppose that might seem like a long time, but the resistance forces were supposed to operate for much longer and train the civilians to resist as well. We did that, but a couple of groups got ambitious and tried to do too much too soon.

"Back then, Frankfort was still just an average city, though occupied by the rebels. The AIs didn't show their ugly hand then, but somehow, they figured out what was going on all over Terra and began hunting the resistance teams.

"One by one, they fell out of contact until there were only a few of us left. My team got ambushed maybe five years after the group here in Frankfort vanished. The last operational group was gone within two years of that."

"I suppose no one will ever know what really happened to them," Talbot said. "Five hundred years is a long time, and over a hundred since the AIs brought the hammer down. I'm sure it was worse in a lot of places."

Carl nodded. "The core worlds were spared some of the most horrible things the AIs did. In some out-of-the-way places, they just dropped people into the Stone Age or blocked the supplies necessary for them to survive. On Avalon, we were lucky."

"Sometimes you make your own luck," Peters said. "It looks like that's what you've done. You should be proud of that."

Once they'd secured the pinnaces, they found their way down to the tunnels underneath the city and began making their way toward the still-occupied sections. It didn't take long at all for them to run into the inhabitants.

Thankfully, the locals had been warned that they were coming. Once everyone was sure that there wasn't going to be violence, the residents quickly escorted them down to the area where the fusion plant was being assembled.

Carl had Kelsey and Talbot hold his arms while he got out of his armor and dressed in clothes the locals scrounged up for him. The people from the palace almost certainly wouldn't recognize him since he'd had his helmet on most of the time he'd been there.

After making sure that his friends and compatriots would go somewhere else while he covertly watched the reassembly and reactivation of the fusion plant, he walked into the large room. As expected, none of the people from the Imperial Palace paid him the slightest bit of attention.

To the uninitiated, it was unbelievable that a fusion plant could be disassembled or reassembled in such a short time frame, but everything was modular. So long as it was done correctly and carefully, the process didn't have to take a long time.

Thankfully, the original mounts were still there in the plascrete floor. Basically, all the technicians had to do was drop the pieces where they needed to be, bolt them down, and add on the modules as they got to that part of the assembly.

Once it was fully assembled and the shielding was installed, the technicians began running tests. Carl made sure to be standing right there and going over everything remotely. They wouldn't know that he was looking over their proverbial shoulders, but he'd see everything.

While he was no expert, he'd had to learn a fair bit about fusion plants over the last several years, and he knew how to let the equipment guide the safety checks for him.

He expected at least a few things to be questionable, but the fusion plant had been shut down in good order and was undamaged. Everything started up just the way it was supposed to. All systems green.

They weren't putting out any power because the technicians had cut all the feeds going out to the rest of the city. It would've been stupid to bring the system online and then have it light up the city for the AI to see from orbit.

Once the work was fully completed, the guards from Frankfort escorted the technicians and fighters from the Imperial Palace to the lift and took them down. From there, they'd be put on the train and sent back to the Imperial Palace. When they arrived, they'd undoubtedly find the place in an uproar, but the deed was done.

Carl turned toward Jebediah once they'd departed. "We're going to need to know where you want power. The closer it is to the surface, the more likely you're going to do something that draws unwanted attention. I suggest you keep the lighting and power to this level and lower to reduce the risk."

The large man nodded. "That's what we were thinking as well. If we can make certain that only those areas and the maglev platform are isolated, that will allow us to operate the way we want.

"Once the others get back to the Imperial Palace, I feel certain that they'll cut power, so we need to spend the time to make certain that we get those areas connected and that nothing else is going to be affected."

"I'll be able to run power down to the area that they're currently energizing without any problems. It should only take a couple of minutes since it's already proven to be isolated. From there, it won't be hard to expand along the levels that we want one step at a time.

"I'll be able to show your people what needs to be done with the fusion plant reasonably quickly. The maintenance processes aren't all that complicated. They just have to be done on time and in a precise manner.

"I've got a lot of files on the operation and maintenance of this kind of equipment that I can upload to your computers now that you can use them. With the files in the fusion plant itself, those will help you keep it running. I'm hoping that the people from the Imperial Palace will come back and you can formalize arrangements with them. If not, I think you can learn what you need and manage."

Connecting just the areas that were now covered by power from the maglev platform was simple enough. Once he'd accomplished that, Carl brought the fusion plant up from standby to its minimal power production settings and verified that everything was working as designed.

When they finally cut the power, the output from this plant would be more than enough to make up for the loss. Since they hadn't died in a kinetic strike, the shielding was doing its job, too.

Because he was linked to the power system, he saw when the power along the maglev line cut out and knew that the train must've made its way all the way back to the Imperial Palace.

He made sure that power to the train systems remained unpowered and tagged the controls to sound an alarm if they powered up again. They'd know if the others were coming back, and they'd be ready for them if they did.

The process of turning the power on in the lower levels of the city was going to take hours, but it should be straightforward. It would easily be dawn by the time he was done, but then they'd finally be able to leave Terra and go back to the stars.

He was so ready for that.

* * *

As DAWN WAS BREAKING, Jared once again met with Mordechai in his high tower overlooking Frankfort. They stood there a while, just staring out over the ruined megacity without saying anything. Jared was content to let the man speak in his own time.

Eventually, Mordechai turned to face him. "You've done

everything that you promised. The lower levels of the city are once again safe to travel, and we have power that we haven't had in a hundred years.

"With the power restored, Carl has shown us how to retrieve the information that we need from the computers that were dead. It's a good beginning. It will take us a long time to return to the level of knowledge that our forefathers had, but we will one day do so.

"Jebediah has turned all of the equipment that once belonged to the Marine Raiders over to your people. My people are even now carrying it to be loaded on your pinnaces."

"We hope to return one day and help you start rebuilding Terra," Jared said. "I wish we could leave someone with the kind of training that you need behind, but we can't afford to spare anyone. Take small steps, Leader Mordechai. Don't take chances with the AI. With any luck, it will be dead or under our control inside a year."

Mordechai cocked his head slightly to the side. "Do you truly believe it will be that easy? That it will only take such a short amount of time?"

"You've got a point," he admitted. "While it might be inside a year, it might be many years. Or it might never happen at all. The fight we're waging is going to be a hard one. We're the underdogs, and we know it.

"The system where the artificial intelligence was created and resides is going to be more strongly defended than anything we've faced thus far. I've got a fleet of warships that will help us, but even that might not be enough. To win this war, we're going to have to take a lot of chances. Chances that under other circumstances I might not take.

"Just like you, we'll have to do the best we can. If you don't hear from us again, I guess that will tell you what happened to us."

The older man stuck out his hand, and Jared took it.

"I wish you well, Admiral Mertz. You and your people have a chance to undo some of the most terrible wrongs that have ever been done to humanity. I hope that you can stop the evil that we caused and once again allow us to live free.

"If there's anything that my people or I can do or provide that would help in your task, you need only ask, and it shall be given to you."

"I appreciate the offer, but I think we have everything we need," Jared said with a smile. "Thank you, Mordechai, and good luck to you and your people."

An hour later, Jared was aboard the pinnace he was piloting, and the ramp was raised. Using short-range communications, he verified that Kelsey was also ready to take off. This was going to be one of the most nerve-racking parts of their escape from Terra. If anything was going to go to hell, now was when it would happen.

He'd had the others bring Major Peters onto the flight deck and strapped him into the copilot's seat beside him. Since he didn't have anyone to help control the pinnace, he might as well talk to their newest associate.

The disabled man looked a bit uncertain, so Jared spoke up. "Having second thoughts?"

Peters shook his head. "No. I want this more than anything, but I feel a little out of my depth. It's been a long time since I've done anything other than merely existing.

"I know that Doctor Stone says that she can get me fitted with artificial limbs and on the road to recovery, but that's a little frightening. I've spent so much time as a cripple that I'm not sure if I know how to be normal again."

Jared checked his console and then nodded. "You can't change the past. You'll never be the man you once were. What you can do is become the man you want to be."

The former Marine Raider nodded appreciatively. "That's deep, Admiral. I suppose with all the trouble that you've been through over the last few years, you've got some experience at coming out the other side now. I appreciate your insight.

"Once we get to Twilight River, how are we going to get into the system and onto the station where the AI is located?"

Jared shrugged slightly. "We'll have to figure that out once we've rendezvoused with my fleet. It may be that we have enough force to break through the inevitable blockade. Or, since the enemy doesn't know about multi-flip points or far flip points—which I'll have to explain to you later—we might be able to find a back door that lets us into the system with them none the wiser.

"Frankly, the latter option is my preferred method. If we can gain access without any of the defenders being aware that we're even there, we can smother the damned machine before it can raise the alarm."

"*Persephone Two*, this is *Persephone One*," Kelsey said over the short-range com. "I'm ready to lift. I'll take the lead as we head north. Once we're far enough out of the orbital coverage pattern, then we'll head straight up."

"I'll be right behind you," Jared responded. "Let's do this."

He brought his controls out of standby and lifted the pinnace off the ground, pivoting it in place slowly to follow Kelsey out into the sunlight.

Once again, they were taking a chance by leaving during the day, but the pinnaces were extremely hard to detect. Rather than wait for night, which wasn't much of an impedance to the AIs, he'd decided that he'd rather be gone.

It was time to end this chapter of their lives.

35

Kelsey took her pinnace northward with Jared close behind her, and Talbot sitting quietly beside her. As they traveled, the ruined cities and towns that they passed transitioned to an untamed wilderness. She crossed a small stretch of ocean and then onto the ice shelf beyond.

She knew roughly where Terra's axis was located, but she didn't need to be over it for this to work. In fact, it might be better if she wasn't so precise. That was the way machines thought.

Once she reached a frozen, isolated area that suited their needs, she double-checked to verify that her stealth systems were fully operational. Then she called Jared to make certain that he'd done the same, even though she knew that he already had. It was far better to be sure.

Only then did she lift the nose of her pinnace and begin rising from the surface of Terra.

Rather than rushing up to orbit, she lifted as slowly as she could while still maintaining good headway. She wasn't going to go fast enough to cause a disturbance in the atmosphere that might give them away.

Long minutes later, they finally exited the atmosphere and were in space. Kelsey didn't dare use active scanners, but her passives told the same story that Angela had passed on to them. The area around the equator, which held all of the orbitals around Terra and the AI, was packed with ships.

Quite a few more than there had been here when they'd arrived, in fact. Though her detection ability was limited on passive scanners, she thought that many of them were bigger than destroyers.

Thankfully, while the enemy had the planet encircled, their coverage at the poles only consisted of a few automated destroyers that were scattered fairly wide. They obviously didn't consider the chances of someone coming out this way very high.

Score one for her outguessing them. The AI was confident that it had destroyed their only means of transport. While it was covering its bases, it thought there was little chance unprotected humans could survive and escape from such an inhospitable place.

In fact, this would've been an excellent place to hide facilities meant to survive the invasion. She wondered if they were traveling over lost habitats deep under the ice where the descendants of the survivors even now lived out their lives.

The possibility couldn't be dismissed out of hand. Not for Terra or any other world. That was something to think about later.

"It looks like we've got a couple of destroyers that could be in position to detect us if we get unlucky," she told Jared over the short-range com. "I'll maneuver to avoid them as best I can. Once we get away from Terra, we should be able to rendezvous with *Persephone* without any issues."

"What do you think our chances are?" he asked, his voice quiet.

"Decent. That doesn't mean we can't have a run of bad luck, but I'm hopeful that we can pull this off. It would really suck to come this far only to have them spot us just as we're getting away."

"Don't jinx us. Positive thoughts only."

She took a deep breath and pushed her worries away. Slowly— ever so slowly—she edged between the destroyers that were farthest apart. The strength of the scanners searching for them rose toward the detection threshold with every second.

When she and Jared were as close to the destroyers as they were going to get, the scanner strength hovered just a few notches below disaster, but the automated vessels didn't react.

She only started breathing easily again once they'd left the blockade around Terra behind them and were in open space and headed for *Persephone*. Their passive scanners wouldn't be capable of picking the ship up as they approached, but she had no doubt *Persephone* would be right where she was supposed to be.

"I see her," Jared finally signaled. "Look off a bit to port and up."

She turned her eyes in the direction indicated. *Persephone* was only a dot at this range, but she was growing steadily larger.

Once her former command had come close, Kelsey lined up with one of the docking cradles. Ten seconds later, the pinnace made contact, and *Persephone* latched on. Kelsey watched as the controls locked everything down and saw the airlock seal go green.

Only then did she let out a ragged breath. "I can't believe that we made it," she muttered.

Talbot reached over and took her hand. "I knew you'd make this work. You always come through."

She laughed a bit shakily. "I had my doubts this time. This mission was worse than anything we've ever been through."

"Come on. Let's get out of this tin can."

Once everyone had exited both of the pinnaces, she headed straight for the bridge and found Angela seated in the command chair. The other woman rose and wrapped her arms around her.

"It's so good to have you back home," the big woman said. "I've been worried sick."

Kelsey squeezed her back. "We've got a lot of stories to tell, but first, we need to get out of here before someone spots us. How long is it going to take us to get to the flip point you found?"

"A while," Angela said as she sat back down. "That's why it's called a *far* flip point. Thankfully, it looks like the outer system is only intermittently patrolled. There are a couple of destroyers that might become problematic, but we won't know that's the case until we get a little farther out."

Kelsey gestured at the main screen in front of the bridge. "All those ships in orbit around Terra. We didn't see anything like them in the system when we arrived. Where did they come from?"

Angela's face scrunched into a frown. "The Alpha Centauri flip point was heavily guarded with both ships and stations. Almost all of them were shut down, and that's why we didn't spot them before you went to Terra.

"Once things started happening, the AI reactivated a bunch of the ships and brought them in. It also increased patrols in the system. It looks like you made them very nervous."

"Why would they have *that* flip point guarded?" Kelsey asked, feeling her brows knit. "Alpha Centauri is a cul-de-sac and not one with any habitable worlds. Why guard it?"

Angela shrugged. "It may be that's where the AI parked the inactive ships that it used during the rebellion. They won the fight, and they probably still had a lot of ships when they were done. They might've taken a lot of them to Alpha Centauri to make certain that no one could get to them, like the wrecks they put around Boxer Station. We don't really have a way to be sure."

"And we've got more pressing matters to attend to," Kelsey agreed. "That mystery is going to have to wait for another time. Right now, we need to get out of here and rendezvous with Jared's fleet."

Angela nodded. "We're already on our way. The nightmare is just about over. Why don't you and the rest go take a hot shower, get something to eat, and relax for a bit. Let me do the driving."

Kelsey was more than willing to do that, but she was worried that something could still go wrong. She wouldn't relax entirely until they'd left the Terra system behind.

* * *

AN HOUR after they'd arrived aboard *Persephone*, Talbot was standing in the cramped medical center. Jake Peters was about to undergo the surgery to install Marine Raider–grade artificial limbs. He figured that he owed it to the man to be there.

He also needed to get Kelsey down here at some point to get her thigh regenerated, but figured that wouldn't happen until they'd made their escape from the Terra system.

Lily quickly had Peters on the table and had applied the somatic stimulator. With him fully asleep, her professional face quickly transitioned to one that looked concerned to Talbot.

"What's wrong?" he asked.

"Unlike replacing Julia's burned-out artificial eye—which went off without a hitch—this surgery is going to be difficult. These injuries have been scarred for a very long time. Longer than I would've imagined possible. They're going to be extremely resistant to regeneration, I suspect.

"I ran him through the regenerator back at the Imperial Palace, but I didn't have the time and equipment that I needed to go through and remove the worst of the scar tissue. Once that's done, I'm going to have to attach the artificial limbs in such a way that they're permanently bonded into place.

"I wasn't lying when I told Major Peters that I can do it, but I'll admit that it's going to be one of the more difficult surgeries that I've attempted. Success is not guaranteed."

She took a deep breath and stretched her back. "His recovery is going to be painful and difficult, too. He's going to have to go through retraining on a similar scale to what Kelsey needed after she was augmented.

"He's going to get frustrated and depressed, but he's still going to have to work his butt off if he expects to make a full recovery. That's where I'm hoping you'll come in. You know how hard it's going to be, and you can help him."

"I'll be there for him," Talbot assured her. "Better yet, Kelsey will be there. She'll shame him into doing the very best he can. After all, can you imagine a big, tough guy like this failing to perform when she's watching?"

Lily chuckled. "No, I suppose that's a pretty good motivator. It's worked for the entirety of human existence, so it'll probably work this time, too."

She took a deep breath and got to work.

As a marine, Talbot had seen more than his fair share of blood and injuries, but the process of opening a man up to get at badly scarred tissue had a kind of gruesome feel to it.

For whatever reason, the work she did on the man's ruined eye socket was the worst. Yes, Peters had had the eye removed after the injury, and a civilian-grade model installed. It had burned out when the AI had used the EMP weapons on Terra a hundred years ago.

That didn't mean that whoever had done the work had done the best job possible. It also didn't mean that someone that had lived as long as Peters had hadn't developed scar tissue where another person might not during an average—or even long—lifetime.

It felt like an hour had passed by the time she finished cleaning up the wound where his eye had once been. A check of his internal chronometer showed Talbot that it was less than half that.

No matter how uncertain Lily said she'd felt, that didn't slow her sure, quick motions as she did the work. Once she'd regenerated the tissue around his eye socket as much as she could, she carefully fitted an artificial replacement into the eye socket and began building the flesh back around it.

Talbot was always amazed at how well Imperial prosthetics could be made to replace something. They looked completely normal to the naked eye. He knew that based on the eye that Julia had. It had all the same abilities as her original Marine Raider augmentation. From what he understood, it even had a few extras.

The man's arm and legs took hours more for Lily to prepare the stumps and fit the prosthetics. Attaching the nerves was kind of gruesome, but Talbot accepted that was just part of doing business.

Then came the man's mangled hand. She cleaned the stumps of the missing fingers and attached prosthetic ones to replace what was lost. Then she opened the hand itself and reconstructed it to mitigate the damage done during the original injury.

Once that was complete, she began working on the other injuries he'd suffered. Some of that involved rebreaking bones that hadn't healed correctly and excising more scar tissue that had formed inside his torso.

It was a grueling, ugly task, but she eventually had him wheel Peters to the big regenerator next to the bulkhead and started it up.

She stretched her back before facing him. "I suspect I'm going to have to do some fine-tuning on just about everything, but I think I've made a good start. I've never dealt with long-term injuries like this before, so I'm going to reserve judgment until I have a better idea of what I'm dealing with, but his prognosis is good.

"I've also taken some tissue samples so that I can try to understand how his body is adapting to such an extended life span. It would be a lot better for us going forward if we really understood the process a lot better. I'm going to have to go over everything with the Imperial Physician, and I want to have the answers."

Talbot clapped a hand on her shoulder. "You did one hell of a job, Lily. I didn't think it was possible to put someone back together that way again. You're amazing."

"I just wish I was back aboard *Caduceus*," she said glumly. "I'd feel a lot better with more facilities and extra hands to help keep an eye on his recovery. If we can rendezvous with the fleet soon, I might take him over there to finish his recovery."

He watched her washing her hands, suspecting that she wasn't done talking. She confirmed that when she turned toward him, her face a mask of worry.

"Do you think we really have a chance at this? I know we've got the override, but defeating the AI in its lair seems so… daunting."

"We're going to beat this thing," he said. "We're going to take back the Empire. Don't doubt that for a second."

She nodded, likely not convinced by his projected confidence. "You should probably go check on your wife and Julia. You know, to make sure that they aren't getting into trouble."

"I'm not sure *anybody* could do that," he said with a chuckle. "But, I'll try."

With that, Talbot left the medical center and went in search of his wife. She'd want a report on what had happened with Peters, and he was finally ready to see this damned mission end.

36

J ulia wandered the corridors of *Persephone* after Doctor Stone replaced her burned-out eye. This was a tiny ship. Significantly smaller than a destroyer. It also had a number of features that she didn't understand.

In particular, there was a room that had a series of large tubes going from floor to ceiling that had openings for large pods to be loaded in. She supposed they were escape pods, but why were they gathered in one place like this? She made a note to ask Kelsey about them once they were safely clear of danger.

At that point, she decided that she'd put off the inevitable for as long as she could and made her way to the bridge. Like the rest of the vessel, it was laid out differently than most Fleet ships. It was a much closer affair, with fewer seats, and it was arranged in such a way that everyone could see everyone else. It felt communal.

Angela was sitting in the center seat. Julia had to stop herself from rushing up to the woman and giving her a big hug because this wasn't *her* Angela. This was the Angela from Kelsey's universe.

While that woman was probably good friends with Kelsey, the two probably weren't as close as she and her Angela were. Though the relationship between her and her Angela had never been romantic, it was as close as Kelsey's relationship with Talbot otherwise.

Angela looked up at Julia and smiled as she rose to her feet. "You must be Julia. I've heard a lot about you, and I feel like I've known you forever. Of course, I feel the same way about Kelsey. Welcome aboard *Persephone*."

"It's good to meet you as well," Julia said. "In my universe, I've known you for years. You were the marine assigned to keep me safe, just like Talbot did for Kelsey, minus the kissing. We're friends, and it feels that way deep in my heart, so if I seem a bit too familiar, I apologize."

That brought a high-amperage smile to the tall woman's face, a grin that Julia remembered very fondly.

"You're not going to bother me with anything like that. Honestly, I hope that one of these days, I'll have an opportunity to visit your universe and meet myself. I think that would be an extraordinary sort of thing. If I might ask, why didn't your version of me come with you?"

"It's complicated, but you were needed there. Honestly, we really didn't expect this to be a long-term sort of thing, and I'd already brought Scott Roche with me."

Her face fell at the memory. "He didn't make it, and you're probably going to be very angry with me when I get back home, but the situation is what it is. Do you mind if we talk in a less public setting?"

Angela gestured toward the corridor that Julia had just come up through. "The wardroom is just this way. They'll call me if anything comes up that needs my attention."

Once they'd made their way to the small room, Angela closed the door and raised an eyebrow. "What can I help you with, Highness?"

Unsure of exactly what the best way to start was, Julia decided to just lay out the entire situation. "I've spent a good amount of time with your husband, and I've made the decision to pursue his doppelgänger in my universe and convince him to become my consort. If he's anything like your husband, he's just the kind of man that I need at my side to help save the Empire."

Angela blinked. "Of all the things you could've said, that's something I'd never have expected to hear. It doesn't surprise me, because Carl is a terrific man and a brilliant scientist, but I've never really pegged him as your type. Isn't he a little... geeky for you?"

"Kelsey and I aren't completely in sync," Julia said with a small shake of her head. "I'm a lot less prone to break things than she is. I think that she found the perfect man for her when she found Talbot, but somebody like that isn't for me. I believe that Carl might be.

"And with that in mind, I'd like to get your advice on how best to pursue him. Plus, I owe you an apology. Circumstances being what they were down on the surface, he had to help me get into my powered armor, and I think that as his wife, you probably should know that I was naked in front of him."

Regardless of what Carl had said, she expected Angela to be upset about that. It shocked her deeply when the big woman laughed and shook her head.

"Highness, I'm a Marine Raider and was a marine before that. I can't even count the number of people who've seen me naked. Also, I have no doubt that my husband was the perfect gentleman. So long as nothing improper happened—and I'm absolutely certain that nothing did—then you've got no reason to be worried about me.

"I'll be happy to tell you all about Carl and give you my best advice. Honestly, it took me a long time to understand the kind of person that he really is. If your version of Carl is anything like mine, you're going to need that information to plan your campaign, because this is not going to be something that happens overnight.

"Now, if that's all, we really should be getting back to the bridge. We're coming up on the area around the far flip point, and there's still a couple of distant patrol ships that we want to make sure don't cross our path before we leave the system."

Somewhat shocked at how easily the conversation had gone, Julia followed Angela back to the bridge and wasn't surprised to find Kelsey and Talbot already there.

Angela sat in the command seat just as one of the people around her looked up from his console. "One of the destroyers patrolling the outer system just changed course and is headed toward the area around the far flip point. It's going to pass within a fair distance of us."

"Can we change course enough to avoid them entirely?" Angela asked.

The man shook his head. "No, ma'am. We don't have enough time at this low rate of speed."

"Then let's hope that they don't see us. If they do, we might manage to blow the hell out of them, but that's going to clue the enemy in on the fact that we're out here. If they ever suspect anything like the far flip points or multi-flip points exist, I can't begin to tell you how screwed humanity is. That's our secret weapon, and we've got to keep news of them to ourselves."

At that moment, Mertz entered the bridge. From his expression, he'd overheard enough to realize the situation they were in. He stepped over to the command chair and put his hand on the seat back.

"It looks like the moment of truth is upon us," he said.

Kelsey clapped Mertz on the shoulder. "It's time to roll the dice. No snake eyes."

Julia shook her head. Where the hell did her doppelgänger keep coming up with all these strange sayings? She'd never understand her.

* * *

JARED STOOD BEHIND ANGELA, and between Kelsey and Julia as the Marine Raider strike ship slowly crept toward the far flip point. It was marked on the screen with a small blue dot.

The red dot approaching *Persephone* represented the Rebel Empire destroyer. Its course wasn't directly toward the flip point, and it was going to come closer to *Persephone* than the flip point itself, which made it a real hazard.

"Can we reduce our detection threshold?" Mertz asked. "What if we stop thrusting entirely and just drift?"

Angela considered that for a moment and then shook her head. "I would suggest, however, that we don't stop moving entirely. Maybe we can just give ourselves a little angular momentum and take ourselves as far away from the destroyer's course as we can.

"At the very least, that will keep us a bit further away from the detection threshold and reduce the time that we're in danger."

Without waiting to see if he agreed, Angela ordered the helmsman to make the course change, and the strike ship turned away from the flip point. Jared watched as the enemy destroyer kept coming closer and closer, waiting for the moment it turned toward them.

And thankfully, that moment never came.

They waited until the destroyer was out of detection range before they resumed their course toward the flip point. A little bit more than an hour later, they were safely there, and at a stop.

"I assume you've already sent a probe to the other side," he said. "What did you find?"

"It's not an occupied system," Angela said, turning to face him slightly. "It's not on any of the old trade routes, so the odds of any vessels detecting us there are low, particularly since we'll be appearing far outside the normal area where any ship would be.

"With any luck, we can wait there for the fleet to join us. It might take them a while to get to our location, but I think it's better if we wait for them than try to meet up somewhere else. We're isolated and need to play defense."

He couldn't argue with that. "Then that's what we'll do. Flip the ship, Major."

Angela gave the order, and moments later, the transition was complete. He waited for the passive scanners to report and relaxed when they said nothing was near them.

"I'm pulling data from the drone we left here," Angela said. "If anyone's been through, it'll have records. And we're good. No ships have transited this system since I put the probe here four days ago. If the system is used as a gateway from one place to another, it's not used very often."

Jared stretched his neck, feeling good for the first time in what felt like months. "Once we get the fleet to our location, our next step has to be Twilight River. We can't go in through the front door, but with our ability to use multi-flip points and far flip points, there's a decent chance that we can get in through the back door.

"It's going to be challenging to find the other end of an

undetected flip point that leads to where we want to go, but we're going to have to spend the time doing just that. We can't count on using a hammer to break our way in."

"What if we can't find a way in?" Julia asked.

"Then we do it the hard way," he admitted. "We'd put the fleet through the flip point that we know leads to Twilight River and force our way through. I'm certain that it's heavily guarded, and if I were the AI, I'd do everything in my power to make sure that that system is invulnerable."

"Say we manage to sneak through a back door," Kelsey said. "You know the station is going to be surrounded by every ship they can stuff in there, just like Terra was. It's going to be impossible to get on board the station without being seen."

He smiled. "Getting on board the station is a Marine Raider job, so I'll leave that to you."

His sister grimaced. "At the moment, we've got three Marine Raiders and a few others that are partially ready. Oh, and one in the medical center. That's not exactly a Marine Raider strike force of old."

"We're not going to get to Twilight River today. We're not even going to get there next week. By the time we finally have a way in, months will have passed.

"Once we get everybody in the fleet together, I believe you can use *Caduceus* to get more of your people transitioned. Hell, there's a ton of marines in the fleet that would kill for an opportunity like this. Pick the very best among them, and you'll have your strike force.

"By the time we're ready, *Persephone* is going to be stuffed to the gills with Marine Raiders. We'll get your crew transitioned as quickly as we can as well, but the main thing is getting our fighting force prepared for the assault.

"We've got to get our people on board that station. All we've got are two Marine Raider pinnaces. If we stack people in armor aboard those, that means we can get almost a hundred and fifty people in regular marine armor. With the smaller Marine Raider version, maybe as many as a hundred and eighty. They're all we're going to have to make this work."

He looked around the bridge and at his friends. "Twilight River is coming, folks. This is a fight we can't afford to lose, and I want everyone's minds fully focused on winning it. When we get there, we're only going to get one chance at this. Let's make it count."

* * *

WANT to get updates from Terry about new books and other general nonsense going on in his life? He promises there will be cats. Go to TerryMixon.com/Mailing-List and sign up.

DID YOU ENJOY THIS BOOK? Please leave a review on Amazon. It only takes a minute to dash off a few words and that kind of thing helps Terry make a living as a writer and gets you new books faster.

WANT the next book in this series? Grab *When Luck Runs Out* today or buy any of Terry's other books, which are listed on the next page.

VISIT TERRY's Patreon page to find out how to get cool rewards and an early look at what he's working on at Patreon.com/TerryMixon.

ALSO BY TERRY MIXON

You can always find the most up to date listing of Terry's titles on his Amazon Author Page.

Note: the links below (ebook only, obviously) redirect you to my website where you can click a button to go to Amazon. This allows me to participate in Amazon's associates program and earn a little more. Sorry for any inconvenience.

The Last Hunter

The Last Hunter

Bonds of Blood

Alpha Strike

The Enemy Revealed

Command Authority

The Grand Conspiracy

Shield of Humanity

Fog of War

Ships of the Line

Operation Liberty

The Empire of Bones Saga

Empire of Bones

Veil of Shadows

Command Decisions

Ghosts of Empire

Paying the Price

Recon in Force

Behind Enemy Lines

The Terra Gambit

Hidden Enemies

Race to Terra

Ruined Terra

Victory on Terra

When Luck Runs Out

Gunboat Diplomacy

The Imperial Marines Saga

Spoils of War

Imperial Recruit

Enemy Action

The Humanity Unlimited Saga

Liberty Station

Freedom Express

Tree of Liberty

Blood of Patriots

Single Novels

Scorched Earth

Storm Divers

The Vigilante Series with Glynn Stewart

Heart of Vengeance

Oath of Vengeance

Bound By Law

Bound By Honor

Bound By Blood

Box Sets

The Empire of Bones Saga Volume 1

The Empire of Bones Saga Volume 2

The Empire of Bones Saga Volume 3

The Empire of Bones Saga Volume 4

Humanity Unlimited Publisher's Pack 1

Humanity Unlimited Publisher's Pack 2

ABOUT TERRY

#1 Bestselling Military Science Fiction author Terry Mixon served as a non-commissioned officer in the United States Army 101st Airborne Division. He later worked alongside the flight controllers in the Mission Control Center at the NASA Johnson Space Center supporting the Space Shuttle, the International Space Station, and other human spaceflight projects.

He now writes full time while living in Texas with his lovely wife and a pounce of cats.

TerryMixon.com

amazon.com/author/terrymixon
facebook.com/TerryLMixon
patreon.com/TerryMixon
bookbub.com/authors/terry-mixon
goodreads.com/TerryMixon

www.ingramcontent.com/pod-product-compliance
Lightning Source LLC
Chambersburg PA
CBHW072104020726
47501CB00003B/704